SWORD OF LIGHT

Heroes of Asgard Book Two

S.M. SCHMITZ

MYTHOLOGY GLOSSARY

If Gavyn gives one of the characters a nickname, I've put it in parentheses right after his or her actual name

Aegis—a shield belonging to Zeus and Athena, which may have conferred special attributes to its bearer.

Aesir—one of the two tribes of gods in Norse mythology, and the tribe associated with most of the Norse gods such as Odin, Thor, and Tyr. The other tribe is the Vanir.

Anhur—Egyptian god of war who was sometimes portrayed with the head of a lion, which is why he can shift into a lion in this series.

Anubis—in Egyptian mythology, Anubis is a god of the dead and is associated with jackals.

Ariadne's Thread—in Greek mythology, Daedalus, the brilliant inventor, is tasked with creating a structure to hold the

Minotaur. He builds the Labyrinth, but he does such a good job, he himself could hardly escape it. In one of the more popular versions of this story, some Athenian kills King Minos's son, so as retribution, the Athenians are required to send seven girls and seven boys as a sacrifice to the Minotaur every seven years. One year, that includes the Greek hero, Theseus, but he's all like, "I'm not just going in there as a sacrifice—I'm going to be one of the most badass heroes ever," and decides to enter the Labyrinth to slay the Minotaur, but Ariadne sees him, thinks, "Whoa...dude. Lust, er, love at first sight!" and gives him a thread to help him find his way back out.

Arnbjorg—isn't a real mythological figure; I made her up for this story. She is the love interest of Havard.

Asalluhi—Mesopotamian god of incantations and magic.

Asclepius—Greek demigod or god associated with healing. His staff has a single serpent wrapped around it, but it has gotten confused with Hermes's over the centuries so that the caduceus (the name of Hermes's staff) is often used in modern medicine instead of the staff of Asclepius.

Asgard—the realm of the Aesir, one of the two races of gods in Norse mythology. The other is the Vanir (who originally lived in Vanaheim).

Badb (Agnes)—Irish goddess of war. One of the triune of goddesses who form the Morrigna.

Balder—son of Odin and Frigg and the most beloved of the Aesir. Balder is killed by a mistletoe arrow that Loki convinces Balder's blind brother, Hödr, to shoot at him. Now wait: it's not *quite* as cruel as it seems. After Balder dreams about his death, his mother has every object swear an oath that it will never harm her son, except she didn't get the oath of mistletoe. Since nothing would hurt him, the gods would take turns hurtling arrows and objects at Balder, which bounced off, leaving the much-loved god unharmed. But when Loki learns about the mistletoe loophole, he makes a dart, spear, or arrow from it (gotta love it when sources conflict), and poor Balder is murdered by his twin brother.

Belatu-Cadros—Celtic god of war. His name is also given as Belatucadros.

Berstuk—an evil Wendish (a Slavic ethnic group of eastern Europe) forest god. Yeah, what else really needs to be said about an evil forest god?

Bukavac—in Slavic mythology, this is a demonic monster that is often portrayed as having six legs and gnarled horns. I made up the halitosis part, but if you think about it, what monster *wouldn't* have horrible breath? They probably don't do a lot of teeth brushing while hanging out in the underworld.

Dagr—in Norse mythology, Dagr is the personification of day. Odin gave him a horse (Skinfaxi), and he and his mother, Nótt (night), would ride around the world bringing day and night.

Drekavac—in Slavic mythology, this is the name of a furry, humanoid forest demon whose name translates as "the screamer."

Elysium—also known as the Elysian fields, it's part of the

ancient Greek concept of the afterlife where those chosen by the gods would spend eternity in happiness and peace.

Erymanthian Boar—in Greek mythology, the Erymanthian boar is a huge boar that terrorized the mountainous region of Arcadia. It is famously killed by Heracles (Hercules) as the fourth of his Twelve Labors, which he completed as penance for killing his wife and son. Now wait: Heracles wasn't a terrible guy—Hera was a terrible goddess. She cursed him, making him insane, and when he regains his sanity, he's grief-stricken over what he's done, and he seeks forgiveness from both mortals and gods alike. Disney left out that part in the movie.

Forseti—in Norse mythology, he is a god of justice. The only mention of him in the *Poetic Edda* discusses his home and identifies him as someone who settles disputes. I've made him the mediator in this series as well.

Frey—Norse god of prosperity, fertility, and peace. He and his sister, Freyja, are members of the Vanir and were brought to Asgard to live among the Aesir when the war between the two tribes ended.

Freyja—Norse goddess of love, sex, fertility, and war. Known for her unparalleled beauty, she's often coveted by different gods and mythological figures, while she tends to covet jewelry, particularly Brísingamen (her necklace).

Gerd—gastroesophageal reflux disease. Just making sure you're paying attention. In Norse mythology, she's Frey's wife. Frey saw her from a distance and instantly fell in love with her.

Gunnr (Keira)—a Valkyrie. In Norse mythology, Valkyries would select which men would fall in battle and bring them to Valhalla.

Havard—isn't a real mythological figure. He's made up for this story, in which he's a god of war. I know his name is a pain in the ass (trust me: I'm the one who's having to type it), but I chose it because of its meaning. It contains old Norse elements that translate as "high defender" and I thought that was fitting for his character. If it helps, I keep pronouncing it as "Hav-ard."

Heimdall—Norse god whose impeccable sight and hearing make him an excellent watchman for the unfolding of Ragnarok. He also possesses the gift of foresight (ability to foretell future events).

Hermes—in Greek mythology, Hermes is the messenger of the gods, whose staff, caduceus, is usually depicted as having two serpents intertwined on it. His staff has mistakenly gotten mixed up with the staff of Asclepius, the Greek mythological figure associated with healing. The caduceus is often used as a medical symbol.

Hildr (Heidi)—one of the Valkyries.

Idun—Norse goddess whose apples grant the gods eternal youth.

Inanna—Sumerian goddess of beauty, love, sex, war, and justice. Yeah, I have no idea why the ancient Sumerians decided to lump all those different characteristics together. Maybe they just ran out of deities.

Inti—in Incan mythology, Inti is a sun god and was one of the most important deities of the Incan civilization.

Ljósálfar—in Norse mythology, it is the realm of the "light elves." In this series, it refers to the Norse's name for Ireland.

Mama Pacha—in Incan mythology, Mama Pacha is an earth and fertility goddess who can cause earthquakes.

Medeina—a Lithuanian goddess of forests who is sometimes depicted as a she-wolf with an escort of wolves...so, of course, she can take the form of a wolf in this series.

Menhit—Egyptian war goddess whose name roughly translates as "she who massacres." Nice, right? She's often depicted as a lion goddess, so she can shapeshift into a lion in this series.

Morrigna—a triune of Irish war goddesses formed the Morrigna. The three goddesses are usually given as Badb, Macha, and Nemain, although Nemain is sometimes replaced with Morrigan or Anand. Each goddess represents a different aspect of war.

Nergal—ancient Mesopotamian god of war and pestilence. He wreaks havoc in *The Guardians of Tara* series, so he's taking a backseat to some other gods at the moment.

Niflheim—in Norse mythology, Niflheim is sometimes used interchangeably with "Hel," the underworld over which the goddess of the same name ruled. It is a land of darkness and cold, and one of the two original realms (the other being fire) from which all other realms were created.

Ninurta—another ancient Mesopotamian war god, Ninurta played a small enough role in *The Unbreakable Sword* series to warrant a bigger part in this series. His enchanted weapon, Sharur (sometimes a talking mace, sometimes a talking spear) will be back in book two, but unfortunately, it doesn't talk to Gavyn.

Odin—the All-Father of the Aesir, Odin is one of the most famous gods of Norse mythology. Although he's a war god, Odin is also associated with magic and wisdom. His wife is the goddess, Frigg.

Paricia—an obscure name in Incan mythology, this god may be synonymous with Pacha Kamaq. He is most known for sending a flood to wipe out people who weren't paying him the proper respect. In this series, he is a water deity since he's sent tidal waves to punish people for not submitting.

Ra—in Egyptian mythology, Ra is one of the sun gods (specifically, god of the noon sun). He is associated with falcons and is often depicted with the head of a falcon.

Róta—one of the Valkyries.

Serpopard—an animal found in Mesopotamian and Egyptian mythology, it's supposed to be half leopard, half snake.

Sharur—Ninurta's enchanted weapon (either a mace or spear), which could supposedly talk...I'm really not sure what good a talking weapon is.

Sif—in Norse mythology, Sif is Thor's wife. An earth goddess, she is best known for her beautiful blond hair, which Loki infamously cut off as a prank...and not surprisingly, Thor didn't take it too well and threatened to kill him. Loki got away with his life after promising Thor he'd have a golden... wig?...made for her. The same dwarfs who make Sif's new hair make Mjollnir as well as several other gifts for the gods.

Sigyn—in Norse mythology, this is Loki's faithful wife who willingly stays with him after he's bound in the cave. Since a venomous snake was hung above Loki and dripped its venom on him, she would hold a bowl over her husband's face.

Supay—in Incan mythology, this god of death rules over Ukhu Pacha (the underworld) and commands an army of demons. Gavyn is not a fan.

Thor—god of thunder, storms, and fertility, Thor probably shares the top-honor of being the most recognizable Norse god along with his father, Odin. He defends Asgard with his hammer, Mjölnir, and is also known for being a protector of humans.

Tuatha Dé—the gods of Irish mythology. Also known as the Tuatha Dé Danaan, which means "tribe of (the goddess) Danu."

Tugarin—in Slavic mythology, this is a concept of evil that often takes the form of a dragon.

Tyr—Norse god of war who lost his right hand when he put it in a wolf's (Fenrir's) mouth so he could be restrained. So look: Fenrir would only allow himself to be restrained if some dumbass stuck a hand in his mouth because he suspected the fetter the gods had brought was enchanted. And Tyr was apparently that dumbass. I mean, the gods *did* bind the wolf that was prophesied to be such a terror, and *supposedly* he's gonna stay bound until Ragnarok just like his dad, Loki (yeah, because Norse mythology is F.R.E.A.K.Y y'all), but he'll just break free then and kill Odin anyway, so what was the point?

Ukhu Pacha—the underworld in Incan mythology.

Ull—Norse god associated with archery. Not much is known about him, but it's always good to have expert archers on your side.

Valaskjalf—one of Odin's halls. While Valhalla is the hall associated with his dead warriors, Valaskjalf is where he watches over all the realms.

Valhalla—one of Odin's halls. Famously portrayed as having a golden roof, slain warriors are brought to Valhalla by Odin's Valkyries. Here, they fight each day in preparation for Ragnarok and those who fall again rise each night when they all dine with Odin himself. Peachy afterlife, huh?

Vanir—one of the two tribes of Norse gods, the other being the Aesir. Frey and Freyja are from the Vanir.

Vigrid—field on which many battles of Ragnarok are prophesied to occur.

Wepwawet (Willy)—Egyptian god of war associated with wolves, which is why he shapeshifts into a wolf in this series.

Yngvarr—doesn't exist in Norse mythology; I made him up for this story. Brother of Havard and also a god of war.

Zababa—ancient Mesopotamian war god.

CHAPTER ONE

Of all the places I'd never wanted to wake up, which I'd cataloged quite a few times considering the drunken dares between Hunter and me, in the hands of a bunch of angry gods had never made it onto the list. Mostly because I'd never even *thought* I'd end up in the hands of a bunch of angry gods. But once I found myself there, it quickly rose to the top of that list. I really don't recommend becoming a prisoner of any kind of god—angry or not.

I slowly sat up and rubbed the back of my head, which throbbed with a dull headache, but I couldn't remember falling or anyone hitting me and there was no lump. The pain extended into my neck, wrapped around through my left ear, and landed behind my eye. Nothing in the room looked real. The walls waved and rippled and shimmered and the floor bubbled like a hot spring, so I squeezed my eyes shut and reopened them. For a brief moment, everything settled into place but I blinked, and the walls began to melt.

A door opened and a woman—no, a goddess whose voice I immediately recognized—entered. "You're finally awake," Inanna said.

She appeared to be melting, too, which was far worse than the walls.

"What did you do to me?" I asked, closing my eyes again because watching a person melt was way too disturbing, even if that person planned to kill me.

"We just sedated you. It'll wear off."

"Why am I alive?" Probably a stupid question, but I *was* kinda known for asking stupid questions, so why stop now?

"Because we think you can lead us to something we want," she said.

I snickered. "First of all, you probably should have told your minions to capture me alive then since quite a few of them tried to kill me. And secondly, the only thing I can lead you to is a lifetime of bad decisions."

She snickered now and sat on the other end of the bed, so I opened one eye just enough to peek at her. Since her face was still melting, I quickly closed it again. "First of all," she said, mimicking my tone, "if they'd managed to kill you in New Orleans, it was no great loss. We simply saw an opportunity and took it. And secondly, you don't know you can lead us to the Sword of Light, but you will."

I inhaled a quick breath and opened my eyes, despite the melting room and melting goddess and my melting brain. "How do you know about that?" I breathed.

She lifted an eyebrow at me, which temporarily shifted her features back into place. "Because it wasn't a Norse sword. It was ours."

I shook my head slowly. No way. That sword had belonged to Havard, and he alone could wield it. It *couldn't* have belonged to the Sumerians. Inanna must have sensed my confusion because she continued, "Our god of magic, Asal-luhi, made the Sword of Light. It's the most powerful weapon among our kind, and with it, we could easily vanquish your new friends."

"It won't work for you," I insisted. I'd suddenly become violently jealous of even the *suggestion* that someone else would be using *my* sword. A tiny voice in my mind reminded me it wasn't really my sword, so I told that voice to shut up and mind its own business. And then that voice told *me* to shut up and mind *my* own business, which I really didn't appreciate considering I'd been drugged and kidnapped—for the second time in a week, I might add—and was now nursing the world's worst hangover. I thought the voice called me a pansy, but Inanna began talking again, and I was forced to listen to her instead of the silent argument in my head.

"What makes you think it won't work for us?" she asked, and by the sound of her voice, she'd had to repeat the question... maybe more than once.

"Because it'll only work for the person it rightly belongs to," I answered.

She folded her arms across her chest, and most likely scowled at me, but her features had begun to melt again, so I wasn't quite sure where her nose and lips and chin actually were. "Who told you that?"

"Um... the dead god it used to belong to?"

This seemed to take her by surprise, and I wondered if I should've kept that a secret. "You're dreaming about Havard?" she asked cautiously.

"You knew him?" I think I was just as surprised now.

"Of course," she said, her voice just above a whisper. "I'm the one who gave him that sword."

When I awoke again, the walls and floor remained stationary and the headache had mostly subsided. I stared at the ceiling for a long time, trying to decide if I should believe Inanna or not, but she had no reason to lie to me. Her announcement that she'd given Havard his sword as a present when he was born had been greeted by my stunned silence—a remarkable feat, even for a goddess. There was something in her brief explanation that seemed to suggest she'd known Havard's father a little too well for my liking, but I'd just sat there, mute and shocked and wanting to throw up but I wasn't sure if it was from the drugs or her story.

The one piece of good information I'd gleaned from her account of the Sword of Light ending up in a Norse god's hands was that she didn't seem to know Havard beyond his presentation as an infant. On the opposite end of the spectrum, my knowledge of this dead ancestor disturbed her, as if somehow, these memories could be dangerous for her and the Sumerians. I couldn't imagine how. The only thing I could be fairly certain of was that she seemed even more motivated to end my life early, even if it meant no chance of ever recovering that sword.

I'd just counted the tiles on the ceiling for the thirteenth time when the door opened again, but this time, it wasn't Inanna. Ninurta had come to see me, and he seemed to carry a storm cloud with him wherever he went. It was probably just my imagination, but the air in the room even seemed to drop twenty degrees, and I shivered and pulled the blanket higher around my throat.

"Can you see?" he asked, his voice silken and smooth, but something slithered beneath it like a current of deadly poison.

I nodded and kept my eyes on the ceiling. "Then get up and follow me," he ordered.

I obeyed and he led me through a maze of hallways and stairwells until we finally emerged in a large room with table after table of desktop computers. Ninurta gestured toward the closest computer and commanded, "Sit."

I gritted my teeth but pulled the chair away from the table and sat down. Straight ahead was a row of windows, and I could just make out the trunks of trees in the distance and a wide lawn with a birdbath in the center before Ninurta forced my attention away from the outdoors. He stood over me and nodded toward the monitor. "Which of these names is familiar?" he asked.

I read the list on the screen but didn't recognize any of them.

"Impossible," he insisted.

"Dude," I sighed, "I can't even *pronounce* any of these names."

He slapped his hand against the table, causing me to jump, and leaned in close to my face. I wanted to back away, but he was obviously trying to intimidate me, and I refused to let him know it was working. "Do not," he said in that icy, silky voice, "waste my time. Your death can be quick or prolonged."

"You want me to lie then?" I shot back. "Because I really don't recognize any of these names."

Ninurta stood up straight, narrowing his eyes at me. "Then look again. Concentrate. When a god has children, it's not only his physical features that get passed down in his genes but his memories."

I scanned the list of names again, but I still didn't recognize any of them. I'd suspected, of course, they had something to do with Havard, but now that Ninurta had confirmed it, I wouldn't have told him the truth anyway. His threat of torturing me to death still hung in the air, but the only emotion that stirred within me was my own stubborn refusal to allow him to win. These assholes had kidnapped my father. Did they really think I'd help them now?

As if reading my mind, he added, "If you think your

father's life doesn't depend on your cooperation, you truly are as stupid as you want others to believe."

"As far as I know, he's already dead."

The corners of Ninurta's lips turned up in the slightest, most sinister of smiles, and he called out, "Bring him in."

Ninurta's order was answered with shuffling in the hallway, the sounds of a struggle, and I leapt to my feet but he pushed me back down. My father was dragged into the room, his eyes wild and angry, but as they settled on me, they took on an intense and crazed mania. "Dad," I croaked.

His face was splattered with dried blood, his shirt torn and stained a deep brownish-red. More blood, I realized.

"Gavyn," he breathed.

"What did you do to him?" I screamed, rising to my feet again only to be forced back down.

My father strained against the two men, presumably more demigods, each gripping one arm. When they'd first dragged him in, they'd been holding him upright, but now, they were holding him back as he struggled to reach me.

"The names, Gavyn," Ninurta said, calm and unaffected.

"I'm going to kill you," I growled. "All of you."

He only smiled again, his eyes flitting to the computer screen as a final warning. Cooperate or watch my father die. I tried to focus on the screen, the letters, strange accents, but they seemed to twitch and dance and refused to stay in place. At first, I thought it was only the adrenaline, the fear, the rage... I couldn't focus because I'd never been so angry in my life. But as the letters shifted and jumped, I realized I *could* read them; they weren't names at all. Not anymore. The letters spelled out a message, and it was directed to me.

Sharur is with Ninurta at all times. Take him hostage with it. He won't resist if he thinks he can get it back.

Sharur, I repeated silently. An image formed in my mind. A spear. Ninurta must have it hidden somehow, in a way only gods could manage. I swallowed and took a deep breath, needing to be able to steal glances at him so I could find it without raising suspicions. I looked at his hands first, telling him, "I'm trying. How long do I have?"

Nothing. His hands appeared just as empty as before.

"Until I'm tired of standing here," he responded as if that answer should satisfy me.

I focused on the screen again, hoping for more insight, or even to see if I'd just lost my grasp of reality, but the letters hadn't changed and still spelled the same message. Even if I could get my hands on a weapon, taking Ninurta prisoner would be damn near impossible. I mean, he was a *god*. I'd have to hope this message was right, that his desire to get Sharur back would force his cooperation. And that Inanna wouldn't burst in with the whole damn Sumerian-hero army. I didn't think I'd get many chances to glance in his direction again. The next one had to count.

"Maybe it would help," I suggested while trying to discreetly search the god who held my father's life in his hands, "if you told me whether these names are people or places."

Ninurta sighed, exasperated. "People, Gavyn."

As I lowered my eyes, prepared to accept that either the drugs or my situation, or maybe the combination, were causing me to hallucinate and there wasn't actually a message on the screen offering me a solution, a chance to escape with my life and my father's, the overhead light reflected off something, glinted, catching my attention. It had been brief, this glimpse of silver in the incandescent lights, but *something* was hidden, animated in midair, constantly awaiting Ninurta's grip.

When we'd first arrived in New Orleans, I'd asked Frey if he always traveled with swords and he'd told me yes. I'd assumed he was just being a smartass—after all, he *was* learning from the best—but perhaps he was telling me the truth. I sat up straighter, pretending something on the screen had caught my attention and Ninurta leaned in closer, just slightly, just enough that when I shifted my attention from the screen to his vicinity, I could see the spear I needed to stand a shot of getting out of here with my dad.

I pointed to a random spot on the screen, and Ninurta leaned a bit closer and began to say something but I twisted in my seat and grabbed the spear. Part of me had expected my fingers to find nothing but air, so when they closed around the smooth shaft, I was almost as surprised as the god Sharur belonged to. Ninurta gasped, but I wrapped my free arm around him, forcing him in front of me like a shield, and pressed the tip of the spear against the base of his skull. "If you want your magic spear back, don't move unless I tell you to," I directed.

Truthfully, I didn't know how to *use* a spear, but I figured as long as I had the sharp, pointy end directed toward the guy I wanted to kill, I was on the right track. The two men holding my father had frozen, immobilized by the sudden turn of events. "Let him go!" I shouted. When they still didn't move, I pressed the tip of the spear into Ninurta's skull until it drew blood, which caused him to cry out in pain. His chest heaved and he hissed, "Do it. Let him go."

The captors released my father's arms, and his knees buckled. He caught himself before his face slammed into the floor, his hands splayed in front of him. But I couldn't help him up. If I let go of Ninurta, my only leverage to get us out of our prison, we'd both be dead before I could reach him. "Dad, you have to get up. You have to stay with me."

My fifty-seven-year-old father was still far stronger than all of the gods and demigods combined. His eyes met mine and he slowly, carefully, painfully pulled himself back to his feet. Each stumbling step physically hurt me. None of these gods or heroes would escape my vengeance.

I forced myself to watch the men who'd held my father prisoner instead. If they made one move toward my dad, I'd spear Ninurta's head. I was certain not even gods could survive a spear through the brain. We couldn't retreat into the hallway. I had no idea how many gods and demigods waited inside this massive labyrinth of a building. Instead, I dragged Ninurta toward the windows and my father set his jaw and somehow, kept pace with me. Perhaps it was the temporary rush of a possible escape after giving up hope that salvation would ever come.

He fumbled with the latches for only a few seconds then managed to swing the windows open. The drop to the ground was only a few feet, but in my father's condition, it would be brutal nonetheless. But he didn't hesitate. He climbed onto the sill and landed with a muffled groan. "Now what?" Ninurta asked me. "Do you really think you can get me outside this way?"

To be honest, I had no idea. We had to get across the lawn, which was a lot of open space to cover without a hostage. I *needed* to get Ninurta out if we were going to survive. I glanced in the demigods' direction one last time. "Get over here. You'll wait by the windows, and if I hear you call for help or see you leave this room, I'll kill your boss."

Ninurta grunted in response but nodded, and the two demigods reluctantly made their way toward us. As so often seemed to happen now, my body began acting before my brain had a chance to catch up. I pushed the Sumerian war god toward the window, punched him, and knocked him over the sill. A gunshot, followed quickly by the splintering of wood as a bullet embedded into the wall right next to my ear, warned me I'd have one chance to get out of this building, so I took it. I jumped through the window just as a second gunshot joined the chorus of shouting behind me, and the most difficult part of our escape began.

CHAPTER TWO

A n injured middle-aged man. An irate war god. And two hundred yards of open space.

Somehow, I had to get us across the lawn to the trees, and those assholes inside had called my bluff. Ninurta groaned and his eyes rolled around for a few seconds as he squinted and blinked. I was tempted to punch him again, just for the hell of it. He placed a hand on the side of the building and forced himself to his knees, so I did the only thing I could think of: I stabbed the bastard.

He turned his dark eyes on me, so filled with surprise that I'd just injured him with his own spear, and his hands touched his side. He held his fingers up and stared at the blood on them as if completely unable to comprehend he was hurt. But if I killed him now, I'd no longer have any leverage at all. The demigods had moved away from the windows, most likely to get help, so I dragged Ninurta closer to me again and yanked him to his feet.

"Come on, Dad. We've got to run."

My dad was still looking at me like I was some alternate-universe version of myself, and honestly, I couldn't blame him.

But I also couldn't worry about *how* I was going to explain what was happening to us, and how Mom had obviously known something was different about me all along. "My supernatural allies need to put a tracking device on me," I muttered.

Ninurta finally got his eyes to focus long enough to glare at the spear in my hand as if Sharur had betrayed him. But my dad nodded toward the trees, indicating he was ready to run. He'd gotten that determined look on his face, the same expression I'd see when he was trying to hook up a modem, or the Blu-Ray player I got him for his birthday and he refused to read instructions or ask for help.

But another gunshot and the shattering of glass prevented us from running. Inanna still hadn't come outside, so I clung to the hope she'd left and had no idea my father and I were trying to escape. Instead of running, we began to inch along the wall. The corner of the building was only twenty feet away, and we'd attempt to find cover on the south side. Ninurta stumbled, forcing me to glance at him. His olive skin had paled to a sickly green. He clutched his side, and I noticed the bloodstain had spread. He was bleeding worse than I'd thought, but in my defense, I didn't exactly have a lot of experience stabbing people so it's not like I *knew* I was killing the bastard.

As we reached the corner, my father finally whispered, "Our hostage isn't going to make it, and he's just slowing us down."

Ninurta lifted his head and recognition briefly lit his features as if he understood he wouldn't survive much longer. I made the terrible mistake of hesitating when I should've killed him, because he placed a bloody palm on the yellow stucco to steady himself just as Inanna and a group of demigods turned the corner. There was nothing I could do now: my father and I had to run.

"Shed," Dad whispered.

The garden shed was close enough for *me* to reach, but in my dad's condition, I doubted he could run fast enough. Given at least four demigods and one goddess were outside with us now, I wasn't even sure he would have been able to reach it if he'd been uninjured. But we had nowhere else to go, and we were out of time.

So we ran.

I heard the gunshot just as I reached the doors and broke open the padlock. I had only a second to think these assholes were extraordinarily bad shots before I realized they hadn't missed this time... not entirely. Dad had fallen.

I think I screamed as my body acted without my ability to think, and I grabbed his arm and dragged him inside the shed. Bullets pelted the door but didn't penetrate, and I fell to my knees at Dad's side. His eyes met mine, and I noticed the sweat on his forehead, the pale, clammy skin. He wasn't going to make it.

Suddenly, I was twelve years old, sitting by my mother's hospital bed, watching her body struggle to take those last breaths. She hadn't been conscious for two days. Dad held one of her hands, and I held the other, and we just watched her in silence until her chest stilled completely. And neither of us moved. I don't know how long we sat like that.

The bullet had entered and exited his side, almost in the exact same place I'd stabbed Ninurta, and he was in immediate danger of bleeding out. I took off my shirt and held it to the exit wound, but I couldn't save him even if there *weren't* a handful of Sumerian demigods outside. I knew nothing about first aid.

Dad's eyebrows pulled together as his gaze shifted away from me to something over my shoulder. Her hand touched my back for a second before she knelt beside me, and I had to blink at her several times before my brain yelled at me, telling us to hurry and get the hell out of here.

"Keira," I gasped. I hadn't even noticed anyone entering the shed.

"Sh," she responded. Outside, I heard the struggle ensuing between our captors and my allies. Finally, the cavalry had arrived. And we had far more gods here than the Sumerians, which meant those guns were useless.

The shed door opened again and Yngvarr hurried inside, nodding to my father. "We called an ambulance. We can't move him like this."

"An ambulance?" I repeated. How surreal it sounded to wait on something so *ordinary* after I'd been kidnapped by *gods*.

But Yngvarr just shot me a strange look and said, "Yeah, how else are we going to get him to the hospital?"

So I just blinked at him like I hadn't understood the question.

Fortunately, we must not have been far from a city because I could already hear the sirens wailing as the ambulance approached. My father closed his eyes, so I focused on him again, urging him to stay awake. I wasn't sure that was really necessary; I just saw them doing it all the time on TV. I talked to him about football, because I honestly didn't know what else to say. I couldn't bring myself to talking about his condition or even mentioning the possibility that he might die. But he occasionally smiled as I ranted about LSU's offense and poor clock management, and soon, paramedics were loading him onto a gurney and we were transported to a hospital.

As we entered the ER, a small group of people in blue scrubs bolted around desks and emerged from somewhere, maybe one of the nine realms where healers and wielders of magical potions hid, and they wheeled my father toward the operating room. Keira shook my shoulder and said, "Gavyn, they're taking him into surgery. He'll be okay."

"How do you know?" I asked.

"Because he has to be," she said. "The universe *can't* be this cruel."

I just nodded and fell into one of the chairs, burying my face in my hands. Keira sat beside me and put a hand on my shoulder again. "What you did... getting away from them like that. Gavyn, that was incredible."

"This happened to him because of *me*."

"Oh, Gavyn. You can't help who you are. This isn't your fault."

I kept my face buried and asked, "How did you find me?"

"I went back to Asgard and had Odin perform a scrying spell," she said.

"You say that like I should know what it is."

"It's how we found you the first time," she said. "He does a spell and looks into a mirror and can see you."

I finally lifted my head and squinted at her. "That's totally pervy."

Keira rolled her eyes and stood up. "Come on. Let's find you a shirt in the gift shop."

Once I was fully dressed again, we got coffee we barely touched and sat in the waiting room. The silence between us was occasionally punctuated by whispers of what the other heroes and a handful of Norse and Irish gods were doing to help the people in New Orleans. At some point, Tyr showed up and sat with us, also holding onto a cup of coffee that he didn't drink.

Finally, a doctor emerged from the double doors and approached me. My legs seemed too weak to hold me up, but somehow, I didn't fall. Maybe because he looked pleased rather than grim. "The surgery went well," he assured me.

"He's in recovery then we'll move him to a room and you can see him."

I exhaled slowly and thanked him, waiting until Keira and Tyr were alone with me again before saying, "Every last one of those bastards is going to die."

CHAPTER THREE

A week passed before the Sumerians resurfaced, perhaps because they were licking their wounds as well, waiting for Ninurta to recover. We brought my father to Asgard as soon as he was released from the hospital then returned to Reykjavik where Agnes *finally* started pulling her weight by bringing in a handful of Irish heroes. I was still trying to convince Hunter that he should go to Asgard, too, but the stubborn ass refused. Neither Cadros nor Agnes would help me convince him, and Tyr and Frey refused to just kidnap him and bring him anyway.

So naturally, I crossed my arms angrily and snapped, "Y'all had no problem kidnapping *me*."

"That was different," Frey argued. "You're Norse."

"And that whole 'fate of the world' thing," Tyr added.

"And it was just more fun that way," Keira also added.

"I hate you," I said, even though that wasn't really true. Not anymore. My feelings for Keira were particularly muddled, but it's not like I had time to sort them out considering the fate of the world really *was* kinda at stake.

But Agnes waved me off anyway and snatched the newspaper off the table. She'd adopted her old witch disguise again, so at least I didn't have to worry about being attracted to her because *that* had been completely unacceptable. "Hunter's fine," she insisted. "Stop worrying."

"Don't you have children to lure into ovens?" I asked.

Agnes cackled then flipped the newspaper, holding it in front of her five-hundred-year-old face so I could no longer see her. I'd learned by now that was her cue she was no longer participating in our conversations, so I turned on Tyr and tried again. "One trip to Asgard will shut me up."

"You'll eventually shut up anyway," he replied.

"But I'll annoy the hell out of you until then."

Yngvarr snickered and took *their* side, the bastard. "You know how you're not supposed to cave when a toddler throws a tantrum over not getting his way? Sets a bad precedent."

"Traitor," I mumbled.

"Stop trying to orchestrate my kidnapping," Hunter demanded.

"Go willingly so I don't have to," I demanded back.

"If I were going anywhere, I'd go to the Otherworld, but since Agnes won't tell me if there's a harem of goddesses awaiting me, I'm staying here."

"All right, you old hag, you heard him," I said. "Whisk him off to the Otherworld."

Agnes turned the page and ignored me.

Cadros turned the volume up on the television, pretending he was completely engrossed in an Icelandic game show in which a host appeared to be asking the contestant trivia questions, but unless those questions involved dead Sumerian gods, I couldn't see why it was so interesting. "Coward," I mumbled at *him* now.

"Gavyn," Keira sighed. She sounded exasperated with me already, and it was only nine a.m.

I gestured toward Hunter and shot her a "Then *do* something" look, but she only shot me her "You're being an annoying asshole" look in return. And Freyja suddenly returning from New Orleans didn't help the atmosphere at all. Keira seemed to remember she was mad at me or just thought I was a selfish pig, which was probably fair, and started scowling at me again while Freyja announced the last of the hostages, if that's what they were, in New Orleans had been rescued.

"The Sumerians just let them go?" I asked.

Freyja shrugged and smiled at me, but for some reason, I just didn't find her that irresistible anymore. "What choice did they have? They'd promised not to kill anyone if they surrendered, but with Ninurta so badly injured, whatever they'd planned got delayed. If they killed those people, no one would believe them again, and the Sumerians don't want to slaughter everyone—who would be left to worship them?"

"So they have to be evil but not *too* evil," I said.

"Exactly," she agreed.

"See?" Hunter interjected. "If I were in Asgard, I'd be missing all this."

"If you were in Asgard, I wouldn't have to worry about a handful of asshole gods abducting you to get to *me*," I argued. "There are very few people in this world I care about, and they know that and they *will* hurt you if they get the chance. Especially since I almost killed one of them."

"How *did* you almost kill a god?"

It was my turn to shrug. "With a spear."

"Not what I meant, dumbass."

"With a *sharp* spear?"

Hunter blinked at me then tapped Agnes's shoulder. "Can I reconsider the Otherworld?"

"They're back," Cadros breathed, pointing to the television.

I groaned because the Sumerians *always* resorted to tele-

vising their stupid demands, so I thought everyone should
know my thoughts about it. "This is why nobody gives a shit
about the Sumerians anymore. They lack originality."

The entire room shushed me, so I added, "But they probably let their demigods speak."

The entire room shushed me again, but before I could
add anything *else*, Keira put a hand over my mouth. I squinted
at her, but she was watching the television.

And not surprisingly, when the Sumerians spoke, they
addressed me directly. Also not surprising was Ninurta's
appearance. We'd all assumed they'd been quiet for the past
week because he was recuperating, but seeing him looking so
healthy irritated the hell out of me. "As you can see, Gavyn,
your attempt to murder me has failed."

I *tried* to say, "If I'd wanted to kill you, you'd be dead," but
Keira still had her hand pressed tightly over my mouth and it
came out sounding more like, "Ehm haunted oo eel oo, oo'ed
ee ed."

And the room *still* shushed me.

"And," Ninurta continued, "your escape indicates we
underestimated you. Rest assured, we won't make that
mistake again. As payback for costing us so much time..."
The camera panned to his left, allowing me to see he was
standing in the parking lot outside Tiger Stadium, which
shuddered then began to collapse.

"Oo summona itch!" I yelled, which wasn't what I yelled
at all, but since Keira still had her hand over my mouth, that's
probably what everyone *heard*. Hunter groaned and ran his
fingers through his hair as we watched our beloved stadium
reduced to a tremendous pile of debris. At first, I thought
they'd at least had the decency to wait until the stadium was
empty before remembering most universities had canceled
the rest of their football games. At least until the Sumerians
stopped taking out their anger on the world by destroying

buildings, but honestly, I figured they might as well just cancel *everything*.

Keira let her hand fall and we braced ourselves for the inevitable ultimatum. But Ninurta was obviously full of surprises that day. "We'll see you soon, Gavyn."

The screen went dark as they cut the feed, and a few seconds later, the Icelandic game show came back on. In a few minutes, the game show would be interrupted again once word spread that the Sumerians had resurfaced, but Cadros muted the television and Tyr muttered, "I *really* hate that guy."

"Our stadium..." Hunter said.

I nodded because words seemed stuck in my throat. Ninurta had accomplished the impossible: he'd rendered me speechless.

"Should we look for them?" Freyja asked.

"Odin is always looking for them," Keira said. "His spells don't work on gods."

"I didn't suggest we rely on Odin," Freyja replied smugly. "I suggested *we* look for them rather than constantly waiting and responding to catastrophe."

Keira crossed her arms angrily and snapped, "If you think they're so easy to track down, be my guest. Go find them."

Freyja crossed *her* arms angrily and snapped back, "That's exactly what I'm proposing, dumbass!"

I snorted over hearing a goddess call someone a dumbass and Hunter shot me a look that said, "*You're* the dumbass."

"I can't believe I'm saying this, but I agree with Freyja," Yngvarr said. "We can't keep waiting for them to destroy some building or kidnap an entire city. We need to be proactive."

"And do what?" Tyr asked. "They could be anywhere in the world, and we don't exactly have a global reach of allies."

"We kinda do though," I said, admittedly a little

impressed that I didn't even need vodka to regain my ability to speak. Tyr raised an eyebrow at me and waited for my explanation so I shuffled my feet nervously for a moment as even Agnes lowered her paper, those beady eyes studying me. I looked away quickly before she turned me to stone or something. "The Sumerians are probably the biggest threat to humanity right now, so why not get the help of mortal agencies? Do you really think the FBI and CIA, and every other acronym you can think of, aren't out there looking for the gods who've already murdered almost two thousand people and caused billions of dollars of property damage?"

"I'm sure they are," Tyr said. "But why would they trust *us*? You didn't trust us at first."

"Of course not. You assholes kidnapped me."

"You were being uncooperative," Keira responded as if that excused my abduction.

"And it's not a good idea for you to show up on the CIA's doorstep," Yngvarr added. "Once they find out you're the hero the Sumerians have targeted, they'll hand you over in the hopes it appeases them enough to stop killing people."

I shook my head and insisted, "We don't negotiate with terrorists. *Everyone* knows that."

"Do you?" Keira said. "Do you *really* know what your government does or just believe that because it's what they tell you?"

I squinted at her because I didn't have an answer for that, and she was right anyway. How did any of us know how the U.S. handled situations like this? And we'd never really encountered a situation like *this*. Gods weren't supposed to exist. These were just stories most people didn't tell anymore.

"So don't admit you know me," I finally offered. "Frey and Cadros can go talk to them, see if we can work together. But I'm done sitting around and letting those assholes hurt people. It's time we put them on the defensive."

Frey and Cadros glanced at each other, and Frey took a deep breath, nodding slowly as he thought about my proposal. "Okay, Gavyn. We'll go."

I noticed Keira staring at me, so I stared back at her and she smiled, but I was a little too freaked out by *how* she was looking at me to smile, too. "What?" I demanded.

"You," she said. "You're finally turning into the hero I always knew you could be."

SLEET FELL against the metal roof of the warehouse where Tyr had set up an impromptu training center since we couldn't fight outside. I stood in front of the table of swords, but I wasn't really studying them or trying to decide which to use. I was too worried I'd made a huge mistake by sending Frey and Cadros to the States; I couldn't bear being responsible for their deaths. Keira lifted the plainest sword on the table and the light reflected off the blade. I blinked at it, temporarily seeing a completely different sword, one that glowed in its owner's hands.

"Try this one," she said. "It's very well balanced."

She handed it to me, and I suddenly felt transported back to my first day in that field when I'd never held a weapon in my life and I almost dropped it. I sheepishly grinned at her and apologized. "Sorry. My head's just not in this today."

"I know. But until they return, there's nothing else we can do."

"Perhaps," Tyr suggested, "you can learn how to handle a few different weapons today. Sword fighting is already in your blood." He gestured to a spear on the table, and I laughed because he'd brought Sharur into the training center.

"If I weren't already Sumerian-Enemy-Number-One," I

said, "stealing that spear would have catapulted me to the top."

Tyr nodded seriously. "Ninurta is really attached to this thing. Like Havard's sword, it's supposedly enchanted. Or maybe he's just crazy for thinking his spear talks to him, but either way, it's just a spear to us."

"You take it," I said. "You're the one who's an expert with a spear."

Tyr just shrugged and plucked Sharur off the table. "It *is* a nice one," he murmured.

I twisted the sword in my hands then slowly studied each one on the table as an idea—or, more accurately, a realization —formed in my mind and I blurted out, "I want to find the Sword of Light."

Keira didn't seem all that surprised by my announcement. She simply picked up a different sword and felt its weight and balance as she considered the possibilities of finding my ancestor's sword. "Do you have any clues as to where we should start?"

"No," I sighed. "But I know the Sumerians want it. Inanna told me some god on their pantheon whose name was..." I bit my lip as I hurt my brain trying to remember this god's name. "Asshole?"

Tyr arched an eyebrow at me. "Asalluhi?"

I pointed the plain sword in my hands at him. "That's it."

"Okay," Keira said. "So what did Asshole have to do with your sword?"

"She claims he made it. He's like their magician, and for some reason, Inanna gave it to Havard when he was born."

"Oh, I think I know *exactly* why she gave it to him," Yngvarr said. He'd snuck up behind me and scared the shit out of me, to be honest. I spun around and pointed my sword at him now.

"Never sneak up on someone holding a sword," I warned. "That's suicidal."

"Probably," he agreed.

"Um..." Tyr interjected. "You think your father and Inanna...?"

"It's my father," Yngvarr sneered. "Of course they had an affair."

"Why would she give such a valuable gift to her lover's son?" Keira asked.

Yngvarr shrugged. "No idea. But it's definitely possible Inanna is telling the truth, especially since she knew about this sword *and* Gavyn's ancestor even though none of us Norse remember him."

"If you're abducted by the Sumerians again, don't wait a week to tell us about super important conversations," Tyr instructed.

I grunted at him and reminded him I'd been kinda busy worrying about my dad surviving a gunshot wound. Keira tossed her sword onto the table and met my gaze. "Where do you want to start looking for your sword?"

"If Havard hid it somewhere before he died, it would have most likely been in one of two places, right?" I answered.

Keira nodded. "Asgard or Norway, neither of which is particularly small."

"True," Yngvarr agreed. "But we *do* know where he lived. If we're going to find his sword, why not start at the most obvious place?"

I smiled at him and threw the plain sword onto the table by the one Keira had dropped. "To your palace then. Because if we're going to defeat Ninurta, I have a feeling we're going to need this sword."

"I think so, too," Keira agreed quietly. "Not because of the sword itself, but because of *you*. When it's in your hands, it'll become the most powerful weapon among our kind."

Goose bumps broke out across my arms, and I rubbed them quickly, trying to coax the skin back into submission. But that feeling I'd been having that I'd *need* this sword in order to defeat the Sumerians had only grown stronger, and part of me already knew Keira was right. Finding the Sword of Light would transform me, and I would transform it, and together, we'd become unstoppable.

HAVARD REVEALS A PROPHECY

(And I think he's one lucky bastard)

Three days had passed since Arnbjorg and I traveled to Midgard and discovered her parents were missing. And in those three days, Arnbjorg had largely kept to herself, no longer harvesting apples or baking treats for my nieces and nephews. I worried she blamed me for her misery, but what could I possibly say to the girl who'd just lost her family?

I was in the stables with Sigurd when she found me, clutching a book to her chest as if it contained the secret to her immortality. I didn't even notice her at first—she was so quiet as she sat on a hay bale and watched me comb his coat. When she spoke, she startled me. "I can't read."

"What?" I said. How did her literacy have anything to do with her family?

She lowered the book, setting it carefully in her lap, and ran her fingers over the embossed cover. It was a collection of our stories, the myths men told about the gods. "Are you in here?" she asked.

I shook my head. "No, I'm too young. And outside of battles, I've mostly tried to avoid the world of mortals."

"Why?"

I knelt in front of her and flipped the book open. "I'm not sure," I admitted. "Maybe because my father was fond of it. He met not only mortals there, but goddesses from other pantheons."

Arnbjorg put a hand over mine to keep me from turning the pages. Her innocent touches always set me on fire, and I quickly looked away from her and kept my attention on the page. "You once told me your sword had a terrible secret," she said. "It's not in here then?"

"No, and I'm not entirely sure how it ended up in my possession."

"What do you mean?"

I sat on the hay bale next to her and pointed to the book. "I can teach you to read if you'd like."

"I'd like you to tell me this secret," she whispered.

I met her gaze again and for the second time, quickly looked away. It was impossible to tell her no when I looked at her. But I hadn't even told Yngvarr all of my dreams. "It grants the gift of prophecy," I whispered back.

"How do you know it's the sword and not one of your natural gifts?"

"Because I only dream about things that involve my sword."

Arnbjorg seemed to consider this then pointed out, "That's not a terrible secret, is it?"

"No," I sighed. "Not really. But it's shown me how I'm going to die. I've never even told Yngvarr about that part, only that one of my descendants will one day wield it. And I thought I would hate him for it, but I don't."

"Oh," she breathed. She ran her fingers over the illustration of Frey holding his own enchanted sword. "Is it awful?"

"Is what?"

"Knowing how you're going to die?"

"It's confusing," I said. "Even in my dream, I know my

death is coming, and I don't fear it. On the contrary, I welcome it. Why would I ever do that?"

"All of the major gods know their fates during Ragnarok, and they'll each go into battle with the very thing that will kill them. At least, that's true of the stories my father..." Arnbjorg bit her lip and studied the picture of Balder, who'd been one of Asgard's most beloved gods, then closed the book, clutching it to her chest again. My heart hurt for her, but what could I do?

"It's true of them," I offered. "Once it's been ordained, death is inescapable, even for us gods."

"Still... what's so terrible about this secret?" she asked.

"My sword is just a sword to anyone but me," I explained carefully. "But in my hands, it's light itself. The more enemies that are around me, the brighter it will glow until its power bursts and slays them all."

"If you can kill your enemies so easily, how can you possibly be defeated?"

"That's what I don't understand. I lay down my sword—I let this god I've never met kill me."

She grabbed my hand and squeezed it, shaking her head, pleading with me. "Then don't. When you see him, kill him instead. Don't give him the chance to even speak to you."

"Arnbjorg—"

"Promise me, Havard. Promise me you'll fight back and not let him murder you."

I never should have made a promise to her that I knew I couldn't keep, but she was so desperate, so sincere, so filled with too much pain already. I could have pointed out her obvious oversight: in my dream about seeing my sword in someone else's hands, I know he's my descendant. And I didn't yet have any children. One day, I would have a family, which meant I'd be intensely vulnerable for the first time in my life. My father's power protected me as a child, and my own had always protected me as an adult. But a wife and children would one day lead me to my grave.

If I told her the truth, that I already knew I was dying for her, would she ever agree to marry me? Knowing that a life without her was no life at all, I said nothing except the words she wanted to hear. "I promise, Arnbjorg."

Her grip on my fingers loosened, and she suddenly leaned toward me, kissing me gently. I was aflame, brighter than my sword, than any fire from any of the nine realms. She pulled back from me but just slightly, so that when she spoke, I could feel her breath on my lips. "I love you, Havard."

I smiled and made her a different promise, one I could actually keep. "And I love you. I always will."

The book slipped from her hands as I kissed her, but neither of us retrieved it from the scattered hay on the stable floor. I had no use for men's legends anyway. The only story I cared about was here with me, and I knew how it would end. But the journey to get there would ultimately be my salvation.

~

ARNBJORG SHOT me a stern look and whispered, "You have to tell him."

"I will," I whispered back, perhaps a little defensively, but truthfully, I feared my sisters. And as soon as I told Yngvarr that Arnbjorg and I were getting married, he'd tell our sisters, and any involvement I thought I'd have in planning my own wedding would be over.

Yngvarr entered the dining hall and tossed a quiver onto the table. "You should have come with me, brother," he said. "The geese were so plentiful, I couldn't miss."

Arnbjorg scowled at me, obviously sensing I was losing my resolve again. I groaned and gave up before she could change her mind about marrying me after all. "Yngvarr, we have news."

He arched an eyebrow at me and waited, but the smile he gave me indicated he already knew. "Arnbjorg has agreed to marry me. We'll have a ceremony here in two weeks."

Yngvarr affected an air of confusion and innocence, so I groaned again, but that didn't stop him. "I don't understand, Arnbjorg. You've had a chance to live with him for over three months now, and you still want to marry him?"

"Don't tease your little brother," she scolded, but she smiled at him as she added, "And a thousand times yes."

"All right then," he laughed. "I'll save the teasing for when you're busy elsewhere."

I'd often thought Asgard itself had ears and delighted in whispering secrets to those you most wanted to hide truths from. As Freyja bounded into the dining hall, her gold bracelets jingling to announce her arrival, I could tell by the expression on her face that she'd overheard us discussing our engagement. She put a hand on her hip and cast a disgusted glance in Arnbjorg's direction before turning her attention to me. "I couldn't help but overhear," she purred. "Congratulations."

I bristled at the obvious condescension in her voice but took Arnbjorg's hand and smiled at the goddess whose affection I'd never return. "Thank you, Freyja. I hope you and Frey are able to attend."

"I wouldn't miss it," she said.

"Did you need something, Freyja?" Yngvarr interjected, and I thought again how grateful I was for my big brother, always looking out for me, always on my side.

"I came to extend an invitation to... well, I suppose your future wife," she cooed. Nothing about Freyja's presence here or her suspicious invitation sat well with me.

"An invitation to what?" I asked.

"To a gathering I'm hosting for the ladies of Asgard," she replied. In all the years I'd known her, she'd never hosted a gathering for only women.

Yngvarr laughed, obviously finding her party just as ridiculous. Freyja rarely regarded women as friends. "And who is attending this party?" he asked her. "Who in this realm have you not estranged?"

Freyja narrowed her eyes at him and crossed her arms defiantly. "Frigg and Idun have already accepted, and Gerd and I frequently visit one another."

"Your sister-in-law is one of the few women in Asgard who doesn't have to worry about you sleeping with her husband," Yngvarr muttered, so I kicked him under the table. I'd been thinking the same thing, but I didn't want to cause more tension between my bride and the goddess who viewed her as an obstacle to be overcome. Yngvarr yelped and glared at me, but I ignored him.

But Freyja ignored him as well. "I hope you'll join us, Arnbjorg," she said sweetly. Too sweetly. Freyja rarely did anything for anyone unless there was something in it for herself.

Arnbjorg was far too kind and gracious to refuse her though. "Thank you, my lady. I'm truly honored."

Freyja's smile broadened, and she gave Arnbjorg a time for the gathering before sweeping out of the dining hall in a musical exit. I exhaled slowly, still clinging to Arnbjorg's hand, but she'd accepted and there was nothing I could do to save her from Freyja's machinations.

She must have sensed the reason for my stormy mood because she kissed my cheek and told me, "Other goddesses will be there. It won't be so bad, Havard."

"Oh, Freyja's up to something," Yngvarr replied. "Just don't feel obligated to stay if you become uncomfortable. Return home and let us deal with her."

Arnbjorg nodded, but I doubted she would tell us the truth. It simply wasn't in her nature to be spiteful and to stir up animosities.

I should have known she was too good for a world like mine.

CHAPTER FIVE

Keira was mid-yawn as she opened her hotel room door. She looked me over quickly and sighed, stepping back to allow me inside. "Please don't tell me you've found the Sumerians *now*. It's two a.m."

"No," I said. "Just had a few questions and didn't really know who I could trust."

She gave me a funny look and gestured to the empty bed, indicating I could sit down if I wanted. Honestly, I felt a little weird about being in her room at all, but when I'd awakened, pissed off at a goddess who'd never given me any reason to be pissed off at her, Keira had been the first person I'd thought of to help me make sense out of Havard's memories. For some reason, I didn't want Yngvarr to know about this particular dream, although I suspected it had something to do with Havard never sharing the specifics of the prophecy regarding his death. Maybe in some indirect way, I also wanted to protect his brother from the truth.

"I know you don't like Freyja," I finally said. "But I guess I just need to know if you think she's capable of doing something truly despicable... like evil-level shit."

Keira had been about to sit on the opposite bed, but she stood up straight again and her fingers curled into fists. "What did she do?"

"I don't know," I admitted. "It was a dream." I shared the entire thing, from their encounter in the stables to Freyja's strange party, which was obviously some sort of ruse to get Arnbjorg away from Havard. Keira listened silently, but her face remained stony as if none of this surprised her. When I'd finished recounting the entire dream, she finally allowed her fingers to relax from the tight fists she'd kept by her sides and sat on the bed, staring at her fingernails for a few seconds before asking, "Why did you do it?"

"Um... wake you up in the middle of the night?" I mean, granted, it was pretty assholish of me to wake her up, but I thought she'd *want* to hear this.

But she shook her head and said, "*Her*. Why'd you sleep with her?"

"Oh," I breathed. She might as well have punched me in the stomach. It probably would have been less painful. "I don't know." That was it? That was the only excuse I could give her? When nothing else came to mind, I sighed and gave up. I honestly didn't even know how I felt about it. Mostly, I just regretted it.

Keira shrugged and tossed her blond hair over a shoulder as if it didn't matter, but by now, I knew better. And maybe I'd ruined whatever chance we might have had by sleeping with Freyja, but Keira couldn't pretend like those feelings didn't exist. "I'm not sure if she would have been capable of hurting Arnbjorg," she said. "Probably, but if her intention was to get rid of her competition, that wouldn't be the way to go. Havard would have been so furious, he would've sought revenge. And it's obvious by now that you're also descended from Arnbjorg or you wouldn't keep dreaming of her, too. Since they haven't had children yet, I'm pretty sure whatever

Freyja was really planning, it didn't kill Arnbjorg or drive her and Havard apart."

I thought about that then acknowledged she had to be right. "But it still doesn't seem innocent at all," I insisted.

"Oh, I'm sure it wasn't," Keira agreed. "But even Freyja's jealousy has its limits."

"Her lust for gold turned her into a war goddess," I argued. "That's not much of a limit."

Keira waved me off. "That's just a story. She was always a war goddess."

"If all of these memories are somehow etched into my DNA, why can't I extract them all at once?" I asked. "Getting snippets like this isn't helpful. In fact, it's just annoying as hell."

Keira shrugged. "I've never actually known anyone this has happened to. I've *heard* about it, but it's so rare..." She seemed to think about my situation then decided, "We'll go back to Odin, see if he can draw the memories out."

"No," I said. "I don't trust him."

"You don't trust *anyone*," she claimed.

"I trust you."

I couldn't quite tell in the dim light of her room, but I thought her cheeks might have darkened as she lowered her eyes again, refusing to hold my gaze for more than a few seconds at a time. "Keira, what's up with this prophecy of mine? You *all* seem to know something else about my fate and no one will tell me what it is. Freyja suggested I might die, but that's it."

"Knowing won't help you."

"How would you feel if everyone else knew something about your future but refused to share it?" She bit her lip but still said nothing, so I sighed angrily and demanded, "I'm going to die, aren't I? It's not a maybe, it's an absolute."

"Gavyn—"

"Just answer my question, Keira!" I yelled.

"Yes," she whispered.

I'd expected to hear my death had been predicted and was unavoidable, but actually *hearing* it still took my breath away as if I'd been body slammed by Thor himself. They'd known all along I wouldn't survive this ordeal, and yet, they'd come for me anyway. And now that I was here, my father and best friend and everyone I cared about was in danger even though I'd never wanted to be a hero.

We sat without speaking for a long time as I tried to process this not-exactly-revelatory revelation, and I couldn't help thinking of my mom and hearing similar words from her oncologist when the cancer returned, metastasized, untreatable. He gave her six months to live. She survived eight.

She'd known her fate, and for eight months, I watched her look at the world differently, as if all the little details held new discoveries and a kind of beauty she'd never noticed before. I doubted the world would look any different to me. And I doubted I could ever forgive Keira for withholding this information from me, for forcing me to accept a role I hadn't wanted and wouldn't have chosen for myself, for sealing my fate.

I finally stood up and murmured, "I'm going back to bed."

"Gavyn, I'm sorry," she said.

But I shook my head and wouldn't look at her. "No, you're not. If you'd really cared about my life, you would've left me alone."

"That's not fair," she cried. "We didn't have a choice! Don't you understand how many people would die?"

"Then *you* deal with the Sumerians," I snapped. "All you've done is drag innocent people into a war I never wanted to be a part of." Not only had we become pawns in their supernatural chess game, but the gods had decided for us that our lives were acceptable losses. And now, I had some dead god's memories harassing me, trying to pull me deeper into Asgard's secrets.

Well, not anymore. They'd try to stop me again, but this time, I wasn't coming back. What was the point? I was going to die anyway. I stormed down the hallway to Hunter's room and beat on the door until he pulled it open, scowling at me, his dark brown hair matted on one side and upright on the other. Cadros grunted at me and mumbled something about bad manners, but I ignored him and told Hunter to put on his shoes.

Cadros jumped out of bed and grabbed Hunter's arm before I could even enter their room. "What are you doing, Gavyn?" he asked.

"What do you think?" I said. "We're leaving."

"Um..." Hunter chimed in. "Is that really a good idea considering a bunch of pissed off gods are looking for you?"

"What difference does it make if I'm going to die anyway?" I retorted.

"Gavyn," Cadros started, but I wanted to hear his excuses even less than Keira's. I grabbed his wrist and twisted his arm, forcing him to let go of Hunter, then pushed him away from us. He stumbled and tripped over his boots, landing on the bed behind him. I snatched Hunter's shoes off the floor and nodded toward the door. But as we left, I called over my shoulder, "Tell your buddies not to follow me, because this time, I'll kill whoever gets in my way."

Hunter didn't speak to me until we were standing outside the hotel, freezing on the sidewalk as sleet stung our faces and arms. Neither of us had the coats we'd been given. A taxi pulled up to the doors, and I realized I didn't even have money for a cab. This was the worst escape plan ever.

"Think we can ponder our next move indoors some-where?" he asked. I shivered along with him and nodded.

We'd die of hypothermia long before the Sumerians had a chance to kill us.

But I didn't want to go back into the hotel, so we crossed the street to a diner that was still open. The waitress shot us a strange look, not that I could blame her considering we were out in the middle of the night without coats, and Hunter was actually wearing Superman pajamas. I wanted to give him a hard time about it, but I was too damn cold.

"Kaffi," I told the waitress. It was the only Icelandic word I'd learned here. She glanced between Hunter and me but brought two white porcelain cups and the carafe. I wondered if I could somehow send the check across the street to Keira's room.

Hunter leaned on the table and arched an eyebrow at me, silently asking me what the hell was going on. I sunk a little lower in my seat and mumbled, "I'm going to die."

"Okay," he said carefully. "Soon?"

I lifted a shoulder. "Soon enough... I'm not going to survive whatever's going on with the Sumerians." I wrapped my fingers around the cup of coffee to warm them. Not grabbing our coats had been one of the dumbest ideas I'd ever had, but in my defense, I hadn't known we were going to make a run for it again until I was beating on Hunter's door.

"What's your plan then? And what about your dad?"

"My plan is to get us away from all of these deified assholes."

"Is deified a word?"

"Of course it is," I said, but I wasn't actually sure.

But Hunter just nodded and asked, "Can we go somewhere warm? A tropical island with nude beaches is preferable."

"You realize all the guys will be naked, too, right?"

Hunter squinted at me and sighed. "Fine. Swimsuits required. But I still want some place tropical."

"We've got nothing, Hunter. No money, no identification, no allies. I don't actually know how to get us out of Iceland. I only knew I had to get away from them." I told him about Keira's admission regarding the prophecy of my death, how they'd always known and had still forced me here and thrown me into this battle with the Sumerians, simply because *they'd* wanted me to fight on their behalf. And while Freyja had suggested the same thing, she'd also told me it was only a possibility and that my future could always change.

"But it's just a prophecy," Hunter argued. "Maybe their seers aren't often wrong, but they *could* be."

I didn't have the heart to tell him I already knew they weren't wrong.

"Besides, it doesn't matter," he continued. "We'll go to the police and tell them the truth. If they get us home, we can get our passports and money and take off on our own."

I sunk even lower in my seat. "The Sumerians know who I am now. They'll follow me."

Hunter rolled his fingers across the table as he considered this. "Any chance we can steal the passports Agnes is using?"

I cringed as I imagined breaking into her room. "You're Celtic. You steal them."

"I'm not a demigod," he argued. "I can't overpower gods."

"Agnes hates me," I lied. "She'll curse me, or worse, she'll make a pass at me."

Hunter snorted as the bells above the diner door opened and a familiar face entered. I couldn't place him at first, but there were few people I would've recognized in Iceland, which meant he was connected to the gods across the street. He spotted me almost immediately, and approached our table, so I reflexively tensed, prepared to fight him so Hunter and I could escape yet again.

"What," I sneered, "they're hoping I'm less likely to kill a hero?"

"Something like that," he responded. I couldn't quite place his accent, but like most of the Norse heroes I'd met here, he had the trademark blond hair and light blue eyes like we'd been carved from the same Scandinavian stone. He motioned to the empty chair next to Hunter, and I grunted as an answer. The bastards had sent a human after me because they'd known I wouldn't kill him. But that didn't mean I was going to sit here and listen to him as he tried to convince me to go die in their war.

But the guy sat down anyway. "I'm Joachim," he said. "From Darmstadt."

"You say that like I should know where it is," I said.

He smiled and shrugged. "Germany. Descendant of Freyja, apparently."

I grimaced because I was sitting across from a guy who looked about my age but was descended from a woman I'd slept with. And there was no amount of brain bleach that could remove *this* knowledge. But Joachim just laughed and told me, "We all know about you two."

"There's nothing going on with us," I stubbornly insisted. "It was just a one-time thing. Okay, technically, a four time thing over the course of one day, but it was never going to happen again, even if I were staying."

"You know," Joachim said. "When she showed up at my apartment door and told me who she was and that I was descended from her, I didn't believe her at first either. Who *would?* And once she proved she was really a goddess, and I started to think she might be telling me the truth, I wanted to gouge my eyes out for having more than a few of the same thoughts you obviously had."

"Dude, your ancestor is like the Helen of Troy of the Norse world," Hunter interjected.

"How do you know who Helen of Troy is?" I shot back.

"Hey, I know things," he said. I crossed my arms and

waited and he finally gave up. "*Troy*. You watched it with me, dumbass."

"Gavyn," Joachim said, "just hear me out. If you want to leave, I'll go back to the hotel and get your things and you can go. No one will try to stop you. The only condition is that you listen to what I need to say."

We really didn't have any other option, but I pretended to think about it anyway and made a big show of reluctantly agreeing to his terms. I don't think we were fooling this German hero, but the guy seemed way too nice to call me on it. He just thanked me and poured his own cup of coffee before taking a deep breath, his eyebrows bunching together and his lips slightly moving as if he were trying to translate his speech in his head before launching into it.

Hunter and I shot each other our "What a whack-job" look, but Joachim must have pieced together all the right English words because he took a sip of his coffee then took another deep breath. "Gavyn, it's not only the Sumerians we have to worry about now. And if you leave... Look, I don't understand how they're so certain that you hold the key to saving the world, but they *are* sure of it. And we're here to help you with—"

"Wait," Hunter interrupted. "Back up. What do you mean it's not only the Sumerians that are worrisome?"

Joachim fidgeted with his coffee and offered me an apologetic glance. "The Egyptians have announced their alliance with the Sumerians. Apparently, they want to take their territory back. They have too many temples to just abandon Egypt altogether, but we can count on more pantheons demanding a return to our pagan pasts. This is going to blow up in our faces really soon."

"How long have you known about this?" I demanded. Just like Keira to keep more information from me. I sat there seething, feeling stupid that I'd actually come to trust her after she rescued my father and me then stayed by us in the hospital, not only for our protection but so that I wouldn't be alone. I wasn't sure if I was angry at how she'd been using me and toying with my emotions, or if I was sick over it.

But Joachim glanced at his watch then said, "About fifteen minutes. Gunnr just told me—"

"Keira," I corrected. As much as I'd hated her adopting my ex-girlfriend's name, it had stuck, and I had a hard time thinking of her as Gunnr now, which really *was* an unfortunate name.

"All right," he agreed slowly as if he were placating a toddler on the verge of throwing a tantrum, which honestly wasn't that far from the truth. "Keira got me up, told me I had to come talk to you and why, shared they'd just learned the Egyptians were starting to cause trouble, and that we *needed* you if we're to have any shot of defeating them."

I shook my head stubbornly. "What they *need* is someone expendable, some schmuck they can send into heavy fire and distract their enemies while they sneak in unnoticed."

"First of all," Hunter said, "you watch too many movies. And secondly, you're way too Southern to say 'schmuck.'"

"I didn't realize my vocabulary was limited by geography," I retorted.

Hunter nodded. "Just like you can't say 'bloody hell.'"

"I *do* say that."

"Yeah, but you *shouldn't*."

"Um..." Joachim cleared his throat and squirmed in his seat as he waited for us to remember he was still there.

"I'm not going back," I told him. "Now, I've heard you out. Please bring us our coats and passports... and go dig through Agnes's purse. See if she has any money."

"Agnes..." he repeated.

"Badb," Hunter explained.

"No way," Joachim said. "I'm not crossing that woman.

She'll probably put a curse on me, and hell, my entire country, and honestly, we did a good enough job cursing ourselves. We don't need her help."

I snickered and thought if our circumstances had been different, I would've actually liked this guy. I mean, he'd probably try to get me to sit through a soccer match, but it's not like Hunter hadn't tried at *least* a hundred times and I usually forgave him. "Okay," I agreed. "Avoid Agnes. That's probably good advice for the rest of the time you're with these people. Dig through Keira's purse."

Joachim nodded and pulled out his wallet, producing a few bills to pay for the coffee, but he didn't get up. He flipped open the photo sleeves and passed it across the table, jutting his chin toward the photo on the right. "My daughter. She just turned three. Her name is Ada and she's obsessed with *Mia and Me*, and anything on wheels. She must have a hundred toy cars."

He extended his hand and I placed his wallet back into it. What was he doing? Resorting to emotional blackmail? But Joachim put his wallet away, and with it, the picture of the beautiful little girl with blond curls and round, pink cheeks and a sunflower yellow dress, a picture-perfect child that could have been painted by whomever the German Norman Rockwell was. "I don't know if I'll see her again," he said. "But I know I can't go home. I can't risk losing. That's not the world she deserves."

He stood up and promised he'd return soon with our things, but the sinking feeling in my stomach already assured me we wouldn't be needing them.

Because I got it, what I would have to do and why.

It was my life for theirs.

CHAPTER SIX

Keira kept trying to get my attention so she could apologize and convince me to forgive her for not telling me I would never be going home, but I wouldn't give her the satisfaction of a clear conscience. I pretended to be immensely interested in Frey's presentation on the Egyptian gods who'd joined the ranks of Asshole Evil Gods Intent on Subversion, or AEGIS for short. And yeah, I'd totally just made that up, but since I'd also recently learned what aegis *was* in the world of Greek gods, I wanted to use it as often as possible.

Frey hadn't assembled us in a conference room but the indoor training area. I noticed Joachim stealing glances in my direction, but I ignored him, too. I wondered if Keira had told him about my prophecy and that by guilting me back into this war, he was just as complicit in my death as she was. Frey occasionally shot me irritated looks, like he knew I wasn't paying attention to his Egyptian god profiles, but honestly, what did he expect? I hadn't yet proven capable of paying attention to anything for more than two minutes.

Frey suddenly stopped speaking, and I realized I hadn't

actually paid attention to *any* of his lecture. A god I hadn't seen since Hunter and I were picked up at the police station approached the weapons' table, selected a bow and quiver, and waited by the archery range. What *was* this god's name? And why were we all standing around to watch his target practice?

"One of these days," I thought, *"I should really learn how to listen when other people are speaking."*

"Archery is one of our best defenses against the Egyptians," Frey said. "It's unlikely you'll be able to get close to them if Menhit is around."

"Why?" I asked. The heavy sighs and impatient shuffling of feet from the heroes and gods told me Frey had already explained all of this.

"Because," he said slowly, "her arrows ignite and her fires spread preternaturally fast."

I wanted to ask what "preternaturally" meant but decided to just use context clues instead. I mean, I'd already been dubbed the village idiot so it's not like I would've changed anyone's opinion of me by asking, but by now, I was curious as to why the god whose name I couldn't remember was standing around with a bow and quiver full of arrows because if all of *his* ignited in the air, that was actually worth being dragged into the training center and having to tune out an entire lecture on Egyptian gods no one had ever heard of.

But my hope that I'd get to see fiery arrows was quickly dashed when Frey said, "We can't fight fire with fire, so our best hope is to kill Menhit first. And the *only* way we're going to do that is by expert archery." He waved a hand toward the god holding the bow and continued, "Ull is one of our best archers. I'd like you each to work with him until you can shoot almost as well as he can."

No wonder I couldn't remember this guy's name. Out of all the gods I'd met, he'd definitely drawn the short stick when it came to names. But Ull pulled an arrow from the quiver, nocked it, and released. He'd moved onto the next target before his arrow embedded into the center of the bullseye. By the time he'd moved onto the third, his second arrow had also hit the center of the target. Down the row of paper circles, twelve in all, he drew an arrow and released it, never once missing his mark. It took him less than a minute to demonstrate he had *preternaturally* excellent aim and *preternatural* speed.

I raised my hand, mostly to be a smartass, and waited for Frey to notice. When he did, he groaned and rubbed his temple like I was giving him a migraine. "Gavyn... what?"

"Just thought I'd point out I'm not a god. I can't move that quickly. And you've seen me shoot arrows. Unless this goddess lives underground, I'm the wrong man for the job."

"You *can* move that quickly and you have," Frey reminded me. "And you don't need to be as perfect as Ull. He has thousands of years of experience. You just need to be good."

I snorted because that still seemed like a tall order.

"Fine," Frey sighed. "Just don't kill any of us, okay?"

"I'm not making any promises," I replied.

Tyr handed me a bow and pointed to a target at the archery range. "Trust me. You don't want to find yourself close enough to Menhit to fight her with a sword. If she's not shooting fiery arrows at you, she's morphed into a vicious lion, and—"

"Wait, she's *what*?" I interrupted.

Tyr blinked at me then ran his good hand over his face. "Did you listen to *anything* Frey just said?"

"Did you just meet me?" I retorted.

Behind me, Thor laughed and clapped my back. "I'm glad you decided to return, Gavyn. Would've been... quiet without you around."

I squinted at him and mumbled, "And I'm so glad all of

you have shown up now. Except your father. That asshole's *still* hiding in Asgard."

I thought Thor would be offended, but he just shrugged and handed his demigod a bow. "He'll be here when we need him. Considering he governs all of Asgard, he can't just leave whenever he wants."

"Never stopped him whenever he wanted to get laid," I said.

"Gavyn, enough," Keira scolded.

But I wouldn't turn around to scowl at her. I pulled an arrow from the quiver Tyr was holding and shot it at the target then watched as my arrow sailed gracefully over the top and into the tarps hanging behind the row of targets. "Well," Tyr offered, "at least you didn't massacre the ground again."

I nodded and took another arrow from him. Ull, who was working his way through all of the practicing heroes, stopped beside me and corrected my stance then asked me to show him my form. "Keep your elbow straight," he instructed. "Draw your string to the same anchor point each time." I'd heard these tips before, of course, but Ull moved around me, studying my feet, my fingers as they kept the string pulled back, turning my elbow just slightly so that it was in optimal position, feeling the tension in both the string and my back. When he told me to shoot, the arrow actually hit the board— not the bullseye, of course, but considering I'd never even hit the target, I was counting this as a win.

"Good," he said. "Now, the key to archery is consistency. You pulled to the left when you released because you allowed your elbow to rotate just slightly. Try it again."

I focused on the bullseye through the sight-pin and released. "Still pulling to the left," I said.

Ull nodded. "But it's better."

I glanced at Tyr and said, "So... this Egyptian goddess. Is

she like the Nemean lion? Will we need to resurrect Hercules?"

"Heracles," Keira and Tyr corrected at the same time. "And no," Tyr added. "Although I'm terribly curious as to how you know anything at all about the Nemean lion."

I lowered my bow to flip him off, although I wasn't sure how I knew that either. Maybe I hadn't slept through as many of my college classes as I'd thought. "Just want to make sure I'm getting this right," I said. "She's just a regular lion then?"

But Tyr shook his head. "Still a goddess. What kills her doesn't change just because she looks different."

"Damn," I sighed. A few targets over from me, Joachim was shooting arrow after arrow into the target, many of them even hitting the center. Freyja stood smiling beside him as if she were taking credit for her progeny's ability to shoot consistently well. She caught me watching them and winked at me, so I set my jaw and glared at the target I was supposed to be impaling.

After what felt like hours of target practice, a hush fell over the room, so naturally, I turned to see what was so fascinating. Agnes, stooped in her black shawl and looking as weak as any nine-hundred-year-old witch, hefted a quiver over her shoulder and snatched a bow off the table. She shuffled to the targets and waved a hand irritably at the hero who'd been practicing there. He scurried out of her way and Agnes lifted her chin as if telling us all, "Now watch as this old hag shows you up. Pansies."

And we did. Arrow after arrow, her arms reaching and pulling and releasing in a blur of black fabric, the center of the target transforming into a porcupine whose quills amassed thicker and thicker. She never faltered or slowed or missed her mark, and when her quiver was empty, she simply dropped it and the bow to the floor, turned around, and shuffled out of the training center.

The room had fallen into an awed silence, so of course, I just *had* to break it. "New plan. We send Agnes into battle with the Egyptians. If she can't kill the lion goddess with arrows, she can just show them her face and they'll turn to stone."

Tyr shot me a funny look and said, "You know a surprising amount of Greek mythology."

"What does that have to do with Greek mythology?" I asked back, completely deadpan.

Tyr's mouth hung open for a moment before he realized I was just messing with him.

Frey, apparently sensing we were getting too close to enjoying ourselves, clapped his hands loudly and redirected everyone's attention to the targets. I obliged but only because I wanted it to end. There was a beer in the lobby's bar that had my name on it.

By the time Frey released us from practice, though, my arms and back were killing me, and I decided to skip the beer and just go to bed. But Keira caught up to me in the hallway and grabbed my arm, and she was back to being the freakishly strong woman whose iron-grip was completely emasculating.

"Gavyn, are you ever going to listen to my apology?"

"I already heard it." I tried to free my arm, but she had her Magic Death Grip on. I only managed to rip a few hairs out of my forearm.

"Your prophecy isn't exactly easy for me to accept either," she claimed. "Do I need to remind you what I do?"

"So bringing my soul to Valhalla is somehow just as bad as actually *dying*?" I snapped. How could she even *compare* the two?

"No," she said softly. "But watching you die and knowing I can't stop it... I don't want this fate either."

I imagined being in her place, and yeah, it was a shitty future to look forward to, but it still didn't excuse her silence.

And yet, I sensed something loosening within me as if the anger I'd been tightly holding onto was slowly unwinding. "Are these prophecies *ever* wrong?" I finally asked her.

She lowered her eyes and let go of my arm. I knew her answer before she even said it. "No."

"Right," I sighed.

"Sometimes, they can be confusing because they have multiple meanings, but there aren't many ways to interpret death."

"And is there any chance y'all could have won without me?"

They'd insisted all along they *needed* me for some reason, but I still couldn't imagine why. They'd found dozens of heroes, most of whom had eagerly accepted their roles in this supernatural civil war. "Not according to the seer," Keira answered. "She insisted we needed you. You won't be the only hero to fall in combat, Gavyn. It's a burden we're *all* bearing."

It had never even occurred to me that she might know the fates of other heroes. I exhaled slowly and ran my fingers through my hair as I glanced toward the training room's door. "Joachim?" I asked quietly. But I was picturing his daughter.

And for the first time in what felt like a long time, Keira offered me good news. "He'll make it home."

"How do you do this?" I asked. "How do you train people and send them into battle knowing they'll die?"

"I've only ever had to do this twice before," she explained. "When they fall, I bring them to either Valhalla or Fólkvangr—"

"To *where*?" I interrupted.

"It's Freyja's realm for fallen soldiers."

I gaped at her for a second before hissing, "You never told me I could end up in *her* clutches forever."

Keira folded her arms over her chest and hissed back,

"Didn't seem like you *minded* being in her clutches a week ago."

Okay, she had me there. But I was apparently destined to spend an eternity—or however long we had before the end of the world—in either Odin's or Freyja's Hall of the Damned... er, Dead... and neither seemed like a good option to me. But Keira's expression softened and she loosened her arms. "Fölkvangr isn't so bad, Gavyn. Just because Freyja rules over it doesn't mean she'll have any more power over you than she does now."

I snorted and rubbed my tired eyes. "And what makes you think she has no power over me now?"

Keira lowered her eyes and lifted a shoulder in response. I hadn't meant to make her feel worse, but I was *so* tired and sore and I just wanted a hot shower and sleep. And I wanted *not* to think about my prophecy or what it would mean for me for a little while.

"I'll see you tomorrow, Keira," I sighed. "After all, I haven't seen you shoot yet. It'll give me something to look forward to." She smiled and this time, when I headed for the exit, she didn't stop me. But as usual, I was wrong. We'd never step foot in our training center again.

CHAPTER SEVEN

Yngvarr whispered my name and shook my shoulder, so naturally, I rolled over and tried to ignore him. But he shook me again and whispered, "Gavyn, get up! We've got company." I groaned and sat up, thinking Tyr or Frey had shown up in the middle of the night for a surprise training session, which honestly, would've been pretty stupid since there was a high enough risk of me hurting someone when I was fully awake.

"Who?" I muttered. I didn't hear anything. Apparently, our late-night visitors were Ninja Gods.

"Egyptians," he said quietly.

For the first time, I noticed he held his sword. I threw the blankets off me, and like Frey in New Orleans, he somehow grabbed another sword from its invisible hiding place. I slipped my shoes on in case we ended up chasing these midnight assassins through the icy streets then followed him to the door where he listened for a moment, but I still didn't hear anything.

He glanced at me and mouthed, "Count of three." I nodded as he reached for the door handle. I should've been terrified about the possibility of fighting a lion goddess with magical arrows that ignited in the air, but mostly, I just wondered if she could shoot those arrows while in lion form and if so, *how*? And would she eat people while a lion? Is that how I was going to die? I didn't even know which god would have the honor of killing me, but if a supernatural lion ate me, I was going to be seriously pissed off. I mean, the dead heroes gathering at Odin's banquet every night probably had these kickass stories with epic sword fights and impressive spear throwing and Xerxes-level amazing archery battles, and I'd be like, "Yeah, a lion bit my face off."

No way. I was going to die with an epic story to tell, too.

Yngvarr pulled the door open and I hurried into the hall-way, suddenly sensing I wasn't alone out there. I spun around and found myself staring into the chillingly vacant eyes of a man with a dark beard and a spear in one hand and a pistol in the other.

Also on my list of ways I refused to die: I was *not* getting shot. If I had to become one of these heroes who fought gods, I wanted a better story than *that*. I swung my blade at his left hand, which held the pistol, but he was remarkably fast. I only managed to open a gash on his wrist. Behind me, Yngvarr clashed with another god that had emerged from the stairwell, and even though I kinda knew an ancient-weapons fight was no time to be a smartass, it didn't stop me. "Dude, what kind of asshole brings a pistol to a fight when he knows his opponent will only have a sword?"

The Egyptian god arched an eyebrow at me and said, "Someone who intends to win."

I was outsmartassed. Not cool.

"That's Anhur, Gavyn," Yngvarr called out to me. "Be careful. He can also take the form of a lion."

I grunted at Anhur, but he obviously didn't want to hear my objections. He raised the pistol, so I lunged again, and the tip of my blade nicked his palm. I had to pivot and swing again at his other hand that held the spear, and he stepped back but didn't drop either weapon. By now, more bodies were pouring into the hallway from the elevator and stairwell, most of whom were likely demigods, but the Norse and Celtic gods and heroes were also emerging from their rooms.

All along the hallway, people shouted in different languages, and bodies slammed into walls as they were pushed or attempted to avoid an attack. But my attention was on this god who'd led the invasion into our sanctuary. After all, we were in *Iceland*. I figured no one would bother looking for us here because who willingly goes to *Iceland*? Admittedly, it had been disappointingly free of ice, but still.

Anhur offered me a smug smile as he inched toward the exit. His own heroes kept getting in my way so I knew I'd lose sight of him soon. But we were in a confined space. With two demigods standing in front of me, brandishing their own swords and eyeing me like a serpopard that needed to be beheaded—don't ask me how I knew about serpopards— Anhur would get away.

I stabbed the demigod closest to me just as Keira appeared at my side to fend off the other Egyptian hero whose sword almost provided the end to my story, but at least I wouldn't have been shot or eaten by a lion. I kicked the body of the slain demigod away from me and chased Anhur, who was slinking into the dimly lit stairwell. But Keira reached me before I could follow him. "Wait," she said, grabbing my arm. "It could be a trap. I haven't seen Menhit here."

I had visions of an entire pride of lions with human eyes waiting for me on the stairs and grimaced. Some of the Egyptian heroes began to retreat into the opposite stairwell but not before a gunshot made my heart leap into my throat. I pushed my way through bodies struggling against each other until the young man's body became visible. Outside the hotel, sirens wailed and the remaining Egyptian gods, who seemed pissed at *us* for not staying asleep while they snuck in and massacred everyone, shouted at their demigods then retreated into both stairwells.

With only the Norse and Celts left, I glanced down the hallway for a body count. Agnes, who'd joined the fight as her young, beautiful redheaded self, beat on Hunter's door, telling him it was time to leave. When he opened the door, he looked shaken and sick. "Will you go to Asgard now?" I asked.

But Agnes answered for him. "I'm taking him to the Otherworld. He'll be safe there."

I wanted to argue with her, to insist he was brought to a world I could at least get to, but Hunter met my eyes and shrugged. "Remember: it was just a prophecy, Gavyn. I'll see you when this is all over. We'll go to Vegas and get completely and totally shitfaced."

I swallowed something painful because I knew the prophecy was right. I'd never actually be seeing him again. But I couldn't tell him that now, not when he was finally agreeing to get off this planet and somewhere safe. Instead, I just smiled and said, "Not sure we're allowed back into Vegas."

"True," he acknowledged. "But maybe you being the hero of the world and all will buy us some goodwill."

"All right," I pretended to agree. "But no tequila this time."

"Deal," he immediately said. Agnes had been watching me, knowing there was no maybe about this prediction, but she didn't betray me. She just took my best friend's arm and disappeared in that way that apparently only worked when gods were traveling between worlds. I stared at the empty doorway, suddenly overwhelmed with self-pity, and whispered, "Goodbye, *Julian*."

Keira touched my hand, reminding me she was still with me, and nodded toward one of the bodies on the floor. "I need to take him home."

I didn't want her to leave. It seemed like everyone I cared about was leaving me. Keira took a deep breath and squeezed my fingers. "Come with me," she suggested.

"Where?" I asked stupidly.

"Valhalla," she answered. "Maybe if you see what it's really like, it won't scare you so much."

She was still holding my hand and standing so close to me that I was convinced she could have asked me to lay down my life right there and I would have. So even though part of me didn't want to venture anywhere near Valhalla, I agreed. Keira let go of me and knelt beside the body of the fallen hero and brushed his sandy blond hair off his forehead. "Are you ready?" she asked him.

Honestly, I half expected this guy, who was obviously dead, to sit up and answer her but nothing happened. She stood up and held out her hand, but she wasn't reaching for me. And suddenly, I was no longer standing in a hotel's hallway but at the base of a brightly colored bridge that spanned a deep chasm, so deep I couldn't see what waited at the bottom. It might have been a river or Hell itself. Trying to find the bottom made me dizzy though, so I backed away from the ledge... and into the dead hero.

Except he wasn't dead anymore. Not really. He was standing and the bloody wound on his chest where he'd been shot was gone. He nodded toward the chasm and in thickly accented English asked, "What's down there?"

"Um..." I stammered. Great. The village idiot was back. "You're dead."

I was going to need a *much* thicker book of dumbest-things-ever-said.

But he just nodded. "Apparently."

"Gavyn, this is Bernt," Keira said. "And you once wanted to cross the Rainbow Bridge, so start walking."

"Why now?" I asked. "Why not show up at the gate like last time?"

"It's a symbolic journey," she said.

"And what if I refuse to take your symbolic journey when *I* die?" I retorted.

Keira rolled her eyes and mumbled, "That wouldn't surprise me at all."

But Bernt didn't seem overly anxious to march across the bridge either. He eyed the chasm warily and said, "I don't like heights. Do we *have* to take the bridge?"

"Would you rather go across on a flying horse?" Keira asked.

Bernt blinked at her then blinked at me. "I'm taking the bridge."

"Good call," I agreed.

We began the trek across the bridge, at first walking down the middle but soon veering toward the right side so we'd have something to hold onto. About halfway across, I became convinced something was moving beneath the bridge and managed to freak out Bernt who joined in my chorus of, "I never signed up to fight trolls!"

Keira shot me a look that I interpreted as regret, and I almost asked her why she'd expected me to be any different than usual on this trip but I didn't want her to leave me alone on the troll bridge. So I flashed her a sheepish grin and pointed to the blackness below us. "I'm just saying there *could* be a troll down there."

"There are no trolls in Asgard," she repeated for the third time.

I jerked a thumb over my shoulder to the bank we'd just left. "What's that land? Maybe there are trolls in it."

"Gavyn," she groaned.

Bernt glanced over the side of the bridge again and shook his head. "I should've taken the flying horse."

Keira put a hand on my back and pushed me toward Asgard. "When it's your turn, I'm not giving you the choice," she muttered. "You're going on horse."

"Don't blame you," I told her.

Bernt was the first of us to step foot on the grassy bank outside the massive wall, and even though he was technically just a spirit, I could've sworn color returned to his face once he was on solid ground again. Part of me regretted never getting to know him while he'd been alive. I suspected we'd have gotten along well. As I joined him by the gate, I glanced back toward the Rainbow Bridge, which looked suspiciously like the Golden Gate Bridge if someone had tie-dyed it. "I don't know what that was supposed to symbolize other than one last emasculating journey for Asgard's heroes."

Bernt nodded solemnly. "I'm dead anyway. Probably don't really need my balls."

"I dunno. I'd like to keep mine when I die," I said.

Heimdall opened the gate and squinted at me like I was already on Asgard's short list of miscreants. To be fair, I probably was and I totally deserved it. "Odin's waiting for you," he told Bernt. As we entered the gate into Asgard, I heard him whispering to Keira, "Why is Gavyn here?"

"Poor judgment on my part," she replied.

Bernt snickered and grinned at me. "No offense, but I'm kinda glad you'll be joining me soon. Not sure how much I'll have in common with demigods who've been dead for centuries."

"I hadn't even thought of that," I admitted.

"Eventually," Keira explained, "everyone who fights with us now will get the chance to come here, even if they die of old age many years from now. It's their reward for helping us when we needed them."

The golden spires of Valhalla reflected the light across Asgard, creating the illusion of a brilliant sunrise. As we reached the top of a hill that overlooked Odin's palace for the dead, I noticed Valhalla wasn't just one castle but a village of homes and squares and its famous field where men and women both fought and played a game that looked an awful lot like soccer. Keira took Bernt's hand and smiled as she looked over Valhalla. "Welcome home, Bernt."

Bernt's eyes had widened as he took in what I'd soon learn was actually an entire city of the dead. Paths wound from the hilltop through the maze of houses and dining halls to the golden palace at the center where Odin presided over his fallen heroes. A woman's voice called out to us in a language I didn't speak, and yet, I somehow understood her. There were few moments in my life I'd been truly speechless, so much so that even vodka wouldn't have loosened my tongue, but this was one of them.

The woman, who must've been another Valkyrie because she looked so much like Keira, waved us over and we followed Keira wordlessly. Bernt had apparently forgotten how to speak as well. Keira introduced us to the Valkyrie named Hildr, who I secretly decided to call Heidi partly because it was easier to remember and partly because she was every bit as hot as Heidi Klum, and she offered to show Bernt around since Keira was babysitting me. Before Bernt could walk away, I forced my mouth to start working again and promised him I'd find him as soon as I came back here, assuming the next time I was in Valhalla I wouldn't be leaving again.

And then Keira and I were alone in a breathtaking city, a tribute to the Norse's war dead. She pointed to a row of houses near the field where mock battles and the soccer match were taking place and said, "That's where we live. The Valkyries."

"You live in Valhalla?" I said.

"Of course. Our whole reason for existing is to bring our heroes home when they die, so why wouldn't we live here with them?"

"I don't know," I admitted. "I guess I just assumed you lived among the other gods."

Keira fidgeted with the hem of her shirt like this topic had suddenly made her uncomfortable. "But we're not gods, Gavyn. We've never really belonged in their world or yours. This is the only place I've ever felt at peace."

I looked out at her home again and offered her what I hoped was a reassuring smile. "You have a beautiful home, Keira. I mean that."

"You know, you're a likable guy when you're not being a pain in the ass," she teased.

"So... you never really like me then," I teased back.

Keira laughed, and I felt kinda awful and very much like the selfish asshole I could definitely be when I realized it was the first time I'd ever seen her really happy. I mean, sure she'd always had a lot on her mind with the Sumerians and all the tragedies they'd been inflicting on us, but I was only just now seeing that part of her always felt out of place, like she was literally trying to exist in a world that was completely hostile and foreign to her.

"Okay, *Gunnr*," I said. "You've got me here. Show me around."

"Keira," she corrected, but she was still smiling, and I found myself thinking I'd do anything to keep it that way, even though that would require me dying.

I let her lead me through Valhalla and was even on my best behavior as she introduced me to other Valkyries, which basically meant I never intentionally embarrassed her. Someone put a sword in my hand and spurred me onto the battlefield where I fought some of Asgard's best swordsmen.

None of them believed me when I told them I'd never even held a sword until ten days ago.

As the sky turned to twilight, the games ended and friends and lovers found each other as they headed toward the giant dining hall. I assumed Keira and I would return to Earth now, but she pulled me along with the crowd, claiming she wanted me to experience all the wonders of Valhalla. But I suspected she was really just reluctant to leave and feel so out of place again.

As we stepped into the hall, I immediately recognized the smell but couldn't place it—a comforting scent, like rain on asphalt, because it reminded me of home. Tables stretched endlessly through the hall, already filling with the men and women who gathered here every evening, and as soon as they sat down, someone set a bowl and stein on the table in front of them.

"There must be thousands of people in here," I murmured.

"Yeah," Keira said. "Every demigod who's ever died on our behalf. Only the bravest join us here."

Despite the voices that accompanied those thousands of bodies, the noise inside the hall wasn't deafening and I could easily hear Keira when she spoke to me. It was as much a mystery as how everybody could be served so quickly. "Here," she said, pointing to two empty chairs at a table where mostly Valkyries had gathered. I sat across from Heidi and before I could even introduce myself to the Valkyries I hadn't met yet, a bowl and stein with dark ale in it appeared in front of me. I blinked stupidly at it as if the food would suddenly explain how it got there. Keira mistook my expression for confusion over what I was about to eat.

"Lapskaus," she explained. "It's a favorite around here."

That was the comforting, familiar smell, although I'd never had this particular kind of stew, which looked a lot better than the name implied. But this scent wasn't from my own memories. I dragged my spoon through the bowl, slightly unsettled by how normal everything in Valhalla already felt, like I was just considering moving to Tampa or something. And for some reason, I thought of Havard and asked, "Where do gods go when they die?"

Keira sipped her ale and shrugged. "Nobody knows. Maybe the same place humans go."

"So gods aren't reincarnated or anything," I said.

"I don't think so. We have legends about certain people being reborn, but it's not something we believe happens regularly." She seemed to sense I didn't like the idea of rebirth at all and gently touched my arm. "Gavyn, Havard is gone. It's only his memories haunting you."

I glanced at her fingers resting on my arm and asked, "Keira, what's going on between us?"

She quickly moved her hand away from me and shook her head, but she wouldn't meet my eyes. "Nothing."

"It's never been *nothing*," I argued.

"That's exactly what it is," she insisted. "I don't want you to feel that way about me."

I sighed, frustrated and hurt, and pushed my chair away from the table. I was no longer hungry at all. "I'll be waiting outside. I'm ready to go home."

Even as I said it, I thought, "*But I am home.*"

I leaned against the side of the dining hall as the cool night air of Valhalla caressed my skin. Lights from within formed warm swaths across the grass, and from the stables at the far end of the village, I heard a horse neigh. And I remembered.

HAVARD'S MEMORY SCARS ME FOR LIFE

(And I learn I need to kick Yngvarr's ass)

When Arnbjorg returned, she wouldn't tell me about Freyja's party, not even what she and the goddesses had discussed. And although she *looked* perfectly fine, happy even, I just knew Freyja was up to something and would attempt to ruin our wedding or hurt the woman I loved. "Won't you even tell me if she discussed our engagement?" I tried again.

"She did," Arnbjorg said. "They toasted our upcoming wedding and welcomed me to Asgard. Honestly, Havard, you're acting like she's conspiring to have us killed."

"Not killed," I clarified. "Just unhappy. She'll have it rain all day for our wedding or—"

But Arnbjorg laughed and cut me off. "Without rain, crops would never grow. If it rains all day, we'll consider it a sign of the many children we'll be blessed with. Now go to Ljósálfar with your brother before you drive me crazy with your worrying."

I smiled at her and kissed her forehead. "We'll be back in a few days," I promised. "Are you *sure* you don't mind me leaving?"

From the doorway behind me, Yngvarr groaned and said, "Give the poor girl three days without you. It's a wedding present to *her*."

"Don't tease him like that," Arnbjorg scolded. "And take care of him, Yngvarr."

"Always," he laughed.

I kissed her hand one last time before following my brother to the stables. We'd decided to take one last hunting trip together, hoping that I would soon not have the time for such frivolities. Arnbjorg and I dreamed about having a large family, and once I became a father, I wouldn't leave them for pastimes, even innocent ones like this. I would always be in Asgard for my wife and children, unlike my own father. And they would never doubt how deeply I loved them.

It had been Yngvarr's idea to spend a few days in Ljósál-far, one of his favorite realms. Mortals had somehow gotten the idea it was a world populated with elves, but we'd never encountered those creatures anywhere. Still, it was a beautiful land with rolling green hills and thick forests, and we could hunt in the woods and eat roasted venison at night and never be disturbed by another god or mortal.

We walked our horses to the gate where we told Heimdall our intentions and he waved us through. Truthfully, I'd never been clear as to *how* the same Rainbow Bridge could bring us to different lands, but I assumed it was part of Heimdall's power over travel and his guardianship of Asgard. Outside the walls, we mounted our stallions and rode across the bridge to Ljósálfar.

A procession of men who looked starved and battle-weary slowed our progress. Most of them didn't give us a second glance, and I thought, "*They won't survive another fight in this shape.*" Sigurd stamped his feet impatiently as we waited for the procession to end. Yngvarr noticed her first, and he motioned to the beautiful redhead who stood on the other side of the retreating army. She wore a sword at her hip and a quiver on her back, but her clothes were pristine as if they'd never seen battle.

"War goddess," I whispered. "Think she chose the wrong side here?"

"Don't know," Yngvarr whispered back. "Their enemy might be in far worse shape."

The goddess stared across the river of men at us, as if she knew who we were and didn't like us infringing on her land. As the last man passed, she waited, watching us, and Yngvarr sighed. "I'll go explain why we're here."

But I wasn't going to let him go alone.

We were careful not to get too close to her, but she never flinched and her feet seemed permanently rooted to the ground. Admittedly, she intimidated me, and I was more than a little envious of her fierce presence. "My lady," Yngvarr said.

She narrowed her eyes at him and said, "Norse. What are you doing here?"

"We're only here to hunt."

"You have your own piece of the world in which to hunt. This is mine."

"We have no intention of interfering in your affairs," Yngvarr promised. "And we'll be gone in a few days."

She tossed her fiery hair over a shoulder and kept her scrutiny on my brother, which made me nervous. "Who are you?" she finally asked.

"Yngvarr and this is my brother, Havard. And we recognize this is the domain of the Tuatha Dé."

The goddess's emerald green eyes flickered briefly toward me before settling on Yngvarr again. "There's an inn over that hill. You can see the smoke rising from its chimney. I'll be there tonight. Ask for Badb."

Yngvarr smiled at the goddess and raised an eyebrow but told her he'd come as she asked then she turned and followed the retreating army without so much as a glance in my direction again. I blinked at her back as my mind scrambled to catch up to the unexpected turn of events. And when it did, I started laughing, so Yngvarr laughed, too. "Brother," I said, "you'll leave hearts broken across all nine worlds."

Yngvarr affected an air of solemnity and insisted, "I have no intention of breaking this beautiful goddess's heart. She requested my company, and she shall have it."

"Come on then," I said. "Let's hunt before you're summoned to her bed."

"Badb," he said thoughtfully. "You know, I think she has sisters."

"Have you forgotten I'm getting married next week?"

"But you're not married *yet*."

I rolled my eyes at him and nodded toward the forest. "I am as good as married to her, and I'll remain faithful for the rest of my life. Now, are we hunting or not?"

We left our stallions by a stream and crept through the woods with our bows, bringing down a magnificent stag that we cleaned and roasted early since Yngvarr was completely serious about meeting Badb at the inn. When I awoke in the morning, I saw him sleeping on the other side of the fire pit and roused him, asking him if she'd been so dissatisfied she wouldn't even let him stay the night.

"No, you ass," he muttered, but he smiled even though he cursed me. "The soldiers moved on early this morning, and she went with them. We're going to meet again tonight if we head in the same direction, so she hardly seems dissatisfied to me."

"Be careful, brother. A scorned goddess is far more dangerous than a mortal woman," I warned.

"I have no intention of causing her to hate me."

"So you won't break her heart by a refusal to commit?"

"Havard," he sighed, "if anyone's heart is in danger, it's my own."

I'D NEVER BEEN SO glad to see my palace as when I returned from that hunting trip, not because I hadn't enjoyed myself but simply because of how much I'd missed Arnbjorg. I swept her into my arms and kissed her and she laughed, a magical sound. I didn't want to let her go, but I had a present for her and had been anxious to give it to her. I pulled the golden torc from my bag and held it out to her.

"We met a goddess while there," I said. "Yngvarr is quite taken by her. She asked me if I was interested in meeting one of her sisters, so I told her all about you and that my heart and body only belonged to you now. She was so impressed by your bravery that she gave me her torc as a gift for you."

"A goddess wanted me to have this?" she gasped. Her fingers danced over the golden braids, and I smiled as I watched her. She was still so oblivious to how extraordinary she was.

"Not just any goddess," I said. "Badb, the most fierce and powerful of the Morrigna, a triune of war goddesses who can strike fear into the hearts of men far faster than I can."

Arnbjorg smiled mischievously back at me. "Well, no wonder Yngvarr is so enamored with her then."

I laughed because she was right—Badb was certainly beautiful, but Yngvarr had been most attracted to her strength. Arnbjorg put the torc around her neck and admired it in the mirror for a moment then turned back toward me. "The past few days while you were gone, I regretted not setting your mind at ease regarding Freyja. She'd asked me to keep our conversation private, and I didn't want to betray her trust."

I tensed as I waited for Arnbjorg to tell me what despicable words Freyja had thrown her way, but she took my hand
and gently squeezed it. "She cannot be my friend, but she has
vowed not to be my enemy either. You shouldn't fear her,
Havard. She won't harm me. The party she held was partly a
gesture of peace between us."

I was certain my expression must have conveyed my
confusion, because I felt terribly confused. "But why can't she
be your friend if she's willing to go through the effort of a
party to make peace with you?"

"Havard, do you really not know?"

Apparently not. There were many things I didn't know,
and among them were the motivations of any woman.

"It's *you*, Havard. Any injury to me is an injury to you, and
she'd never hurt you."

My mouth fell open, but I couldn't believe Freyja had any
real love for me... could she? Surely, I just intrigued her
because I was the only man to turn her down, an ultimate
conquest for a goddess used to getting her way. But Arnbjorg
had already shared more than she'd ever planned, so I didn't
press her for more information. And really, if I learned Freyja's feelings were genuine, I'd only pity her, and she wouldn't
want me to. I smiled and kissed her forehead, wanting to ask
my brother about this development but not wanting to betray
Arnbjorg.

So I would say nothing to him about Freyja's love for me,
even though I feared a goddess in love was far more
dangerous than a spiteful one. Because of all the emotions to
consume me, only love had driven me to desperation. And
only love had driven me to act recklessly, not caring about the
casualties along the way.

CHAPTER NINE

Keira and I had been gone an entire day, giving the Norse and Celtic gods and heroes time to relocate. I stood over Yngvarr as he slept in his new bed, wondering if I was about to get myself killed but not once thinking I should reconsider. I held up the metal tray I'd snatched from the dining room in the lobby and hit it with the serving spoon.

Not surprisingly, Yngvarr leapt from the bed. Also not surprisingly, he already had a sword in his hand in that way only gods could manage. His chest heaved as he looked from my eyes to the tray to my eyes again. "Gavyn... what the hell?"

"That's what I'm here to ask *you*," I snapped. "Why didn't you warn me about you and Agnes? How could you let me get bowled over by that memory?"

"What memory?" he asked innocently, and for the first time, I wanted to hit him. I genuinely *liked* this guy, and not because of Havard's memories but because *I* liked him, but how could he and Agnes have gone around pretending they didn't even know each other? And Agnes had insisted she never knew Havard either. She wasn't only a witch, she was a *lying* witch, but really, I assumed most witches were.

"You and Havard," I said, attempting to remain at least somewhat calm. "You went to some land where people thought elves lived—"

"Ireland?" he interrupted.

"No," I sighed irritably. "That's leprechauns."

"No, Gavyn," he laughed. "The names for all of our realms except Asgard are actually parts of Europe, the parts of Earth we most often traveled. Midgard is today Sweden and Norway and Ireland was known as Ljósálfar."

I pointed the serving spoon at him. "That's it. So you both went hunting there, only you met Agnes—not the old witchy Agnes but the young super-hot one—and y'all hooked up a couple of times. And I was just hanging out in Valhalla minding my own business and had to get knocked on my ass with *that* memory!"

Yngvarr blinked at me then rubbed his eyes with the heel of his hand. "You'd think I'd remember sleeping with Badb, because her young self *is* hot. Like crazy hot."

"And she's a witch," I added. But then I realized I really was convinced she was at least part witch, and Yngvarr seemed sincere about not remembering this affair he'd had with her. "And as a witch, I'm willing to bet she could force everyone to forget certain things."

"You think Badb—"

"Agnes," I corrected.

He grunted at me but said, "You think *Agnes* would force us all to forget my brother? But why?"

"Because she's a witch!" I reiterated, a little louder this time in case he usually woke up deaf.

"Pretty sure she's just a regular goddess," he said. "And if she were looking for vengeance against me, forcing me to forget my brother wouldn't be the way to do it. Since I didn't know he was gone, I haven't been able to miss him, you know?"

I reluctantly admitted he had a point but quickly reminded him Agnes was still a witch, so I wasn't putting anything past her. And then, in an attempt to prove she *wasn't* a witch, he grabbed my arm and dragged me to her room. I tried to run away before she could open her door, but the bastard wouldn't let me go.

"If she turns me to stone, just remember you'll be on your own fighting the Sumerians and Egyptians," I hissed at him.

"Fair enough."

Agnes opened her door, and I reminded Yngvarr, "I hate you." Because the old witch-goddess stood there in nothing but a t-shirt that barely concealed her cotton panties and *definitely* didn't conceal her thin, wrinkled legs, which were criss-crossed with thick, ropey veins.

"I kinda hate myself right now," he whispered back.

"What do you boys want?" she barked. "You see the time?"

"Um..." I stammered. "Any chance you remember having an affair with Yngvarr? Presumably not looking like this, because dude."

"I've decided I hate you, too," Yngvarr told me.

Agnes narrowed her eyes at me like she was once again trying to see through so much stupid. But then she looked Yngvarr over and shrugged. "Don't remember. Seems like I'd remember *you*."

"Ew," I mumbled. "I think I just threw up in my mouth."

But Yngvarr *still* didn't let go of my arm. "While he was in Valhalla, he remembered this time Havard and I went to Ireland for a hunting trip, but apparently, we met and you and I spent the night together and planned to see each other again. But I don't remember this either."

Agnes drummed her crooked fingers against the door then motioned us into her room, which was the *last* place I wanted to go. But since I also wanted to know if Hunter had gone to the Otherworld and if he were all right, I followed her anyway. Not like I had a *choice* since Yngvarr still gripped my arm like it had become attached to him, but still. She grabbed the black robe she liked to wear off the back of a chair and slipped it on, and my mouth started working again before I could stop it. "Why do you always go around looking like this when your other self is so gorgeous?"

Agnes waved me off like that was the dumbest question she'd ever heard. "And if I looked that way right now, what would you two be thinking? Would you be paying attention to what I say?"

I thought about it for a minute, as well as lying because I hated that she was right, but conceded her point and sat on the empty bed. Yngvarr sat next to me, watching the Irish goddess as if he could somehow force those memories to resurface. But honestly, whatever had happened between them in the past was better off in the past forever because no way did I want Agnes and Yngvarr hooking up *again*. The memories were bad enough without having to experience it in real-time.

"So," Agnes said, "I met Havard, too. Did you know our friendship with the Norse isn't that old? Not for gods anyway."

Yngvarr and I exchanged uneasy glances then we both shook our heads. I'd never been told anything about their friendship, and Yngvarr claimed he'd never really thought about it. Agnes just shrugged. "About eight hundred years, I think. But I can't actually remember *how* our families became friends."

I snorted and said, "I have an idea."

But Agnes just shrugged at me again. "Maybe. If our friendship *does* somehow tie into Havard's story, it would explain a lot, like why none of us can even recall his name.

But if our families forged an alliance based on Yngvarr's and my relationship, I'm guessing it wasn't a short-lived affair."

Yngvarr grimaced and begged, "If we're going to discuss our affair, do you *have* to stay an old woman?"

"Ass," she muttered, but she also transformed into the redhead with long legs, an ivory thigh peeking out from beneath the robe. She waved a hand in my direction and said, "See? *That's* the problem."

"I'll stop staring," I hurriedly promised, although I wasn't sure I could actually *keep* my promise. I mean, the only woman I'd ever met who was more attractive than Agnes when she wasn't pretending to be an old witch was Keira, who never pretended to be a witch, so even if Agnes *didn't* scare the shit out of me, Keira easily won out.

Agnes watched me carefully for a few seconds to see if I could manage not to objectify her for three whole minutes then focused on Yngvarr again. I thought he was undressing her in his mind now, too, but she didn't threaten to turn back into the old hag when *he* did it. So I stopped lusting after her and pouted instead. "When I'm back in the Otherworld, I'll consult with our own seers about figuring out this curse. But it's unlikely they'll be able to tell us more than yours can."

"Speaking of the Otherworld, Hunter's okay?" I asked.

Agnes flipped her hair over a shoulder, just like she had in Havard's memory, and I felt a bit nostalgic over a life that had never been mine. "Of course he is. When I left him, he had two goddesses fighting for his attention. I'll have a terrible time trying to get him *out* of the Otherworld when this is over."

"So leave him there," I said. "I'm pretty sure Copeland's can find another bartender."

"Not my decision," she told me then looked Yngvarr over again and smiled. "And believe me—I wish I remembered *you*."

"That's only slightly less disturbing now," I said.

"If you're done, I'm going back to bed," she replied, although she flashed a disconcertingly sexy smile at Yngvarr again and added, "But if you like, I don't have to go alone."

"Yep, time to leave," I announced, dragging Yngvarr behind me. As we left Agnes's room, we bumped into Freyja, who glanced at the door then each of us, one perfectly shaped eyebrow rising as if to say, "I won't judge. Much."

"It's not what you think," I protested. "We just had to ask her something."

"Both of you," Freyja said slowly. "At the same time. In the middle of the night."

Well, now I was just feeling a bit defensive. "It couldn't wait. What's your excuse? Where are you slinking off to?"

Freyja brushed her fingertips down my arm and purred, "Looking for you."

"And that's my cue to leave," Yngvarr said.

"You don't—" I started, but apparently, my objections meant nothing, because he turned around and slipped back into Agnes's room while she still held the door open. "He *is* an ass," I complained.

"Come on," Freyja laughed, tugging on my hand, but I didn't budge. Something about Havard's discovery that she may have been in love with him, his fear that she'd end up even more of a threat because of it, and my own guilt that I'd hurt Keira by sleeping with her only made me want to disappear, to free myself from Freyja's sights forever.

"I'm tired. I walked all over Valhalla and fought a bunch of dead people. I'm going to sleep. Alone."

Freyja sighed at me and blocked my path. "It's never going to happen between you and Gunnr. She's already vowed it won't, so you might as well move on."

"What?" I breathed. I was certain my voice sounded as wounded as I felt. Sure, Keira had told me the same thing in the dining hall of Valhalla, but she was *vowing* never to be with me and making that vow common knowledge? It wasn't only hurtful—it was humiliating.

"She should've told you the truth from the beginning," Freyja said. "She had no right to string you along like this."

I stared at the forest green carpet by my feet and nodded. She hadn't really been stringing me along though. When I'd asked her about us, she'd told me the truth. But it was a truth I wasn't ready to accept. "I'm going to bed," I mumbled. "Goodnight, Freyja."

I stepped around her, and she tried to stop me again but I yanked my arm away from her. But I doubted I'd be able to sleep, because for the first time in my life, I *knew* I desperately wanted someone and *only* this one person and she'd apparently vowed never to accept my love.

And I refused to die without finding out *why*.

∾

MY FIRST ENCOUNTER with a shapeshifting deity was every bit as bizarre—and embarrassing—as I'd expected. Sure, Agnes transformed between an old witch and a young hot one, but every time someone mentioned a god turning into an animal, I kinda thought they were just being metaphorical or something. Because lion gods just seemed a hundred shades of wrong.

In the morning, Yngvarr—who'd mysteriously turned up in our room again, claiming he and Agnes had only *talked* when he went back the night before—and I walked to a coffee and donut shop near the hotel. After spending the past two weeks in Iceland, Phoenix was a paradise—a warm, "hello t-shirts and shorts even though it's November" paradise. He suggested we get donuts to bring back for the others, but I was still mad at Keira for going around telling everyone she'd never be in a relationship with me so I sat my stubborn ass at one of the tables and drank my coffee as slowly as possible.

And because I'd gotten so little sleep the night before, when I first noticed the wolf staring at me from across the street, I thought it was fake, even though I couldn't really come up with a good reason for anyone to put a wolf statue in the middle of a sidewalk. "Um, Yngvarr?"

He looked up from his crawler and just as quickly returned his attention to it. "Is there a wolf by that bank or am I finally losing my mind?" I asked.

Yngvarr set his pastry on the plate and followed my gaze. "Damn it," he sighed.

"*Why* is there a wolf in Phoenix?" I pressed. "And why isn't anyone else freaking out about a wild animal prowling the streets?"

"To them, he probably still looks like a man," Yngvarr said, his eyes narrowing at the wolf like he was trying to curse it. Admittedly, I really wanted to see someone get cursed so I was disappointed when nothing else came of his narrowed eyes and intense stare.

"Wait, a *man*?" I whispered.

"Well, god," Yngvarr explained. "Specifically, Wepwawet."

"Wep..." I exhaled heavily and squinted at the wolf, too. "Okay, so Willy is a god. Sumerian or Egyptian?"

"Willy doesn't sound anything like Wepwawet," Yngvarr pointed out.

"Dude," I hissed. "Priorities. What's up with the wolf-god?"

"I'm guessing he's waiting for us to leave so he can maul us."

I nodded toward his phone on the table. "It's too early to get mauled. Call Tyr. He's an expert on fighting wolves, right?"

Yngvarr blinked at me and slowly pushed his phone across the table. "*You* call him and tell him to come fight the wolf."

"Can't," I lied. "I have a severe cellphone allergy."

"Shit," Yngvarr muttered as he looked out the window again. So of course I looked, too, and jumped a little when the damn wolf was right in front of the donut shop now, statuesque and still staring at me like some canine version of Chucky.

"Make it go away," I whispered. "This is worse than Cujo."

Yngvarr nodded. "By the way he's staring at you, I'd think you were putting off some serious wolf pheromones."

I risked looking away from Willy to warn him never to say that again. I'd just turned back to the window when he leapt at the glass, snarling and baring his fangs at me. With his paws pressed against the pane, I noticed how *huge* this wolf was—they were nearly the size of a grown man's hands. And Willy had apparently decided to show himself to the diners, because they screamed and moved as far from the window as possible. Not that I blamed them. I wanted to scream and move away from the window, too, but if Willy survived this encounter, I couldn't ruin my street cred. I wasn't quite sure I *had* any street cred, but until I learned otherwise, I intended to act as if I did.

"Rock, paper, scissors for who has to go out there and fight him?" I suggested.

Willy lowered his massive paws from the window and began to pace back and forth. The asshole was just taunting us now. But unless he morphed back into Power Ranger Willy, he lacked opposable thumbs and there was no way he was getting through the door. Yngvarr watched him pace for a few seconds then shrugged. "Or we could outwait him. We've got donuts and coffee. We're set up for a contest of endurance in here."

"Sure," I pretended to agree. "That doesn't sound

remotely dangerous for all the humans outside who don't realize they're sharing a sidewalk with a pissed off Egyptian god."

Yngvarr waved a hand toward the prowling wolf and said, "Well, they can't think it's *normal* to have a giant wolf stalking a donut shop. And if they *do* and end up getting killed, that's just natural selection at work."

I groaned and held out my hand. "Give me a sword. I'll take care of Willy. If I survive, this should impress the hell out of the hot brunette behind the counter, right?"

Yngvarr stood up with me and handed me a sword, which only seemed to cause a new wave of panicked screams from the diners. "No way you're getting all the glory yourself. Besides, even as a wolf it would be suicidal for him to confront us both alone. He's got to have company out there somewhere."

I pushed the door open, much to the loud protests of the humans inside the donut shop, and hackles raised along Willy's neck and back. He showed me his monstrously long fangs and his eyes only briefly flickered toward the sword in my right hand.

"Okay," I said to Yngvarr. "One wolf and a lion probably lurking in the shadows. Naturally, I'm the Scarecrow, so I guess that makes you the Tin Man."

"I don't think there are any wolves in *The Wizard of Oz.*"

Willy snarled in what I assumed was agreement, so obviously, I did the only thing I *could*: I snarled back. And that's when the lion decided to join Phoenix's supernatural zoo and announced its arrival by roaring at me.

Honestly, I'm not sure how I didn't piss all over myself.

"New plan," I whispered. "We run back into the donut shop and call Agnes. If that doesn't scare them away, nothing will."

"Hey, apparently Agnes and I were lovers so I can't be involved in any plot that will likely result in her death."

I wanted to tell him this whole feud with the Sumerians and Egyptians constituted a plot that would likely result in her death, but Willy and the lion lunged at us, forcing us to shut up and defend ourselves. I pivoted on my right foot, swinging the blade of my sword back toward Willy's neck. He howled as I made contact, but supernatural wolves were apparently a hell of a lot faster than normal wolves—not that I'd ever fought a normal wolf to know how fast they were but Willy *seemed* impossibly fast. Maybe even *preternaturally* fast.

The tip of my sword ended up only nicking him, cutting his ear and a small part of his face, but it was hardly lethal. The lion, which I assumed was Anhur because it had a mane, roared again as it leapt at Yngvarr, slicing the air with its claws. Yngvarr managed to avoid having his leg torn to shreds by sidestepping the lion's attack, but the zoological army was closing in on us.

"Gavyn, get out of here!" he shouted.

That was the last thing I'd ever do. Even if Havard's memories didn't compel me to think of Yngvarr as my own brother, he was my friend and I'd never abandon him, especially if it meant dying by mauling. But the animal gods had forced us into a tight corner, and we might *both* die by mauling, which I'd already decided was a completely unacceptable cause of death.

Willy leapt at me again, but this time, I held my ground and thrust my sword just as his torso appeared within reach. His razor sharp claws dug into my left shoulder, and I screamed in pain but drove my blade in farther, which was the only reason those obscenely long fangs didn't rip my face off.

The claws that had attempted to sever my arm relaxed, and I pushed the wolf's body to the ground. The lion backed away, looking as pissed off as a lion can possibly look, but it gave me one last roar then turned and ran down the street.

Black spots floated across my vision and I leaned against the wall, willing myself not to pass out. I stupidly wondered if Willy had poisonous claws or something because nothing had ever hurt this badly. Yngvarr took the sword from my right hand and put an arm around me. The last thing I heard was him begging me to stay with him. Instead, I closed my eyes and slipped into total darkness.

CHAPTER TEN

Keira sat in a chair with a book in her hands but her attention was on the window. She seemed so lost in thought that I didn't want to disturb her, but my shoulder hurt like hell so I groaned and felt around my hospital bed for one of those buttons that would release morphine. Of course, I stood a better shot of finding that button if I'd actually *had* a morphine pump.

Keira put her book down and called for a nurse then sat beside me on the bed. "We're moving again," she said.

"Not back to Iceland," I begged.

"No," she promised. "But Frey and Cadros finally returned. The CIA is going to help us. Apparently, it took so long because they were coordinating a plan with other intelligence agencies across the globe."

I rubbed my eyes and noticed how scratchy my face felt. "How long was I out?"

"Almost twenty-four hours. You woke up briefly in the middle of the night, but you were pretty out of it."

I lifted my left hand and was relieved to find my arm was still attached. And because I was still a bit drugged or because I was just the resident village idiot, I asked, "If I lose a limb, will I get it back when I die and go to Valhalla?"

Keira snickered and said, "Yeah. Limbless heroes won't do us much good at Ragnarok."

"Did Willy have poisonous claws or something?"

"Who?"

I mean, seriously, Yngvarr? I pass out and get carted off to the hospital for emergency surgery on my shoulder and you couldn't even fill everyone in on my epically badass fight against a supernatural wolf conveniently renamed for my pronunciation benefit?

"The wolf," I explained. "And speaking of, what did you tell the hospital? Or the cops, for that matter?"

Keira reached over to my face and pushed back the hair that had fallen near my eyes. As soon as she realized what she was doing, she moved her hand away and returned to her chair, and I *wanted* to stop her, to beg her to just *talk* to me about whatever was going on with us that she clearly had such a problem with, but the nurse finally came into my room with a beautiful syringe of synthetic morphine.

Neither of us spoke until the nurse was gone and my door had been closed then Keira said, "The hospital knows who you are and who attacked you. A wolf and lion stalking the streets of Phoenix aren't going to go unnoticed anyway."

The painkiller must have already kicked in because I sighed and asked her, "Are you *ever* going to talk to me about us? You have to know I'm crazy about you. Are you telling everyone we'll never happen because I slept with Freyja?"

"Gavyn—" she tried, but her tone already told me she was going to avoid this conversation again so I interrupted her.

"I know you have feelings for me, too. And maybe you hate that you feel that way, but don't I deserve an explanation?" I wasn't actually sure I *did*, but if it worked, I'd roll with it.

Keira shook her head and looked out the window again. "It's so complicated, Gavyn."

"How?" I demanded. "It would be complicated if we knew I was going to live because that's one hell of a long-distance relationship, but—"

"But maybe I don't want you to die, okay?" she cried.

I thought about telling her, "Well, good, that makes two of us," but she seemed pretty upset already, so I decided not to intentionally make it worse. Instead, I just asked her where the CIA was sending us, and I wiggled my fingers on my left hand just to make sure it was *really* still attached.

"The gods have spread out, but the CIA seems pretty sure at least two of them are still in Louisiana."

I groaned and sighed at the same time, which made an odd, slightly erotic sound. Judging by Keira's reaction, she agreed with me. "Everybody's expecting the Sumerians to leave New Orleans," she said. "It actually wouldn't be a terrible idea for them to stay and just relocate buildings, especially if they're well set up there."

And since the fake morphine was clearly kicking in, I blurted out, "You should totally dress up as Little Red Riding Hood for me."

Not surprisingly, that earned me a well-deserved sigh and an exasperated, "Gavyn... *what?*"

"You know, I'm like the huntsman. I slayed the wolf." But then, because the drugs were clearly affecting my already impaired ability to think, I repeated the world "slayed" several times before asking, "Is that even a word?"

Keira laughed and kissed my forehead, which would have surprised me more if I hadn't been a little high from the painkiller. "I'm going to the cafeteria, but I'll be back soon. Tyr is right outside if you need anything."

"Yeah," I told her, so naturally, she stopped as if I were

about to request something monumentally important. "Ask him if 'slayed' is a word."

"Get some rest," she ordered, and even though that's all I'd been doing for the past twenty-four hours, I drifted into darkness anyway.

When I awoke again, I had an entire supernatural squad of cheerleaders in the room with me. Or just Keira, Tyr, and Yngvarr, but since it makes me seem way cooler and more popular, I'm going with an entire squad. Anyway, Yngvarr told me the doctor was ready to release me, which I suspected was at least partly due to their concerns the lion would return in an attempt to finish me off, and Keira held up a white paper bag with a blue caduceus on it. "Got painkillers to go," she said.

I was about to tell her that was my kind of Happy Meal when I realized I'd just given a *name* to the serpent staff on the bag, and I was certain I shouldn't have known that. And not only did I have a name for the staff, but I knew it belonged to Hermes and really didn't belong on medical supplies but had gotten mixed up with the Staff of Asclepius.

"Whoa," I exclaimed, sitting up and scaring the hell out of my cheerleading squad. "Why do I know anything about a caduceus and Hermes and Asclepius? What did y'all *do* to me while I was out?"

"Um... brain damage?" Tyr guessed.

"Not brain damage," Keira said. "Either you know a lot more about mythology than you thought or the more Havard's memories are triggered, the more you'll be able to draw on everything he knew as well."

"We all know it's not because I ever learned a ton of mythology on my own," I countered.

I felt a little slighted when they all nodded in agreement.

"This is why I kept telling you in the practice field that sword fighting is in your DNA," Keira added. "It's all there, like a reflex. Did it ever occur to you that when you dream about Havard, he's not even speaking English?"

I waved her off because of *course* he was speaking English. It was the only language I knew. But she reminded me that the Valkyries in Valhalla all spoke an ancient, dead language and I'd understood them. And I may or may not have freaked out a little.

"Is this really any more disturbing than reliving Havard's memories?" Tyr asked.

"Yeah," I shot back. "I might lose my village idiot title if I come across as... *knowledgeable*."

Keira tossed a large plastic bag at me and told me to get dressed, so of course, I asked for her help. And, of course, she rolled her eyes and said she'd send in Freyja. So clearly, she was over *that* whole thing.

Somewhere over Texas on the flight back to New Orleans, I got Tyr to switch seats with me so I could talk to Keira without her walking out on me. I mean, she could *try*, but I was pretty sure even Valkyries couldn't survive that fall. "Two questions," I said as soon as I sat down.

"You get one," she replied, like that would actually stop me.

"First, do you get Paranormal Frequent Flyer Miles?"

Keira lowered her magazine and blinked at me, so I just shrugged. "What's your second question, Gavyn?"

"Is that a no on the Paranormal Frequent Flyer Miles then?"

"Gavyn," she warned.

"Fine, but you should really look into those. I'll be dead soon, but you can totally hit up Elysium—"

"Gavyn," she groaned.

"Second question. Why are you telling everyone about your vow to never be with me?"

It might have just been my imagination, but I thought she paled. "Who said that?"

I didn't want to bring up Freyja right now, but I also didn't want to lie. "Does it matter?" I said instead. "It's obviously true. It's one thing to feel that way, but why are you—"

"Freyja," she interrupted, turning away from me so she could glare at the back of the seat in front of us. I sensed she was going to ignore me yet again so I started this big long speech I had prepared—or was just making up on the spot—about how my one screw-up didn't justify her treating me like this, but she shook her head and grabbed my hand, releasing it just as quickly. "The seer had a prophecy for me too, Gavyn. And you were a part of it. I'm trying to protect you."

Tyr, who was obviously eavesdropping, grunted in response so Keira flashed him an admittedly terrifying "keep your mouth shut" scowl. I mean, not as terrifying as Agnes's scowls, but terrifying enough that Tyr kept his mouth shut. She glanced at me one last time before returning her attention to her magazine, although she seemed to have lost interest in it. "I don't want you to hate me, Gavyn. But we just can't work out. I'm sorry."

Tyr sighed this time, so Keira reached across me to poke him in the ribs, and he let out an exaggerated "oompf" and pretended to be mortally wounded for good measure. I'm pretty sure I taught him that.

"Still doesn't explain why you're going around publicly *vowing* that you and I are never gonna happen," I pointed out.

"I'm not," she insisted. "Shortly after receiving my prophecy, I vowed not to date you, hoping this would change the course of events. That's all. I promise."

That didn't make it any easier to accept, and she clearly had no intention of sharing her prophecy with me, but Yngvarr decided to be *super* helpful at that exact moment by butting in with, "If you have no intention of ever dating him, then maybe stop being such an ass about him hooking up with Freyja."

Keira's cheeks flushed, and Tyr and I just stared at Yngvarr like he'd reached across the aisle and slapped her. If the roles had been reversed, I would have *hated* any guy she'd hooked up with, so it's not like I'd ever blamed her for reacting the way she had. But Yngvarr had put it out there, and Keira was already whispering, "Okay. He's right. I'm sorry, Gavyn," before I could tell her not to worry about it, that I probably would've handled it much worse. Actually, there's no "probably" here... I *definitely* would've handled it much worse.

We all fell into an awkward silence for most of the remaining flight. New Orleans was really just getting back to normal after the Sumerians abducted thousands of people and magically immobilized them, and there we were, riding back into the city to cause havoc once again. As soon as the plane landed, we each dug out our phones to turn them back on, and I was immediately greeted with thirteen missed calls and voicemails, all of them from Frey. I glanced at Keira's screen and noticed Agnes had become her personal stalker.

"How about we *not* listen and pretend like we never got their messages?" I suggested.

"And if there's an ambush in the city and these messages could have saved our lives?" Tyr retorted.

"Then fire your seers for not *prophesying* about it and warning us not to be dumbasses," I shot back.

"Or," Yngvarr countered, "we could not be, you know... dumbasses."

"Easy for you to say," I mumbled, but I pressed the voice-mail icon anyway and listened to Frey's messages. But Frey's message had nothing to do with our presence in New Orleans, and everything to do with the Egyptians and their messed up ideas of vengeance. Keira, who'd been listening to her own messages, whispered, "Oh, my God," and I just nodded because what else could I do?

Anhur and Menhit, the lion deities, had attacked a group of tourists awaiting a bus that would bring them to the Grand Canyon—a dozen injured, three dead. They didn't need to be in their human form for us to understand their message perfectly. This had been an act of revenge for Willy's death. Tyr and Yngvarr cursed and suggested we return to Phoenix immediately, but what was the point? Wouldn't *our* revenge just lead to the Egyptians retaliating again, hurting more innocent people, and causing a never-ending cycle of violence and death?

"Gavyn's right," Keira said. "We need to be smart about this. Someone is supposed to be picking us up who most likely has ample experience with terrorists, and that's exactly what these gods are now. Let's defer to his judgment."

I expected a guy in a black suit and dark sunglasses with one of those white poster boards and our names scrawled across it... but I got a guy in blue jeans and a Metallica t-shirt scrolling on his phone and looking decidedly bored with his assignment. He obviously recognized me though, because as we made our way out of the airport, he just fell in line with us and started talking like he'd always been part of our entourage and was just returning from the bathroom.

"Heard about Phoenix?" he asked.

I slowed down to stare at the guy, and he shot me a strange look like *I* was the one completely out of place here. "Who the hell are you?" I demanded.

"John. Can you keep walking now?"

I crossed my arms and glanced at Tyr for a little assistance, but the bastard never even lowered his phone and kept tapping away at his Facebook status update. Yeah, gods used Facebook—who knew?

"You'd better not be telling everyone we're back in New Orleans," I hissed at Tyr.

"Nope," he murmured but still didn't look up from his phone. "Need help on this level of *Gods of War*."

I glanced at the screen of his phone, and he was totally serious. He'd also chosen himself as his avatar. "Okay, first of all, we kinda have a global crisis here so think you can give us a *little* attention? And secondly... dude, I love that game. What's your screen name? I'll add you."

Keira groaned and grabbed my arm, scolding us both like naughty children, so I grinned at her and asked, "Want to punish me?"

But I regretted it as soon as she smiled back at me, a little *too* sweetly, and said, "Yes, actually. Agnes is waiting on us, and I know she'd be happy to spank you."

I grimaced and quickly apologized, but Yngvarr just *had* to remind me about his forgotten past by complaining, "Hey, if Badb's going to spank anyone, it's going to be *me*."

"Dude," I complained back. "You've just rendered me permanently impotent."

"Are you really the gods that are supposed to save the world?" John asked.

"No, just Gavyn really," Tyr answered. "Either way, it's not boding well for us."

John nodded, and I would have been more than a little insulted if it weren't so true. "Come on," he said. "Badb *is* waiting on us, and—"

"Agnes," I interrupted. "She goes by Agnes now."

John blinked at me then said, "From now on, you're not allowed to talk. And—"

So naturally, I laughed and told him, "Good luck with that."

He blinked at me again, so Tyr helpfully added, "We've

found it's usually better just to ignore him. He occasionally keeps talking anyway, but it'll save your own sanity."

"Ninurta," John sighed. "We're pretty sure we've found him."

He squinted at me, but I feigned innocence. Truthfully, I was hoping he'd say "and" again so I could interrupt him *then*, but apparently, a person has to be pretty smart to get into the CIA, because he carefully avoided it. "We don't think he's in New Orleans anymore, so let's hit the road, kids. We're going to Baton Rouge."

CHAPTER ELEVEN

E ven before John told me where they thought Ninurta was hanging out these days, I had a horrible feeling I knew exactly where we'd find him. Apparently, stealing a god's weapon made war personal, and Ninurta thought I needed to know how he felt about that. But when we arrived at our hotel in Baton Rouge, Agnes, who was hanging out in her room as the witch who tried to eat Hansel and Gretel, informed us that Ninurta had a whole host of demigods with him, too, so we were waiting on our own host of demigods to show up before confronting him.

And, of course, I had to ask, "Exactly how many demigods are in a host?"

"I think it can vary," Yngvarr said smartly.

"From what to what?" I pressed. "This is critical information."

He nodded just as smartly and lifted an eyebrow at Agnes, but I cringed a little when I thought it might be a little suggestive rather than the acceptable smartassive. Agnes waved one of her nine-thousand-year-old hands at us and said, "Two dozen. Give or take a dozen."

So *I* nodded smartly and said, "Seems legit."

"We could get in some archery practice while we wait," Keira suggested.

I groaned and shook my head. "I have a better idea. Let's go back to Asgard and look for my sword."

"I'll stay here with Agnes," Tyr offered.

"It might not even be in Asgard," Keira argued. "We have no idea where Havard might have hidden it."

"Yeah, but Asgard seems like the most obvious place," I said. "That's where he lived. And if he really knew I was going to need it someday, he wouldn't have made it impossible for me to find, right?"

Yngvarr nodded and agreed with me, so Keira relented and asked Tyr to call her as soon as they were ready to confront Ninurta. As we returned to Asgard, another seemingly instantaneous trip, I finally said, "Okay, I give up. Where the hell are we? And don't say Asgard."

Keira arched an eyebrow at me and asked, "Where do you want me to say then?"

"I mean where is Asgard in relation to Earth? And where is the Otherworld? Can Agnes get there just as easily as you can get to Asgard? Can you travel from Asgard to the Otherworld like this? It's all giving me a headache."

Yngvarr laughed and clapped me on the back. "The science of the supernatural will do that."

Even Keira smiled as she waved me on. She was obviously anxious to begin our search for this sword, most likely so we could return to Agnes and Tyr in case they were caught off-guard by a surprise attack in a far less posh hotel than the one in Reykjavik, and really, if I was going to get caught off-guard by a surprise attack, I'd want it to be in a posh hotel. "The world of the gods is separated from Earth by what we call 'the veil,'" she explained. "Once we're in either world, we have to travel just like everyone else, so to get to the Otherworld, we'd have to go by horse and ship or, yeah, even a flying animal. All of the gods live here and can cross the veil between worlds, so I guess it's kind of like a parallel universe?"

I stopped short and gaped at her. "A parallel universe? Like Asgard is really on a planet that looks just like Earth but is inhabited by gods and flying mammals and shit?"

"Basically," she answered.

"Great," I sighed. "That means if Havard hid his sword outside of Asgard, we'll never find it."

"Afraid so," Keira said. "But the good news is that gods almost never venture into other gods' territory. If it's not in Asgard, it's most likely on Earth somewhere."

"That really doesn't narrow it down," I muttered.

"You're back again?" Odin asked, stepping out of the shadows of a nearby palace.

I jumped and twisted on my heels to face him, pointing an accusatory finger in his direction. "Don't sneak up on demigods. We're fragile, you know."

"Maybe mentally," Yngvarr added helpfully.

Keira snorted then told Odin, "We had some time, so we wanted to search for Havard's sword."

"Ah," Odin replied. "Well, if you find it, bring it to me before returning to Earth. If it's the same sword as I think, I'd love to see it."

Yngvarr tensed and turned his back on the All-Father, who obviously noticed, and his eyes narrowed slightly at the insult. Keira promised Odin they'd bring the sword to him if we found it, which led to Yngvarr scoffing and walking away. I wasn't exactly sure what I was supposed to be doing so after a few seconds of paralyzing indecision, I followed my friend, whom I'd loved like a brother since the moment I met him because *his* dead brother's DNA had decided to flare up and become a pain in the ass.

Behind me, I could hear Keira apologizing quietly, but Yngvarr likely overheard her as well. And I had a feeling that was only going to lead to an argument between them. "Hey," I said. "If we find it, I can just lie. I don't care if Odin gets pissed off at me. I don't even know the guy."

Yngvarr glanced in my direction but didn't slow down. "I do know him, and I have no problem lying to him. Don't you think it's suspicious that he wants us to promise we'll take a sword to him that only he knows anything about?"

"Yeah," I admitted. "*Really* suspicious, actually. The whole thing kinda unsettled me, too, but I'm not entirely sure if it's because Havard hated him or because my own instincts are telling me not to trust him."

"Probably both. But be careful what you say around Keira. As a Valkyrie, her loyalty is always going to be with her father."

I looked over my shoulder at her and Odin then asked, "Is he literally her father?"

Honestly, I expected Yngvarr to tell me it was just what they called him, so when he nodded and said all of the Valkyries were his daughters he'd had with mortal women, I stopped short again. Yngvarr shot me a strained smile, because he knew how I felt about her, of course, and he also knew that I'd find her relationship with Odin troubling. "For as long as anyone can remember, Odin would bring his infant daughters to Asgard to train as Valkyries as soon as they could hold a sword. Technically, they're all demigoddesses, but being Valkyries, they're given special gifts, including the ability to cross the veil."

"And if they don't want to be a Valkyrie?" I asked. Keira had finally broken away from Odin and was heading toward us. I watched her as she offered me a small wave, but I was burdened now with the knowledge that she'd been forced into a life she may not have wanted. And what made it worse was that her own father had forced her into that life.

Yngvarr sighed and shrugged. "They don't exactly have a choice, Gavyn. And while Valkyries have always taken lovers, they're not allowed to marry or have children or anything that could interfere with their loyalty to Odin."

"They're his slaves," I murmured. "He enslaved his own daughters."

Yngvarr just nodded and sighed again. "Now you're starting to see why Havard hated him. And why I still hate him, too. He takes whatever he wants and doesn't care who gets hurt."

I looked away from Keira and asked him, "Do you think he could've killed your brother and stolen this sword?"

"Could he?" Yngvarr repeated. "Yeah, he's definitely capable of something like that. And it would explain why none of us can remember Havard—if everyone knew Odin had murdered one of the Aesir just to steal his weapon or his wife, all of Asgard would turn on him."

Keira had finally walked within earshot, so I decided to drop the topic of her father possibly murdering my ancestor and smiled at her as if we'd just been hanging out to wait for her. "Ready to ransack Yngvarr's palace?" I asked her.

"Hey!" he protested.

Keira laughed and nodded. "Ransacking is my favorite pastime."

"Just remember," Yngvarr said. "You break it, you buy it."

I reached into my pocket and held a crumpled ten-dollar bill out to him. "Where can I exchange my Earth currency for Asgardian currency?"

And that bastard actually snatched my money out of my hand and stuffed it into his own pocket. "I accept American money."

"Down payment on anticipated damage to property?" Keira asked.

Yngvarr snickered. "Something like that. Plus, I get to aggravate Gavyn, which is always a bonus."

"Definitely," Keira agreed. "He's going to cover me for any damage I may cause, by the way."

"Pay for your own ransacking," I told her. We'd reached Yngvarr's palace, but I wanted to check the stables first. I suspected it had more to do with Havard's love of them than any real sense that I'd find an enchanted sword hidden with a bunch of horses, but Keira and Yngvarr followed me anyway. I moved heavy bags of sweet oats to check the walls for loose panels while Yngvarr and Keira emptied the saddle room. We eventually conceded the sword wasn't in the stables, but as we were leaving, I passed a horse that looked awfully familiar. I stopped and stroked his face and his nostrils flared briefly then he nuzzled my hand.

"Is this Sigurd?" I asked. "Can horses be immortal, too?"

"Yeah," Yngvarr said. "They can be immortal if we feed them Idun's apples."

"Why didn't you tell me you still had your brother's horse?"

"I don't know," he admitted. "Sometimes, I still have a hard time believing any of this is real. And other times, I hate that it is, because I know I'll never get him back."

I let my hand fall and took a deep breath, but Sigurd didn't seem to like that I planned to leave. He whinnied at me, and I promised I'd return, although I wasn't sure I'd ever be able to. I mean, how long did I have before I became a permanent resident of Valhalla? I doubted there were many leisurely trips to Asgard left in my future.

Keira scratched Sigurd between his ears and smiled at me. "You must remind him of an owner he'd once been attached to."

"Yeah," I sighed. Great. Someone else terribly disappointed that I wasn't Havard and I couldn't bring him back.

We did our best *not* to ransack Yngvarr's palace, although it was awfully tempting. I mean, we were looking for an enchanted sword in a god's palace in Asgard, which just happened to exist in some parallel universe. I had to do a *little* ransacking.

Keira put her hands on her hips and looked around the messy room. "I don't think it's here," she said smartly.

So I put my hands on *my* hips and, just as smartly, said, "We should tear down a few walls, just to make sure."

"They're stone, dumbass," Yngvarr teased. But then he put *his* hands on *his* hips and added, "But maybe Thor could break down one... you know, just to be sure."

"It would be criminal if we weren't completely thorough," I agreed.

"We're not destroying Yngvarr's palace," Keira scolded.

"Killjoy," Yngvarr and I both muttered.

But we listened to her anyway, and as we headed out into the warm sunshine of early afternoon in Asgard, I had a sudden, and quite possibly insane, idea. "Let's search Odin's palace."

Keira and Yngvarr stared at me with their mouths open as if they were *both* trying to see through so much stupid. "Gavyn, if he stole Havard's sword, he's never going to allow us to search his palace," Yngvarr argued. "And we can't just break into Odin's home, especially without any evidence he's done something wrong."

"I'm afraid Yngvarr's right," Keira said. "We can't—"

"I'm not suggesting we break into Odin's palace," I interrupted. "Theoretically, he should want us to find this sword as badly as we do, right? So let's ask him if we can search his pad, and if he says no, we'll be on our way to building a case against him."

Yngvarr snorted and said, "I think you watched too much *Law & Order*."

"No, smartass," I snapped. "*CSI*."

Keira nodded and agreed with me. "Much better show, especially the one set in Miami."

Apparently, Asgard had excellent cable packages.

But since Tyr still hadn't called, we decided to head to Odin's palace anyway, provided I wasn't the one asking him if we could search it. I would've been a little offended if I didn't know exactly why Keira made me promise she could do the talking.

Honestly, I expected Odin to slam the door in our faces, even if it was just a metaphorical door and he was really just telling us to stuff it. So when he held his door open for us to enter, I tried not to look *too* surprised. I sauntered in and gave him a cool, "What's up?" and a "Nice digs" and thought, "*Nailed it.*"

Keira rolled her eyes at me and I blurted out, "So how do you feel about us knocking down a few walls?"

Odin squinted at me and asked, "Were you dropped a lot as a baby?"

I shrugged and reminded him my dad was around here somewhere, so he could go straight to the source and find out. Keira grabbed my arm and pulled me away from her father before I embarrassed her even more than I already had. I thought she should've known by now that there was an extraordinarily high chance of that, but when I pointed out her oversight, namely that I *always* embarrassed her, she just smiled and said, "Not *always*. Occasionally, I'm actually proud of you."

"Odin's palace is much bigger than mine," Yngvarr sighed. "We'll never be able to search the entire thing."

"Yeah," I agreed. "He was probably counting on that."

"Or," Keira countered, "he didn't have anything to do with Havard's death."

"This would be so much easier if I could control these memories. Why do they have to come to me in chronological order?" I complained.

"It's almost like someone's controlling them and only wants to reveal pieces of a story at a time," Keira said.

We blinked at each other then laughed and waved off such a crazy idea.

The first floor of Odin's palace was mostly an enormous library and an even more enormous hall where he apparently held feasts and parties. I nudged Yngvarr and whispered, "Come February, we're having a Super Bowl party in here."

Yngvarr nodded and whispered back, "Let's do it, but only if we don't invite Odin."

"Send him to Freyja's," I suggested. "She'll distract him."

I probably shouldn't have mentioned the goddess Keira had issues with because she set her jaw and walked away, leaving me feeling guilty once again. And the craziest part was that I *still* had no idea why I'd slept with Freyja in the first place. Yngvarr quickly filled the awkward silence by asking me what Havard's sword looked like even though I'd already told him. He hadn't really forgotten, of course, but I provided as much detail as I could, from the way its blade shimmered and both reflected light and emitted it to the intricate silver carvings on the hilt.

Yngvarr listened attentively anyway and as I described the carvings, none of which I recognized, his hand froze over a chest against the wall. I peeked inside it, but much to my disappointment, it only contained table linens. Who knew Odin had *table linens*?

"Gavyn," Yngvarr said, "those carvings sound like Norse runes. If that's what they are, there's no way this sword was ever Sumerian."

Something inside me agreed with him, but I wasn't quite sure if that was because I *wanted* to or Havard's DNA was already telling me those inscriptions were Norse. I concentrated on the details of those symbols then said, "Okay, so the one that looks like a stick figure trying to hug a child... I'm thinking this one is definitely Norse."

By now, Keira had returned and was listening attentively as well. "Follow me," she instructed. "I think we can solve at least one puzzle."

She led us to Odin's impressive, but definitely overcompensating, library and pulled a book that looked *almost* as old as Agnes from the shelf. "Can you find symbols in here like the ones you've seen?"

I flipped the book open and immediately spotted the stick figure trying to hug a child. Yngvarr and Keira glanced at each other and she said, "That's a rune for the gods. It literally means 'one of the Aesir.'"

I flipped through the book and pointed to a few more symbols that looked familiar, and each time Keira told me its meaning, I nodded because it just felt right and truthful. But the one symbol I wanted to find the most appeared to be absent, and toward the end of the book, I noticed a page seemed to have been ripped out.

"None of these runes are quite like the 'N' on Havard's sword," I told her. "Yet that symbol is at the center of the others, like it's the most important."

"Why is there a page missing?" Yngvarr asked.

Keira's eyebrows pulled together and she murmured, "Hm. I've never even noticed that before."

"Are there any other books we can check?" I asked.

"Not like this one," she answered. "It's like our family tree."

"Um... is this where Havard *would* have been?" I pressed.

Yngvarr immediately nodded. "Most likely. It's in chronological order and based on where that should be, he would have been born around 300 AD."

I snickered and *had* to point out, "You're a pagan god and use *anno Domini* to mark the passage of time?"

But he just shrugged and said, "The rest of the western world does."

Keira looked unsettled by this development—the missing page, not Yngvarr's use of the Gregorian calendar—so I suggested we continue our search for the sword. Yngvarr agreed and suggested, "Perhaps we should search the sword room?"

I folded my arms over my chest and scowled at him. "Odin has a *sword room* and we've been wasting our time searching a library and hall?"

He squirmed a bit and crossed *his* arms defensively. "Seemed too obvious a place to keep a stolen sword."

"Next time we're searching for a stolen sword, lead with 'Our suspect has a *sword room*,'" I said.

Keira led us upstairs to a room that was, not surprisingly, filled with display cases containing swords. I tapped my fingers against the glass and asked, "Can I ransack *this* room?"

"All this glass seems highly likely to result in our disfigurement," Yngvarr said smartly.

Keira had frozen in front of an illuminated case, so I glanced inside and froze beside her. A strikingly ornate sword with a silver hilt and familiar runes embossed on it lay on a red velvet cushion, light reflecting from its slender blade and creating the illusion that the sword itself was glowing. I reached for the door on the display case but hesitated as I realized there was an important distinction between the sword in my dreams and this one. "It's missing that 'N,'" I said.

"Maybe it's on the other side?" Yngvarr suggested.

"Why would he let us roam through his palace if he has the sword just *sitting* here?" I asked.

"He can always claim he had no idea he had a murdered god's sword," Keira said softly. She looked pale and defeated, and I suddenly wanted to insist this sword didn't look like the Sword of Light at all and we should leave. But my Valkyrie slid the door open and lifted the sword from its bed. She held it in her hands for a moment before holding it out to me, and I wanted to back away from it but I carefully held out my hands. As the cool metal touched my skin, I flinched and waited for something to happen, some explosion of light or overwhelming feeling that this sword had long ago been etched into my DNA. So when nothing happened, I grinned at Yngvarr and said, "It's not glowing because I'm not in battle mode. Wanna see if you can survive decapitation?"

"Can *anyone* survive decapitation?" he asked.

Keira nodded at the sword and said, "Flip it over. See if the 'N' is on the other side."

I complied and was actually relieved when I didn't see an 'N' on that side either. "Except for that rune, is it the same as in your dreams?" Yngvarr asked.

"Yeah," I acknowledged. "Extremely close."

But a voice from deep within me whispered, *"This isn't mine. This isn't the sword that comes alive in my hands."*

"What do you think?" Yngvarr asked. "Is this a replica?"

I flipped it over a few times and shook my head. "No. I think it was made by the same blacksmith, but this isn't the Sword of Light."

"Let's find out who made this one," Keira said. "We'll talk to them next."

I was about to agree when her cellphone rang. Yngvarr and I both leaned closer to see who was calling, and when I saw Tyr's name, I knew our search would be suspended.

Our host of demigods had arrived.

CHAPTER TWELVE

Have you ever been on your way to an epic showdown between supernatural good and evil and got held up by Baton Rouge rush hour traffic?

Yeah, me too.

Keira glanced at me in the backseat and asked me, "What the hell is wrong with your city?"

So I shrugged and said, "I don't think we planned appropriately for a supernatural battle of the ages."

"*Is* this a battle of the ages?" Tyr asked. "If so, I should have worn my lucky socks."

"You have lucky socks?" I asked back.

"Doesn't everyone?"

I thought about it then shrugged again. "Point taken. But in the future, *always* wear your lucky socks when heading into battle, whether it's one for the ages or not."

We inched down Airline Highway and Agnes scowled at the sea of red taillights in front of us. "Can't you do something about this?" I said. "Surely witches have some sort of spell for clearing traffic jams."

Agnes, who'd decided to confront Ninurta and his

minions as the smoking hot redheaded witch, scowled at me now. "If I had the ability to cast spells, I'd have done it on you a long time ago."

And, really, that seemed completely fair so I nodded and told her as long as I didn't wake up in her bed, I wouldn't even hold it against her. After an hour of being stuffed into a sedan with two gods and a Valkyrie, I was anxious for freedom, even if that meant having to fight an entire host of demigods. It was another half hour before we made it to the oak-lined streets of one of Baton Rouge's oldest neighborhoods, where I'd grown up and my father still lived.

Tyr turned onto my dad's street and immediately pulled over to park. We could see his house from here, and his front lawn teemed with armed men and women as if they'd been waiting on us. And seeing them in front of the house where my mother spent her final days ignited a fire within me. What had they been doing to her home, to the possessions she'd once held dear, to the memories we'd created together? Keira turned in her seat so she could see me and grabbed my hand, squeezing it quickly before she just as quickly let go. "We'll make them regret coming here, Gavyn."

"Yeah," I sighed, but I didn't really believe it. Even with the arrival of some of the heroes I'd trained with in Iceland, we seemed outnumbered and the only leverage we had against Ninurta was his spear. And this bastard had kidnapped and beaten my father and invaded our home, making this war intensely personal for me. It was no longer just about saving the world, but maybe it had never only been about saving the world. Maybe it had always been about an old score between the Sumerians and *me*.

Keira's hand was on the door handle when I stopped her and asked to speak to her alone. Behind us, car doors slammed as Yngvarr and the heroes waited for the rest of us to shut up and join them. I thought they could be waiting a while.

But Agnes and Tyr spilled out of the car, and Keira shot me an expectant look as if reminding me I kinda needed to make this quick. "I've been thinking about Havard and his sword ever since I saw Odin's sword that looked so similar. I think the Sumerians are lying because it doesn't make any sense to have Norse runes on them, right?"

She nodded and agreed with me.

"But Inanna *did* know about it. How?"

"I have no idea, Gavyn. If she was really having an affair with Havard's father, she might have learned about it from him."

"And when the affair ended, maybe the Sumerians tried to steal it. And maybe Havard defeated them, which is why they hate me so much."

Keira looked out the front windshield toward my dad's house and narrowed her eyes. "Don't worry, Gavyn. We've got your back."

I couldn't be sure, but it sounded to me like what she'd *really* wanted to say was that *she* had my back. And I wanted to tell her I had hers, too. I wouldn't let those assholes hurt her.

But she offered me a small smile and nodded toward our allies still waiting outside for us. "Let's get them out of your father's house then return to Asgard to find out who made that sword. We'll get the answers we need."

We stepped onto the sidewalk with the others, and I jumped when Tyr pressed the button on his car key to lock the doors, which made the horn beep loudly beside me. I threw my hands up and exclaimed, "We're about to fight a bunch of demigods, and you're worried about someone breaking into your car?"

Tyr shot me a defensive look and said, "It's a rental. I want my deposit back."

I really didn't know what to say to that, so I turned on my heels and headed toward my dad's house.

It was like walking up to the O.K. Corral, only I hoped no one would pull out their guns. Trying to survive sword fights was bad enough, but since the chance of shooting *myself* in the ass—or worse, my face—still seemed exponentially high, I didn't want to reenact any Wild West showdowns. And yes, the only reason I knew anything about the showdown was because Hunter and I had seen *Tombstone* at least half a dozen times.

As soon as we were within earshot, Ninurta stepped out of the crowd of demigods and held up a hand, stopping us. "Let's fight with honor," he called out. "No firearms."

"Agreed," Tyr immediately responded. And even though I'd *just* been thinking the same thing, I kinda wanted to punch him for answering without consulting us. But Keira seemed to agree, too, so I figured this was in that ancient epic-supernatural-battle-and-showdowns' handbook they still refused to show me.

Ninurta focused his attention on me and said, "I'd like to barter with you."

"Um..." I shuffled my feet awkwardly, because who knew bartering was a part of said epic-supernatural-battle-and-showdown? But he glanced over his shoulder and shouted a command at an actual giant of a man, who reached behind him and yanked two bound hostages in front of him. By their appearances, I guessed they were teenagers, maybe college students, one girl and one boy.

"Sharur for their lives," Ninurta said.

Of course. Being an evil villain *had* to be so much easier than playing superhero, because they got to run around kidnapping people to force us to concede and we actually had to play by the rules of normal civility and decency.

Bastards.

And since Tyr hadn't bothered to consult me about the whole no-guns thing, I didn't bother asking him if I should immediately accept or try to negotiate. I mean, those were peoples' *kids*. "Deal," I said. "But just so you know, if you hurt them or squelch on our agreement, I'll not only steal Sharur back, I'll break it this time."

Ninurta laughed and waved to the giant to make the exchange. "I have no use for them."

Tyr handed me Ninurta's spear, and I carefully approached the giant who pushed the teenagers toward me. I caught the girl with my left arm as she stumbled, which caused the stitches in my shoulder to scream in angry protest, reminding me, "Hey, dumbass! You've got stitches in this shoulder!" Since I held Sharur in my right hand, I couldn't catch the poor guy, who fell forward, but Keira hurried to his side to help him rise. As the giant snatched Sharur out of my hands and handed him to Ninurta, I thought I heard it whispering, and for the first time since stealing the damn thing, I was *really* glad to be rid of it.

I never signed up for possessed weapons.

Ninurta's face lit up in this kind of orgasmic ecstasy as that spear touched his hand, and I cringed and jutted my chin toward Goliath. "So... where's David?"

Goliath just blinked at me, so I turned to Keira and asked, "Any chance you have a huge stone and a slingshot?"

"Do you actually know what to *do* with a slingshot?" she retorted. "Or would you just shoot *yourself* in the head?"

I wanted to make a smartass reply, but she was probably right.

And besides, Goliath looked like he was ready to disembowel me, and that's really something I needed to pay attention to because being disemboweled *would* put a crimp in the epic-ness of my supernatural battle of the ages. Keira handed me the same sword I'd used in New Orleans and I parried to block his swing. A brief clinking of blades was soon followed by the impact, and in case you've never been attacked by a giant with a sword, they can apparently pack a lot of force in their swings. I don't recommend fighting giants, whether they have a sword or not.

Tyr shouted at one of our heroes to get the now released hostages to safety as the lawn erupted into the frenzied chaos of battle. And I had just enough time to think, "*See? Epic supernatural battle of the ages,*" before Goliath charged me, swinging toward my midsection. I had to pivot and retreat, but by the time I faced him again, he'd already redirected and thrust the blade at my chest.

There was no way I could gain the upper hand by over-powering him, and I doubted I could outrun him either. I was most likely faster, but his size meant he'd be able to cover more ground with fewer steps. I honestly had no clue how to fight this guy because unlike David, *I* didn't have a slingshot. And Keira had been right: even if I did, I'd just hurt myself with it, so what would be the point?

I heard Sharur making that ridiculously creepy whispering noise again and just had time to catch Ninurta's pervy, creepy smile in response before he threw it at one of our heroes. It impaled him and he collapsed, and I'm pretty sure I made some croaking sound that only Goliath heard.

And suddenly, I remembered a guy I really liked was on this lawn with me, and he *had* to go home to his daughter. "Joachim," I whispered.

I backed up to the house to give myself a second to find his tall, blond head and spotted him by the street, shooting arrows at a pack of Sumerian demigods who'd formed the Roman's famous testudo formation with their shields so they wouldn't get arrows through their brains. Admittedly, that didn't seem like a particularly pleasant way to die, but I also wasn't convinced any way of dying would be particularly pleasant.

Goliath leapt onto the porch with me, and this time, his attempt to disembowel me hit a little too close to home. The tip of his blade caught on my shirt, ripping a four-inch gash into it, and a sharp pinch warned me he'd gotten some skin, too. Of course, being me, I yelled, "This is my favorite shirt, asshole!"

He grinned like ruining my favorite shirt had been his plan all along.

I'd been so focused a moment before on ensuring Joachim was okay that I'd stupidly backed myself into a corner. Literally. The entire porch had a waist high railing—my waist, not Goliath's—and to my left stood the wall of the house. I could dive over the railing, but if Goliath had even half a brain, which I doubted, to be honest, he'd take two giant steps toward me and spear me in the back as I tumbled to the ground. And harpooning *definitely* seemed like a shitty way to die, so I decided against jumping ship.

By this point, I'd begun having a difficult time remembering what I myself had learned and what I'd only recently unlocked in my weirdo "there's a dead guy living inside me" genes. And in that brief moment before deciding on how I could *possibly* get out of this alive, I remembered that David hadn't actually killed Goliath with a slingshot and stone but only caused him to fall then beheaded him. And even giants can't survive beheading, which was good news for me if I could somehow decapitate this bastard.

I pressed my back against the railing and bumped into a table where my dad kept the same potted ivy my mom had begun growing from a clipping in our backyard. It was the last plant she'd potted before she got too sick to garden anymore.

I lifted it with my left hand, and at the same time, silently prayed, "*I'm so sorry, Mom*," then hefted it at Goliath's head.

My shoulder screamed in protest again, only this time, far louder and something warm and sticky dripped down my arm. I'd popped the stitches, but I'd also hit Goliath in the head with a heavy, clay pot. He stumbled backward but didn't fall. Still, I'd thrown him off balance, which gave me a narrow window to attack. I ran forward and sliced, my blade making contact with the thick, sinewy neck of the beast of a man who'd been trying to kill me for the past several minutes. And since he was quite likely a Nephilim or something, I had to use both hands to grip and swing, which my shoulder *really* didn't like.

Goliath's neck was so thick and filled with rope-like bands of muscle and tendons that his head didn't fall though. My blade got stuck somewhere around his spinal cord, and supernatural swords are a hell of a lot sharper than human swords, or so I was told. And his head *didn't fall*. I yanked it free and kicked him away from me as his eyes bulged and one massive hand reached up to his throat as if he could stem the flow of blood with his thumb.

For the record, it didn't work.

As he stumbled away from me, I inched around him to make a run for it, but I'd barely reached the steps when two demigods charged me. Now, my shoulder was still bleeding and hurt like hell, and I had a dying giant behind me making these incredibly disturbing warbling noises. But I wasn't putting it past him that he'd somehow find a way to disembowel me still. So I retreated to the opposite side of the porch where a quick glance over the railing told me no one would be waiting for me if I made a break for it that way.

But I never got the chance to find out if my escape plan would've worked. One of the two demigods who'd joined the fight lifted a throwing knife and threw it at my face. I managed to avoid becoming Pinhead by ducking, and thought, "*Well, thank the gods for those demigod reflexes,*" but *then* I thought, "*Wait a minute, dumbass. You wouldn't even* be *here if it weren't for those demigod genes and reflexes.*" So I retracted my thanks and prepared to fight two demigods who likely weren't arguing with the voices in their heads.

Keira appeared from a brawl behind the demigods and ran her sword through one, which gave me the opportunity to concentrate on the guy who'd tried to turn me into a life-sized voodoo doll. "I don't," I shouted at him as I thrust my blade into that indentation between the clavicles, which probably had a name but Havard must not have ever learned it either, "appreciate people throwing knives at my face!"

As I retracted my blade, Goliath hit the wooden planks of the porch and it actually shook, so I stared, dumbfounded, at his body for a few seconds before Keira yelled, "Gavyn, hurry! Ninurta's getting away!"

And because that was one bastard I wanted to kill myself, I snapped out of it and ran down the stairs, but I was already too late. He and his remaining demigods jumped into three separate vans that hardly slowed down as they screeched past us on the street, and the Sumerian war god once again disappeared.

HAVARD GETS HITCHED

(And I discover I'm a little too attracted to my great-great-grandmother)

Yngvarr laughed as I nervously paced the orchard, occasionally pulling apple blossoms from a low-hanging tree branch and twisting off petals to scatter on the ground at my feet. "She's already agreed to marry you," he teased. "Are you afraid she won't show?"

"I'm afraid of a lot of things, brother," I answered. "But Arnbjorg changing her mind isn't one of them."

"Then why don't you leave some of the blossoms on the trees," he suggested. "After all, Idun brought back the flowers just for your wedding."

I dropped the petals and sighed, stuffing my hands into my pockets so I wouldn't strip the trees. "Do you think I could ever end up a husband like our father?"

"No," Yngvarr immediately answered. "Never. You're a far better man than he ever was."

"But we didn't know him when he was young," I argued.

"We know of his reputation," he pointed out. "You would never hurt Arnbjorg the way he destroyed our mother."

Voices interrupted our conversation as Arnbjorg's entourage arrived, my sisters forming a wall in front of her.

Yngvarr and our sisters were the only guests at the ceremony itself. Afterward, we'd return to the palace where all of Asgard would gather for a celebration, but we'd decided this brief moment when our union was consecrated would be for our family only, in part because hers had disappeared and couldn't mark this occasion with her. And if her parents and brothers couldn't be with us, we wouldn't invite gods who were strangers to witness our marriage either.

My sisters approached me and one by one kissed my cheek then I finally let myself look at my bride, a glowing vision of white silk with soft apple blossoms woven into the braid around her head. She was resplendent. And I'd never seen her so happy. Behind Arnbjorg, Frigg—who, as the goddess of marriage, would perform the rites—placed a kiss on my cheek then my bride's and put a hand over ours. She blessed us, praying that our marriage would be fruitful, and we swore our allegiance to one another in Arnbjorg's favorite place in Asgard. Somehow, Idun seemed to know the marriage was almost complete because apple blossoms began to gently break away from the trees, creating a shower of fragrant white petals.

In one of the few customs we gods shared with the mortals who invoked us, Frigg asked me to present my new bride with an ancestral sword—a symbol of our union as it would be given to our firstborn son. My Sword of Light and Prophecy had been modeled after the one I placed in Arnbjorg's hands, but this sword lacked the enchantments of mine. Still, it was exquisitely crafted and one of the finest swords in all of Asgard. Finally, we exchanged rings and Frigg declared our marriage sacred and permanent. She then led us back to our palace where almost everyone in Asgard awaited the elaborate celebration my sisters had planned.

I quickly scanned the crowd for Freyja, and I'd asked Yngvarr to watch for her as well. I wouldn't allow anything to spoil this day, especially a petty and jealous goddess like her. But I didn't spot her, and I was soon pulled away from Yngvarr's side as friends embraced me and congratulated us. Thor and Sif brought us such large steins of ale that I suspected I paled at the prospect of having to drink it, which the large god found quite funny, while Sif helped Arnbjorg sip from her own. Soon, both women were giggling and I was finally beginning to find the entire situation funny myself.

Dagr kept the sun shining brightly above us for a long time, so that our wedding feast extended into what should have been night. But no one was in any hurry to return to their homes. We danced until our feet ached, and even Odin himself appeared to congratulate us. Admittedly, it bothered me that Arnbjorg seemed so flattered by this gesture, but I simply thanked the All-Father and returned to my guests. After countless hours of revelry, I heard a familiar voice calling my name and turned to see Gunnr waving at me. I'd seen her around, dancing and drinking with the other Valkyries, but she was attempting to get my attention now so I excused myself from Arnbjorg's company and joined her and my brother.

"Havard," she exclaimed, hugging me quickly, "who would have thought you could convince a woman as lovely as she to marry you?"

I laughed because Gunnr and I were old friends, and we both knew she was only teasing. "Certainly not me," I agreed.

"Gunnr says she has news," Yngvarr said.

I stood up straighter, because I'd asked her to find Arnbjorg's family.

"I've located her younger brother," she said. "No sign of her parents or older brother. If they've been taken from Midgard, they're beyond my reach."

"So her younger brother, Finn, you've found him in Midgard?"

Gunnr nodded. "He's on a farm along with nearly a hundred captives of this war. They're not being fed particularly well, Havard, to say nothing of their treatment."

I glanced over my shoulder toward my new wife who laughed as Tyr twirled her to the music and my chest ached. I didn't want to leave her already, but I *had* to rescue her brother. Yngvarr, as usual, seemed to guess my thoughts and said, "We'll leave in the morning. Lay off the ale, little brother. It could be a long journey."

"I can't tell her where I'm going," I said quietly. "I can't get her hopes up if we fail. So what do I tell her?"

"Only that you have business in Midgard you must attend to and you'll return to her as quickly as possible," he answered. "I'll get the specifics from Gunnr. Enjoy the rest of your celebration." He winked at me and added, "And don't stay up too late tonight either."

Dagr eventually allowed the sun to set and our revelry came to an end. The sun returned far too quickly though, and as its earliest rays peeked into our bedroom, I groaned and rolled over before remembering I needed to leave. I hadn't even told Arnbjorg yet that I was going to Midgard. I kissed her forehead and she opened one sleepy eye at me. "I have to help Yngvarr with something important in Midgard. I'll return as soon as I can."

Arnbjorg sat up, gaping at me. "Now? What could possibly be so important, Havard? We've only been married a day!"

"I know, but we think a friend may be in trouble." I didn't think that should count as lying to my wife since Finn was certainly in trouble and needed our help.

Arnbjorg reluctantly allowed me to leave without too much argument, and I found Yngvarr in the stables, waiting for me with a surprise. Gunnr stood next to him, stroking her beloved winged horse. "Are you anticipating fallen heroes, Gunnr?" I asked.

"I'm anticipating you and Yngvarr needing my assistance," she answered.

As a Valkyrie, Gunnr couldn't travel to Midgard unless she had a purpose there, so her belief that Yngvarr and I may need her help was probably rooted in her desire to travel rather than any anticipation of trouble two war gods couldn't handle. But knowing her boredom and resentment over her entrapment here, I pretended to agree with her and we set out to Midgard.

It was winter here, and snow blanketed the barren fields. With work there suspended for the season, Finn and the other male slaves were most likely herding sheep, and as we stopped to give our horses a break, we discussed taking a number of the herd back to Asgard with us as tribute. We had our own livestock, of course, but we all agreed men should never think they could challenge us gods by breaking our laws.

By the time we reached the land where Finn now lived, the sun had almost set. Gunnr pointed to the west and said, "There. You see the smoke rising from the lord's chimney? That's where you'll find the mortal who bought freemen who'd committed no crimes, which we should never abide."

I nodded in agreement. Men so often fashioned their behavior and laws to avoid incurring our wrath, but perhaps we'd neglected Midgard too much lately. They'd forgotten the kind of vengeance we could unleash. "We'll remind them what happens when they ignore our rules."

"By the time the sun rises again, this land will lie in ruins," Yngvarr added. "And men will think twice before making enemies of us."

"My wedding present to my bride," I said, "is the vindication of her family's fate. This lord will not survive."

Yngvarr nudged his horse's flanks, and we rode up to the lord's home, his oil lamps illuminating the windows with a soft, flickering light. A wolf howled in the distance, and sheep bleated in response, which gave me an idea as to where I might find Finn. I dismounted and pulled my sword, and it immediately glowed in response to my touch. All around me, the air filled with the charge of an impending battle. It was wildly intoxicating in a way no ale could ever match.

Scuffling inside the home made us each pause in our approach, and Yngvarr waved Gunnr to the rear so no one could escape. We waited until she had reached her position then knocked the door from its hinges and entered the warm home that smelled of lamb stew and spiced apples. The lord of the house and his grown sons attacked, but Yngvarr and I easily repelled them, sending them retreating into the kitchen where they'd have no escape.

From the back, Gunnr emerged, pushing a woman and a child in front of her. "What do you want me to do with them, my lord?" she asked me.

I had no use for survivors. "Kill them."

"Even the child?"

"What will become of him if we allow him to live? There will be no one left to care for him."

"Please," the man begged, "don't hurt my children."

"You," I hissed, "had no qualms about hurting the children you purchased, including a fifteen-year-old boy. He was a freeman's son. You violated our laws."

"We were desperate for labor," the man stuttered.

But Yngvarr grew impatient with the man's excuses and beheaded one of the men we'd forced to retreat. The boy screamed and Gunnr grabbed his arm, dragging him from the house along with his mother. The blade of my sword was alight with the ferocity of the sun now, its power merging with my own so that I could no longer tell where the power originated. "You will watch," I ordered the man, "as each of your sons fall. And when you die, you'll leave Midgard in disgrace and everyone in Niflheim will know your shame."

Yngvarr beheaded another young man and I a third before turning to the lord of the house and running my sword through his heart. Outside, screams joined the panicked bleating of the sheep as the herd became disrupted. "Help Gunnr find Finn," I said to Yngvarr. "I'll bring down the house."

He urged me to hurry and slipped out, and I held my sword in both hands, willing its power into the most destructive force in any of the nine realms, which exploded from the sword and my body, leveling the walls and sending rubble and fire into the night sky. As the air cleared, I stepped over the rubble and used the tip of my sword to etch a warning to others in the charred remains of a table: This is the consequence of men believing themselves as the equals of gods.

CHAPTER FOURTEEN

Keira sat across from me and gently removed the bandage on my shoulder so she could put a clean one over my new stitches. I kept shooting her disturbed glances, and she kept returning them like I was the one who'd participated in the slaughter of an entire family. Of course, I hadn't *told* her about my dream yet, so she had no idea why I was looking at her so funny, but details like that seemed totally unimportant.

She taped the new bandage down and gave up. "You've been looking at me like I'm the anti-Christ all morning."

"I think maybe you *are*," I shot back.

She blinked at me and asked, "You think I'm the anti-Christ now?"

I shrugged then yelped because, like the dumbass I was, I'd already forgotten I'd had my shoulder stitched up *twice* now and shrugging hurt like hell. "I think I'd completely misjudged you, because anyone who can murder a child has to be evil."

Keira narrowed her eyes and threw the medical tape into

the first aid kit. "I've *never* hurt a child, and I never would. How can you say that?"

"You did!" I argued. "You want me to believe every one of these dreams is a memory of Havard's, right? So you don't get to claim only some of them are accurate just because you don't like what I'm dreaming about now."

Keira gasped and stood up, backing away from me. "But I would never do something like that..." she whispered.

"And yet, you did," I snapped. I recounted the entire dream for her, and as she listened, the color drained from her face. "And Havard's message. *That's* the way gods think, isn't it? We're gods and we're more powerful than you humans so we can do whatever we want?"

She shook her head but her mind seemed trapped in a past she clearly couldn't remember. "I've never been so cruel, Gavyn. I don't understand why I'd do something like that."

And she sounded so sincere, so *sick* over this forgotten memory that I actually felt sorry for her. "Maybe because Havard ordered you to. But at least you still have a mind of your own. Imagine having this asshole's DNA in you and having to worry about it taking over."

"It won't," she promised, but she no longer sounded so sure.

"And Yngvarr was so casual about the whole thing. I think that bothers me the most," I admitted. I mean, this guy was my *friend*. And thanks to Havard constantly butting in with his feelings, I loved him like my own brother. How the hell was I supposed to reconcile his past actions with the man I knew?

"It won't do any good to talk to him about it," Keira said. "He won't remember this either. But we know now what the Sword of Light can do, and we *have* to keep it out of the Sumerians' hands, just in case they can figure out how to make it work."

"About that..." I took a deep breath. "I could see the sword Havard gave Arnbjorg so clearly. And it's the same one that's in your father's sword room."

"I'm not surprised," she sighed, and while that may have been true, she *did* look sad and disappointed. I mean, the guy was a total asshole, but he was still her father.

Agnes, disguised again as an old witch, entered the room and waved a wrinkled, spotted hand at us. "Come. We have visitors."

"Stay. I don't care," I retorted.

She put her hands on her hips, which made her robe billow around her like bat wings, and I nodded to myself in complete agreement that she *would* make a terrifying vampire. But then I wondered if there were a vampire dentist somewhere who'd make fang-dentures for the ancient blood-suckers among them, or if vampires were like sharks and constantly regrew fangs.

Agnes squinted at me and snapped, "You'd better not be undressing me with your eyes."

"Oh, my God," I groaned. "Keira, kill me now. Here, you can use my sword." I handed her the sword leaning against the wall, and she turned around and handed it to Agnes. "Traitor," I muttered.

"Up," she ordered. "This might actually be important."

"Probably," I agreed. "Which is exactly why I want to stay in here."

I followed them back to Agnes's room anyway where Tyr sat at the table with an unfamiliar man and woman. They each wore grave expressions, which I didn't think boded well for my secret hope that our mysterious visitors had come to whisk me off to Vegas for an extended weekend as thanks for killing Willy. And then I snorted because "killing Willy" sounded like something I should snort at, and Keira just sighed and moved away from me, but really, it was too late to pretend like she didn't know me.

"Gavyn," Tyr said, "this is Mama Pacha, and—"

"Mama... Pacha..." I repeated slowly. She lifted an eyebrow at me, and the corners of her lips turned into the slightest of smiles. "Do I *have* to call you Mama or will you answer to Pacha? Never mind. Everyone else ignores me, you may as well, too."

"I can't imagine why," she said.

"You finished?" Tyr asked me.

I gestured for him to continue, but he really should've known by now I was *never* finished.

"And this is Inti." Tyr held up his hand before I could say anything. "They're Incan, and no, you can't give them nicknames."

What happened next must have been preplanned and rehearsed, because Keira and Agnes took turns welcoming the Incan gods and asking them questions about their flight, and Agnes even seemed ready to break into song if that didn't keep me quiet. I crossed my arms and pouted, deciding to make up for lost time at the earliest opportunity by breaking into my own rendition of "Sweet Child of Mine." But when Agnes said, "There's been an uprising among the Incans," I lost interest in singing.

"An uprising? What exactly does that mean?" I asked.

"It means," Pacha explained, "that some of the gods from our pantheon are following the example created by the Sumerians. They want to be worshipped again, and would rather rule through fear than not rule at all."

"Supay and Paricia have already begun terrorizing the western coast of South America," Inti added. "There was an earthquake off the coast of Chile yesterday, and today, a tidal wave slammed ashore. Almost a hundred people were killed."

"But how do you know that's your rogue gods? Earthquakes can cause tidal waves," I argued.

"Because they've taken responsibility for it," he replied. "And the Peruvian military has engaged with them as well, but modern militaries can't fight gods, especially when one of them commands a legion of demons."

"Whoa," I interjected. "A legion of *what*?"

"Demons," Keira supplied helpfully.

"And Paricia is the god of floods," Agnes added.

"Why do you know that?" I demanded.

Agnes shrugged. "I know things."

"So is South America just filled with demons now?" I asked. Did they really think I was going anywhere *near* that continent after telling me something like that?

"There might be a few," Inti said carefully, but what I *heard* was, "The gates of Hell have been opened, and now is a good time to take up residence in Asgard."

So I grabbed Keira's hand and begged, "Take me to Valhalla now. You can even kill me first if you want."

"We're not actually going to South America to fight demons," Keira said then she looked at Tyr hopefully and added, "Are we?"

"I don't really know *how* to fight demons," Tyr answered.

"What exactly *are* demons?" I asked. "And will guns work on *them*? Because I'm getting really tired of carrying around a weapon that doesn't even work on anything."

"It works on demigods," Keira reminded me.

"Yeah, but the gods' archaic rules of warfare prohibit us from using them," I said smartly. Keira even arched an eyebrow at me as if waiting to see if I could define the fancy words I'd just used.

"I don't think we can shoot demons," Yngvarr announced from behind me, which startled me because he hadn't been in the room with us before now.

I dropped Keira's hand so I could spin around and point accusingly at him. "How many times do I have to tell you not to sneak up on people?"

"Technically," he corrected, "you've warned me not to sneak up on you when you're armed. You're not armed."

"I could be," I argued, even though everyone could plainly see my hands were empty, and it's not like I could hide a sword in my pocket. I did, however, think that sounded kinda dirty, so I leaned toward Keira and whispered, "Want to see if that's really a sword in my pocket?"

Not surprisingly, she pushed me away from her and mumbled something about reconsidering taking me to Valhalla now.

"And," Yngvarr said, "I think we *have* to go to South America. I mean, demons running around the streets of Lima? If we don't go, it'll set a bad precedent."

"Dying will set a bad precedent," I retorted.

"We're not the Winchesters," Keira added. "We don't know how to fight demons."

"We can't really fight them," Pacha said. "They're malevolent spirits, so they're not alive. We can only send them back to Supay's realm."

"Again," I reiterated, "we're not the Winchesters. I don't do exorcisms."

"That's only if someone is possessed," Yngvarr corrected.

I blinked at him then snapped, "I *definitely* didn't sign up for possession. I'm out."

"Actually," Inti said, "exorcisms are performed if a demon is haunting a house or something, too. And Mama Pacha and I can cast them back to Ukhu Pacha—"

"Is that like Mama Pacha's asshole ex-husband?" I interrupted.

"Can I bribe you not to speak again?" he asked.

Tyr laughed so I flipped him off before telling Inti I could totally be bribed, but I hoped he wasn't a cheapskate like Frey.

"Ukhu Pacha is Supay's realm," Inti explained. "Mama Pacha and I can send the demons back if we have a bit of help in warding off attacks by their own demigod armies."

"Please don't make me go demon hunting," I groaned.

I suddenly found myself missing Hunter, maybe because he'd made me sit through *The Exorcist* when we were in high school, and I'd never really recovered. To pay him back, I'd sometimes call him in the middle of the night, yell, "The power of Christ compels you!" and hang up. Remembering Keira had been able to receive phone calls in Asgard, I pulled my cellphone from my pocket, dialed Hunter's number, yelled, "The power of Christ compels you!" as soon as he answered then hung up.

Everyone in the room stared at me for a few seconds before resuming their conversation as if I weren't even there.

My phone chimed with the notification I had a new text message, and I smiled as I glanced at the screen. Hunter had texted, "What an excellent day for an exorcism."

And suddenly, going to Peru to fight demons didn't seem like such a terrible idea. Yeah, my dad and best friend were in some parallel universe where they'd be safe from whatever hell was unleashed on Earth, but billions of dads and best friends and moms and siblings and lovers weren't, and maybe I could actually do something to change that. "Okay," I said. "I'd like Joachim to come with me. He's a total badass with that bow. Maybe if we dip the arrows in holy water, it'll slow those demons down."

"Doubt it," Inti said. "These aren't Catholic demons."

"Are any demons Catholic?" I asked.

"We'll send Joachim with your team," Tyr hurriedly interjected before I could derail us on a ridiculous argument about the religion of demons.

Yngvarr and Keira also volunteered to stay with me, and to my surprise, Inti offered to go with us through the streets of Lima and cast Supay's demons back to their underworld. I thought there was an exceptionally good chance he'd regret his offer before we even landed, but Tyr and Keira smartly kept me away from him on the plane. Instead, I once again sat sandwiched between them and Keira even tried to convince me to read some Incan mythology on her iPad. I thought it was kinda strange they *had* all these mythology books on their tablets, but Keira just said *some* people didn't like everyone else thinking they were the village idiot, which honestly, I found hard to believe.

After landing in Lima and renting several cars for our demon-hunting party, we were greeted by tanks and armored vehicles rolling down the streets, so we figured they probably knew how to find Supay and Paricia and followed them. Loudspeakers blasted warnings to the civilians, but since they were in Spanish, I had no idea what they were saying. Probably something about not picking up demon hitchhikers and avoiding any gods that looked like the Devil.

It didn't take long before a swarm of military vehicles stopped us, but the somewhat terrifying moment of having a herd of soldiers with automatic rifles pointed at our car quickly faded into a lot of shouting in Spanish and waving our convoy through. I shot Keira my "What the bloody hell?" look, and she explained, "They recognized Mama Pacha in the lead car. And I'm assuming she told them why we're here."

Inti, who was sitting in the passenger seat upfront, turned toward me and added, "The military has been trying to subdue Supay and Paricia, and not surprisingly, the results have been deadly for both soldiers and civilians. Paricia retaliated with a devastating flood on the coast that wiped out entire villages."

"Oh, my God," Keira whispered. I instinctively reached for her hand to comfort her, and by the time I realized what I was doing, I'd already woven my fingers through hers. Fully expecting her to yank her hand away from me, I prepared an apology in my mind, but she only looked at me, wide-eyed and sad and maybe even a little hopeful that I could somehow undo the damage these forgotten gods had caused.

"We need to start setting an example," I decided. "No survivors. But we need to make a show of it, let the other gods considering a violent comeback know what fates await them if they murder innocent people."

"You want to abduct these gods?" Yngvarr asked. "And do what with them?"

"Take them to Asgard. Hell, bind them in Loki's cave. I don't care as long as it sends a clear message they're going to regret not staying in the shadows."

"Do we *have* an official torturer?" Keira asked.

Yngvarr nodded and muttered, "Odin," then seemed to remember he was talking about Keira's father so he shot her an apologetic smile.

Inti pointed to the vehicles in front of us and announced, "They're pulling over in the Plaza Mayor. I suspect Supay and Paricia have taken up residence in the Government Palace."

"Well, yeah," I agreed. "If I were going to stage a supernatural coup, I'd totally take up residence in a palace, too."

As soon as our car stopped, I pushed my door open and scowled at the Government Palace, irrationally hoping Supay and Paricia would just save me the trouble of having to go in there by venturing outside and surrendering. Not surprisingly, that didn't happen. But as car doors slammed closed all around me, I thought I saw dark shapes slithering down the walls of the palace, slick like oil but with sharp, jagged edges. "Um, am I the only one who sees the building bleeding?"

"No," Inti replied. "And it's not bleeding. Supay's demons are coming to greet us."

CHAPTER FIFTEEN

Okay, here's the deal: I'm not going to say I ran down the street screaming, but I may not have stayed by the Government Palace either. I'd been expecting Supay's demons to look *kinda* human at least, but what dropped from the sides of the building and formed into distinct shapes was most certainly *not* humanoid. Instead, I found myself staring at elongated bodies that stood upright, but their spindly legs seemed too thin to support their weight, and their heads were straight out of a cheesy 80's horror movie. Long, bony snouts sniffed the air and thick horns—which appeared awfully sharp, I might add—curved upward from their grotesque heads.

Each long, thin arm ended in three fingers... scratch that, three *talons*. And honestly, who *would* stick around to find out how easily those demons could sink their claws into soft human flesh? Unfortunately, their equally long legs made them extraordinarily fast runners so I didn't get very far.

Keira shouted my name, and by the time I spun around, the demon was already in the air, leaping toward me with its talons spread and its snout wide open, and I had the sudden, absurd thought, "*I wonder if they eat people? I mean, vegetarian demons seem pretty unlikely.*" And in that precious, split second before being mauled by a demon, I also thought, "*Being eaten alive is* definitely *an unacceptable way to die.*"

I slashed my sword through the air, expecting the blade to pass through the beast lunging toward me, but surprisingly, it made contact with a firm body and knocked it to the ground. The demon screeched and the hair on my neck and arms stood on end. It was every bit as unholy a sound as you'd expect, considering it *was* a demon and all.

I quickly regained my footing as the demon sprang to its feet, its arm bearing the gash from the blade of my sword. The wound didn't bleed or ooze though. Instead, a strange yellow glow peeked out from beneath the open skin of the demon. "Inti!" Keira yelled. "Cast them back to the Underworld!"

Inti raised his hands and murmured, "I command you to return to your permanent residence, and to leave the servants of the supreme ruler, Inti, alone and unharmed." At this point, I *wanted* to interrupt and remind him I sure as hell didn't serve him, but since he was trying to banish the demon who still looked at me like I was lunch, I wisely kept my mouth shut.

The demons that had surrounded us shrieked in response, and if I *hadn't* been completely surrounded by demons, I really would have run off screaming, and even though I know it's not possible, I would have tried to run all the way back to Baton Rouge. "I command you—" Inti began again, but a man's voice stopped him. And if there were ever a time to describe a voice as sinister, this was it.

"Supay," Inti hissed.

Now, considering an actual *demon* had just tried to rip my throat out, I fully expected their boss to look like Dante's devil—horns, spiked tail, pitchfork, the works. But he was

just this tall dude with an ill-advised goatee that was *so* early
1990s, and really, it should have stayed there. But maybe he
was channeling his inner hipster, which also would have
explained a lot about this guy's evil vibe.

Supay had a bow slung over one shoulder and a single
arrow in his hand. And being me, I nodded toward it and
said, "Is that like the magic bullet that murdered JFK? One
arrow's going to fly around in circles and kill us all?"

"Gavyn," Keira whispered, "shut up!"

Joachim kept his bow lowered but an arrow nocked and
ready so that he'd only have to lift it to send a deadly projec-
tile at Supay's heart. And I'd seen that guy shoot. If I were
putting money on who could shoot faster, I'd bet on
Joachim.

"This land isn't your concern, Norse," Supay said. "I'm
simply giving you the opportunity to leave before the blood-
bath begins."

Personally, I thought that sounded like a *great* idea, but
since no one else hurried back to our cars, I just stood there
stupidly wondering what the hell was *wrong* with us. I mean,
did the words "blood" and "bath" *not* scare the shit out of
gods? Maybe not so much the bath part, but if it was a bath
filled with blood—

"'Gavyn," Keira scolded. "Snap out of it."

"I'm snapped," I lied.

Supay shrugged and said, "Stay and die then. It makes no
difference to me."

Perhaps the guy had some kind of demon-whistle that
only evil minions of dark lords could hear because they
suddenly broke out of their stupor and lunged at us. Arrows
flitted from bowstrings and swords carved the air, occasionally bringing squealing monsters to the hot pavement. But
nothing actually *killed* them. Gashes opened, allowing that
strange yellow light to peek through, but the demons always

sprang back to their elongated feet—which also had talons at the end, by the way—and hurled themselves at us again.

"Inti," I yelled, "cast them back to Hell!"

And yeah, they hadn't technically come from Hell, but close enough.

"I'm trying," he yelled back. "It's not working."

"It's not *what*?" Keira and I *both* yelled at the same time.

And because everything was already going especially well for us, Paricia decided to saunter out of the Government Palace and watch the melee, so naturally, I decided I *definitely* had to kill that guy first. It's not that I *wanted* more gods to fight; it just pissed me off that he found our impending dismemberment amusing.

The demons had closed in on us, forcing us to form a tightly packed circle with our backs pressed together. If Inti couldn't banish them to the Underworld, we'd have to find another way to fight back. Remembering Yngvarr had carried my pistol with him in that admittedly super-cool magic trick way gods had of transporting weapons, I pulled it from my waistband and marveled again at how I'd miraculously not shot myself in the ass.

I aimed at the nearest demon, and even though bullets apparently couldn't kill them either, they *did* create the same kind of wounds that allowed the yellow light to escape. I had the sudden idea that if we could open gashes, letting that light seep out, we might at least weaken them enough for Inti to exorcize them. And guns were a hell of a lot faster than arrows, which took time to reload, plus they had the advantage of allowing us to fire from a distance. I wasn't exactly eager to get close enough to these assholes to repeatedly stab them with my sword. "Shoot them," I shouted. "Get as many bullet holes in them as you can."

All around me, gods and demigods put swords and arrows away so they could retrieve handguns, and if they didn't have one, Yngvarr or Agnes seemed to pull one from thin air, which honestly, was a superpower I really wanted to have. We riddled the demons' bodies with bullets, opening jagged wounds all over their furry gray torsos, but the bullets never seemed to exit. Maybe the light inside them was like molten lava or something.

I emptied the entire magazine then stared at the handgun in disgust like it was the gun's fault I'd run out of bullets and hadn't even killed the damn demon. Inti held up his hands and shouted, "I command you to return to your permanent residence, and to leave the servants of the supreme ruler, Inti, alone and unharmed."

Now, I might have just imagined what happened next. I mean, it was almost summer in the southern hemisphere so I was hot and battling demons in what felt like *the* Hell, so who could really say what was real or not? But all those holes I'd created in the wolf-demon I'd emptied my magazine into began to glow brighter as if it really *had* been filled with molten lava and was about to erupt.

And if the wolf-demon was about to erupt, I was standing way too close. No way did I want to get covered in molten demon juice. I glanced at Keira, and she glanced just as nervously back at me. If I'd had more time, I would have told her I was pretty sure I was falling in love with her and that I was sorry we had to die by demon-juice-drowning, which was definitely *not* a dignified way to die, but the damn thing *did* explode.

I braced myself for the inevitable acid demon rain, but only a brief moment of warmth passed over me. When I opened my eyes, the demon was gone. Some of the others had begun to vibrate like they were about to explode, too, so this time, I watched as the odd yellow light burst from their bodies and scattered around the Plaza Mayor before disappearing altogether.

Supay sighed irritably and scowled at me. "Do you have any idea how long it's going to take for them to regenerate now?"

"Um... am I really supposed to care?"

"Yes," he snapped. "Because it pisses me off and you should care about pissing off the gods who are trying to kill you!"

I threw my hands up in exasperation. "I want to piss you off *because* you're going to kill me, dumbass!"

Keira nudged my arm to get my attention and handed me a sword. "In the future, make sure you're armed before insulting a god who's threatening to kill you."

Supay responded by lifting his bow, but an arrow flew past me before I could even raise my sword. I didn't need to turn around to know Joachim had shot that arrow. Even though my new friend was a total badass marksman, his arrow embedded in Supay's shoulder, simply because gods could move so quickly. Before Joachim could nock another arrow, the Incan demigods who'd been recruited by Supay and Paricia spilled into the Plaza Mayor as if every building had come alive with the heroes of an ancient religion.

"Well, this seems ominous," I said smartly.

"Gavyn, stay behind me," Yngvarr demanded.

"What?" I demanded back. "No way."

"If they shoot at us, bullets can't kill me," he insisted. "And you're too important to die at the hands of demigods who were dumb enough to follow the Incan devil."

Sure, what he was saying sounded logical, but Havard's ridiculously powerful and annoying genes refused to allow me to put Yngvarr in harm's way. So as soon as the Incan demigods reached the street, I drew my sword on the closest one. Yngvarr cursed at me, but quickly became preoccupied by some asshole trying to turn him into a paraplegic.

Mama Pacha, who'd been quietly observing this whole

time, stamped her foot on the ground and extended her arms, and I thought, *"If this is your idea of helping, you could have stayed in the car. Because a getaway driver would be kinda nice right about now, as long as it's not Agnes."*

I really don't know how I always have so much time to have such stupid thoughts when I'm in the middle of a battle.

But as it turned out, Mama Pacha wasn't just trying to cause a distraction by looking silly, because the ground rumbled and shook, gently at first, but soon, none of the Incan demigods could remain standing. And perhaps most shocking was that her earthquake didn't affect us. Instead, we were like the eye of a hurricane where winds were calm but causing massive damage all around the eyewall.

As Supay's and Paricia's heroes fell helplessly to the ground, I grasped what would most likely be my only opportunity to get close to Supay. He noticed me charging him, of course, and raised his bow. Behind me, Keira cried out a warning as Supay released the string and the arrow sailed toward me. And somehow, I slid to the pavement and the arrow went over my head. I stopped only two feet away from Supay's legs and swung my blade at his knee, forcing him to the ground before leaping to my feet and holding my sword above his neck.

"Let this be a warning to every god who tries to rule through fear and violence," I said. "I'm coming for you next."

CHAPTER SIXTEEN

News of the takeover in Russia reached us before we could even get to the airport. Two more gods I'd never heard of and whose names I couldn't pronounce had followed the lead of other forgotten gods and resurfaced, destroying villages and marching into Moscow in a surprising coup. Berstuk and Medeina now held one of the most powerful countries in the world in their dangerous hands.

"Can't you gods get a better hobby?" I whined as we prepared to board a different flight. Instead of going back to Baton Rouge, we—and by we, I mean Tyr and Agnes—decided to head to Moscow so we could liberate yet another country from the clutches of evil deities whose egos were really too inflated for their own good.

"I had a better hobby until the Sumerians started causing trouble," Tyr replied, his chin lifting just slightly like he was getting defensive about my frustration with *all* of the gods.

I waited for a few moments to see if he was going to volunteer the information or if I'd have to annoy the hell out of him first. And apparently, he thought we needed a little annoyance because he didn't elaborate on this mysterious hobby. "Drowning kittens?" I pretended to guess.

He blinked at me so I continued. "Playing triple-dog-dare with wolves?"

More blinking. Okay, he asked for it.

"Dressing up Loki like a dominatrix?"

"I think that's a term for women," Keira interjected helpfully.

"Loki turned into a mare to fool around with a stallion," I replied. "He can totally pull off a dominatrix."

Keira nodded. "Good point."

"Although, he's already bound. I'm thinking he's the submissive and Tyr is the dominator," I said.

I had no idea what got into Keira, but she decided to play along. "True, and given how laid back Tyr is, he's probably a total wild man in that cave."

"And Loki's *definitely* into some kinky shit," I added.

"Please stop," Agnes begged.

But Tyr still hadn't cracked, and I couldn't let him win. And besides, I had an ally. She so rarely let her guard down enough to joke around. I didn't want her falling back into Valkyrie mode. "What do you think Sigyn's doing the whole time?"

"She's been stuck in that cave with Loki for centuries," Keira said. "She's probably hoping Tyr conveniently forgets Loki's safe word."

I choked on the breath I'd just taken and Tyr finally groaned and snapped, "I paint, okay?"

"Paint," I repeated flatly.

"Paint," Keira also repeated flatly.

"Shut up," Tyr sighed.

But I had no intention of shutting up. In fact, I was going to do the exact opposite. "Let me guess. You paint nudes. Like Loki. As a woman. In leather."

"And straps," Keira added. "Don't forget the bondage part."

"Yeah," I agreed.

"Wait," Yngvarr interjected. "If Loki's wearing leather, how can Tyr paint nudes?"

"I hate you all," Tyr said.

"None of you sit next to me on the plane," Agnes ordered.

"Not even Yngvarr?" I asked. "Just gonna meet him in the bathroom, huh?"

But Agnes wasn't easily rattled like Tyr. She glanced at Yngvarr, shrugged, and said, "Maybe. I'll let you know."

And since she hadn't transformed back into the five-hundred-year-old witch, Yngvarr just arched an eyebrow at her and said, "I'll be waiting."

And none of that was okay. Since I doubted brain bleach actually existed, even in Asgard, I decided I really needed to take a different flight. Keira laughed and told me it was my fault for starting all of this, but she offered to sit with me on the plane to distract me. Naturally, I had to tell her I'd be totally willing to meet *her* in the bathroom, but she just rolled her eyes and mumbled something that sounded like "village idiot."

Our flight, which included a layover in Amsterdam, would take nearly eighteen hours, which meant the people of Russia were trapped under the rule of at least two quite likely evil gods for an entire day. And Berstuk and Medeina weren't only pissed off about being forgotten—they were angry about the destruction of their forests. I didn't know anything about them, of course, but Keira did and as soon as we reached our cruising altitude, she pulled out her iPad and handed it to me. "Berstuk has always had an evil side to him," she explained, gesturing to the picture on the screen.

"Are you kidding me? Another devil?" I mean, the guy had horns and everything.

"That's only how mortals imagined him," Keira explained. "But the image of a horned man may have come from his ability to shapeshift, especially into a huge, tusked boar."

"Boar," I said. "Now I have to fight a pig. A *pig*, Keira."

"A boar, Gavyn," she corrected. "And he's no ordinary boar either. He'll be much bigger and unbelievably fierce. Not to mention, his bristles are supposedly venomous."

I stared at her for a few seconds to see if she was just messing with me, because a pig with poisonous hair sounded like something that was *literally* out of a child's nightmare. Or mine, for that matter. But Keira stared back at me like she *hadn't* just told me we'd be fighting a poisonous-pig-monster, so I looked across the aisle to where Yngvarr and Tyr were sitting and hissed, "Did you know Berstuk turns into a poisonous pig?"

"Yes," they both answered, neither bothering to look up from their own tablets where they were probably watching Loki porn.

I twisted around to glare at Agnes, who'd sat behind me, but she'd decided to travel as Hatshepsut's mummy and her nine-thousand-year-old mouth hung open as she snored in what may have been fake sleep. Not that I blamed her. I'd ignore us, too.

But Joachim was sitting next to her, so I hissed at *him*. "Dude, he's a poisonous *pig*."

"Apparently," he agreed.

"Gavyn," Keira said. "We haven't even talked about Medeina yet."

I groaned and sank back in my seat. "Let me guess. She's a poisonous bear."

"Nope."

"Deer?"

"Why would anyone ever be a poisonous deer?"

I shrugged, because really, why would anyone ever want to be a poisonous pig?

"Wolf," she said.

I groaned again. "Not another one."

My shoulder still ached from my last encounter with a supernatural wolf. At least I hadn't popped the stitches again, but at some point, I really needed not to be attacked by supernatural animals that thought I looked like a ribeye. "Any chance Frey and the rest of our allies are going to join us in Moscow?" I asked. "Because they can get off their lazy asses and help us here."

"They can't," Keira argued. "They're still helping the CIA track down the Sumerians, who've set their sights on the U.S. Maybe the Sumerians figure it's only fair to take over America now. Or maybe it's payback for how many temples have been destroyed."

I waved her off because it's not like I'd had anything to do with *that* decision. I mean, I hadn't even been old enough to vote yet. And it didn't really matter *why* the Sumerians wanted the United States so badly. They clearly had no intention of leaving my country. "They've been a little too quiet since the showdown in Baton Rouge with Ninurta," I said. "What do you think they're up to?"

Keira took a deep breath and lowered her eyes. We were all exhausted, but at the same time, with so many threats all over the world and so much uncertainty hanging over our heads, none of us could really rest. Except Agnes, but that was probably because she was a witch. "I honestly don't know, Gavyn. But I'm afraid we're going to find out soon enough."

AS WE DESCENDED INTO MOSCOW, the pilot reminded us that the city could be dangerous and advised us to use caution. I thought it was kinda stupid to remind a plane full of people that the city he'd just flown us to was under siege and we could all die, but then again, I was one of the idiots on the plane that had just voluntarily entered that city, so what did I know? I'd expected Moscow to appear deserted, much like New Orleans when the Sumerians took over, but it was the exact opposite. As our taxis slowly headed toward the Kremlin, the streets became thicker with angry mobs that refused to accept a new religion or government.

I guessed Russians were just used to revolutions because they had no intention of allowing Berstuk and Medeina to rule them.

Our taxis finally stopped when the wall of protestors no longer parted to allow traffic through. In broken English, our cab driver told us, "Six blocks toward the Moskva."

We'd have to look for the Slavic gods on foot.

Our small group of gods and demigods squeezed through tightly packed bodies, all screaming and shouting in a language I didn't understand, but I could easily imagine what they were saying. Probably a lot of what I would be saying, and maybe even with the same amount of profanity. I mean, they were Russian. And Russians know how to curse. But as we turned a corner to head toward the Kremlin, Tyr, who'd been leading the way, suddenly stopped and I bumped into him then was shoved from behind by the swell of humans pushing in the same direction. Keira grabbed my hand so we wouldn't get separated, and it was about that time I noticed why Tyr had stopped so unexpectedly.

Ahead of us, hanging from the trees that surrounded the Kremlin, were the disfigured bodies of what I could only assume had been the leaders of the Russian government.

Most were missing limbs, and their faces were largely unrecognizable. Berstuk and Medeina had not only taken over this country, they'd sent their own message to its people:

submit or face the same fate. "My God," I whispered as I stared helplessly at the bloody, mangled body dangling above us.

"The people are rising up against the gods," Keira said. "If we don't defeat them soon, it could be catastrophic."

I couldn't even guess how many people had packed the streets surrounding the complex. Hundreds of thousands, maybe? And the gods who wanted to rule them would be just as content to wipe them out.

"Why isn't anyone going beyond the woods?" I asked.

As if to answer me, a snarl erupted from the trees, and was quickly joined by a roar and something that *sounded* like a small child screeching at the top of their lungs. And, honestly, that was the sound that scared the shit out of me and made me want to turn and run, even though I risked being trampled by the mob that was already turning and running. Joachim groaned and swayed next to me as bodies beat against us, and his clear blue eyes swept over the crowd. "They're going to crush people, and we can't stop it."

Those noises erupted from the trees again, and this time, leaves rustled. Whatever was roaming around in there was coming for us.

"Run into the woods," I shouted. "Don't let those monsters out!"

A sword was thrust into my hand, and I didn't even notice who put it there. We were already fighting against the panicked masses, and as soon as we broke free from the crowd, we ran. The trees shook again and that shrieking sound *almost* made me pivot and follow the others away from the Kremlin. But whatever was making that noise would soon emerge from the trees, and I seriously doubted it was coming for hugs.

I reached the tree line first, and although it seemed impossible, it was like stepping into another reality, like I'd somehow crossed this veil that separated my world from the supernatural. Behind me, daylight still shone on the grass, but in front of me, the world became as dark as an abyss in the ocean. Not that I'd ever *been* in an abyss at the bottom of the ocean, but I imagined it was awfully dark. Agnes inhaled a slow, deep breath and quietly announced, "We've got company."

I followed her gaze and may or may not have screamed a bit when I noticed the blood-red eyes staring at me from a tree branch above us. A furry body that was vaguely humanoid leapt at me, that ear-splitting shriek echoing through the small forest. I slashed wildly at the little bastard, and may or may not have screamed again when the damn thing *landed on me*.

"Gavyn," Keira cried. Her sword impaled the psychotic monkey that was trying to eat my brain, which, of course, only made me think it must be a zombie monkey, and I wasn't really sure how to kill a zombie monkey. But impaling its chest obviously didn't work. Keira had managed to get it off me, but the creature immediately sprang to its feet, its fangs bared as it shrieked at us.

And if possessed zombie monkeys weren't bad enough, its friends burst through the dense growth of trees and I found myself staring at an honest-to-God *dragon* and a six-legged beast with curvy, gnarled horns and breath so heinous, I swear it left a yellow, vaporous cloud around its face. So quite naturally, I pointed my sword at it and told Agnes, "Look. Your boyfriend's here."

The monster seemed just as insulted as Agnes.

The dragon roared and flapped its wings, which snapped several branches from nearby trees, and my zombie monkey flung himself at my face again. At least, I assumed it was a he, but I had no intention of checking. I slashed at the creature as it made its descent and figured decapitation often worked on zombies in the movies, so why not on zombie monkeys? And really, what *could* survive decapitation?

But as so often happened in these supernatural battles, I got thrown off my game by something completely unexpected. The dragon opened its mouth, a stream of fire spewing forth, and *ignited the evil little bastard in mid-air*. So now, I not only had a zombie hurling itself at me, but an *on-fire* zombie, and if you've never been attacked by a demonic primate, let me tell you, the blazing kind are much worse.

And perhaps strangest of all was that the fire didn't seem to hurt the weird monkey thing. I mean, maybe it did, but how could I tell when its normal scream sounded like Agnes had grabbed him by the balls?

Again, not that I was checking to see if Agnes *could* emasculate it.

I dove out of the fiery fur-ball's way and rolled onto my shoulder that had *just* stopped throbbing from the last time I popped the stitches. Both the pain and the warm, sticky sensation told me I'd done it again, but the creature had landed and was stalking toward me, still dripping flames from its body. The brief thought that it must not be *real* fire vanished when the leaves caught on fire and flames spread across the ground.

So, let me recap: we had a dragon, a demonic zombie monkey, a weird six-legged horned beast that most likely killed its victims with the world's worst halitosis, *and* a fire that was quickly spreading all around us. Our odds weren't exactly tipping in our favor.

"Can't one of you gods make it rain?" I shouted.

"We're *war* gods," Yngvarr shouted back. "How the hell are we supposed to control the weather?"

"Drekavac," Agnes shouted, which I assumed was some Gaelic curse word for, "*Goddamn zombie monkeys!*"

So I nodded in agreement and raised my sword in the air

like I was William Wallace about to lead a tribe of Scots against the English and yelled, "Yeah, Drekavac!"

Agnes squinted at me, and even though she was the smoking hot redhead again, she had the *exact* same look she'd once given me when she was convinced she'd kidnapped the village idiot. "No, dumbass. That," she paused to point her sword at the possessed primate who happened to be on fire still, "is the forest demon, Drekavac."

I nodded again like I'd known that all along. "And the other two?"

She gestured to the weird six-legged monster that honestly didn't resemble *anything* that existed in this world. "Bukavac and the dragon is Tugarin."

"And knowing their names helps us how?"

Agnes shrugged. "It doesn't."

So I shot *her* my best impersonation of her village-idiot look. "Then why the hell do you think we needed to know that right now?"

She shrugged again. "You didn't."

"I hate you," I sighed.

Drekavac shrieked as if he agreed with me and crouched like he was about to leap again, and my heart threatened to burst from my chest. I'd already backed up against a tree, so I had nowhere else to go. But worse, Keira stood right next to me, and he could just as easily decide to leap on *her*. Before he could become airborne, something shifted within me, just like the time I'd knocked out Tyr and escaped from a room full of gods. I was only vaguely aware of what my own body was doing as I moved toward Drekavac to keep his attention on me.

He sprang into the air and I dropped to the ground, swinging my sword upwards into the flaming belly of the monster. His hide was deceptively thick, but I forced the tip of my blade farther into its body, opening a wide gash in his abdomen. I braced myself for the inevitable downpour of blood and guts and God knows what else was inside something that could survive being set on fire, but only the same unnatural yellow light that had filled the demons in Peru emptied from this forest demon.

Moscow filled with the unholy shrieks of the beast, and I rolled over, freeing my blade and spinning around to stab the demon again. My friends engaged the other two Russian monsters, but as the demon died or returned to whatever the Russian Hell was, I heard a *new* sound coming toward us from the edge of the woods where the buildings that comprised the Kremlin were. The snorting, snuffling sound seemed to alarm the two surviving monsters, because they backed away from us.

Or so I thought.

But as the sound became clearer and revealed itself as the snuffling of a giant boar, I realized the dragon and horned beast were smiling.

CHAPTER SEVENTEEN

Berstuk burst through a growth of trees, snapping branches as he stormed into the small clearing where we'd been battling his demonic minions. Sure, the zombie monkey was dead, or exorcised or whatever, but it had been replaced by a boar the size of a minivan that just happened to have poisonous bristles all over its body. And really, if my choices were between a flaming zombie monkey and an enormous poisonous pig, I would've taken an entire army of flaming zombie monkeys.

Joachim unleashed a volley of arrows at Berstuk, but that only seemed to piss him off. He pawed the ground before lunging toward us, which seemed to snap Bukavac and Tugarin out of their happy daze because *they* lunged at us, too. And of course I was closest to the poisonous pig, which was actually worse than a regular poisonous pig since he was a *godly* poisonous pig, so I braced myself for the impact of getting hit by a bus with bristles that would probably turn *me* into a flaming zombie monkey.

Just as my body reacted to defend Keira, it reacted to the

threat of Berstuk barreling toward me. I jumped out of his path and landed on my shoulder again, and at this point, I wasn't really sure if the damn thing was going to stay attached. But as it turned out, Berstuk's size had one distinct disadvantage: he couldn't pivot quickly, which gave me a chance to injure him from behind.

Wait: that sounded totally pervy. Let me try again.

Berstuk couldn't pivot quickly, which gave me a chance to slice the blade of my sword across his hind leg. He made this awful squealing sound as he turned on me, those bristles along his neck and back standing upright. His eyes still looked completely human, which was worse than the tusks or bristles or his size, and they narrowed slightly as he fixed me in his gaze. I rose to my feet, vaguely aware that my shoulder seemed to be gushing like a burst water pipe, and yelled, "Come on, asshole!"

Not exactly clever, but give me a break: I was in pain and bleeding and squaring off with an evil pig that would have given the Erymanthian boar a run for his money. I had a brief moment of surprise that I even knew what the Erymanthian boar *was* before remembering I actually *didn't* know—Havard had known all about Heracles and his Labors. But Berstuk charged me, and I did the only thing I could: I ran.

Ahead of me was the wall that surrounded the Kremlin, and even if I'd been near one of the lower sections of the wall, I wouldn't have been able to scale it. But Berstuk was gaining on me, and I had nowhere else to go. I could try to evade him in the trees all around us, but with his size and strength, he easily broke limbs and trampled any bushes in his path. I had only one idea, and it was either a crazy one or a stupid one or maybe both.

I spilled into the open space between the trees and wall, but didn't stop until I stood directly beneath one of the towers, a closed gate to one side and a long expanse of wall to the other. The pounding of Berstuk's hooves against the hard ground matched the pounding of my heart as I spun around to face him, holding the hilt of my sword with both hands. He made that angry squealing noise and lowered his head just as I dove out of his way.

I never expected the impact to kill him, and being a supernatural pig, it didn't. But running headfirst into a dense brick wall *did* daze him, and as he stumbled backward, shaking his head as if literally trying to chase away the stars, I drove my blade deep into his neck, slashing downward as best as I could, hoping to find the jugular and bleed this bastard to death.

But I hadn't stopped bleeding either, and by now, the exertion of running and the adrenaline of the battle had caught up to me. As I pulled my sword free, I tripped, falling onto the ground but I couldn't stand again. Moscow grew dark and quiet, and when I closed my eyes, it disappeared.

I ONCE AGAIN AWOKE IN a hospital and sighed loudly when I heard the television, because it sounded like they were speaking Russian and I *really* wanted out of Russia. Keira touched my hand and I smiled up at her, asking, "Here to give me a sponge bath?"

She rolled her eyes and pulled her hand away. "You needed a blood transfusion. They want to keep you overnight."

"Why? To make sure I'm not allergic to someone else's blood?"

Keira shrugged. "It's one night. I'm pretty sure the world won't burn before then."

"Have you been paying attention to what's going on?" I shot back.

"Yeah, about that..." she said carefully, so I groaned and

told her I didn't have enough Demerol in me for this conversation. She just shrugged again and said that had to be true because they hadn't given me *any* Demerol. Given that I was in Russia and all, I thought there was a fairly good chance of at least scoring some vodka, but Keira told me what I'd missed even though I was still completely sober. "Forgotten gods are emerging all over the world, Gavyn. We can't possibly fight them all. We've tried recruiting help, but the Olympians are still refusing to leave Olympus, and almost every other pantheon in the world has these gods trying to reassert their control over pieces of Earth."

"Except the Sumerians," I said. "They want all of it."

Keira nodded and sat on the edge of my bed. "If this turns into a supernatural civil war, we're all going to lose."

I took a deep breath and asked, "And Medeina? Did she ever show up?"

"No. What you did with Berstuk... Gavyn, that was incredible."

I waved her off because it's not like I'd engaged in some brilliant battle—I'd run from the bastard then seized a small opportunity to stab him while he was disoriented.

"Fine," she relented. "You never seem to want us making a big deal about what an amazing hero you are, so I won't. But Russia is still under Medeina's control, and uprisings are erupting all over the country."

"Are you seriously going to make me go back to the Kremlin to fight her?" I complained.

She shook her head, and her eyes already told me she was losing hope. "That's what I've been trying to tell you. We can't fight them all. We're on our own against a world filled with angry gods, and we're so badly outnumbered, what's the point in trying to liberate one area when ten more are falling?"

I sat up and winced from the pain in my left arm, but they'd forced me into this role I'd never wanted, they'd insisted I become a hero willing to die to defend Earth, and now they were giving up? No way. "Keira, I don't care if we're outnumbered. I don't care if I have to fight every god that ever existed. I am *not* quitting. You don't want to help me? Go back to Asgard. But this is my home, and I'm going to defend it."

She smiled at me, but it was still a sad smile as if her heart was breaking and she was trying to get through life while carrying a tremendous burden, weighed down by centuries of pain. She touched my hand again and lowered her eyes. "I knew you were the greatest hero Asgard has ever known. I won't leave you."

And I thought we were about to have this wonderful moment, this outpouring of how we really felt about one another, but the hospital door opened and Tyr bounded in, causing Keira to quickly retract her hand and rise from the edge of my bed. So I scowled at the war god and attempted to send telepathic messages along the lines of, "Get lost, asshole," and "*Why* are you wearing a Hawaiian shirt?" but apparently, he wasn't telepathic because he neither got lost nor explained why he was wearing a Hawaiian shirt.

"You're not going to believe this," he said.

"You raided Don Ho's wardrobe?" I guessed.

Tyr blinked at me then said, "Isn't he dead?"

I gestured toward his shirt. "Apparently not."

So he just blinked at me again then turned his attention to Keira. "I finally found gods willing to help us."

"The Greeks changed their minds?" Keira asked. For the first time since I'd woken up, she sounded hopeful.

Tyr shook his head. "No, but not exactly surprising. They've always been a selfish lot."

"Let me guess," I interjected. "The Polynesians, which explains why you're paying homage to their pantheon."

Tyr sighed *and* grunted at the same time, so I was feeling pretty proud of myself for being able to evoke such a complicated reaction. "Just as Mama Pacha and Inti wanted to get their own gods under control, some of the Egyptians do as well, and—"

"Then why the hell are you sucking up to the Polynesians?" I interrupted.

"Gavyn, shut up about his shirt," Keira scolded.

Tyr shot me a suspicious glance like he *knew* I wouldn't keep my mouth shut, so I decided to prove him wrong even though that was exactly what they wanted. Talk about a Catch-22.

"Ra and Anubis contacted me," Tyr explained. "They want their rogue gods captured so they can deal with them how they see fit. But if they pull stunts like they did in Phoenix, they don't hold us accountable for the deaths of any Egyptian god who's harming or threatening to harm innocent people."

"So are they actively helping us or not?" I asked.

"In a way, yes," Tyr answered. "They're hunting down Menhit and Anhur, and considering how many gods are causing problems, having any help at all is encouraging."

"But Menhit and Anhur are probably hunting *me* down," I argued. "And why are we responsible for cleaning up this supernatural mess even though no Norse gods are involved?"

"The Tuatha Dé are helping us," Keira reminded me. "Not all gods are turning against mortals."

"And the Sumerians?" I asked. "What have they been up to?"

Tyr and Keira exchanged a nervous glance and shrugged. "We haven't heard from them since the battle with Ninurta and his demigods."

"That can't be good," I decided.

They both agreed with me, but apparently, Frey hadn't called with any news, and given how long it took the CIA to find bin Laden, I wasn't holding out hope they'd be calling anytime soon. "So what now?" I asked.

"Now," Tyr said, "we find out just how powerful we really are."

GUNNR IS A TOTAL BADASS

(And the plot with Odin thickens)

The ruins of the farm stretched before me as I searched for my brother and Gunnr. I occasionally heard shouting in the distance, but otherwise, it seemed a wasteland now, blackened and charred and emptied of life. I reached a row of huts where the slaves lived, but they appeared abandoned. Or so I thought. Whimpering from inside surprised me so I carefully pushed the door open to find a boy huddled in the corner of a dark room.

"You're all right, child," I said.

He shook with fear so I tried again to reassure him I wouldn't hurt him. And that's when he lifted his head and I saw that the child I was talking to was supposed to be dead.

"Havard," Gunnr said, emerging from the shadows. "Leave this child alone. You've come for Finn, so go find him."

"He's orphaned now anyway," I said, trying to stem my anger that Gunnr had disobeyed me. "And he'll inherit this land and grow up to be just like his father."

"And have you grown up to be just like your father?" Gunnr demanded.

Her question was biting, and for a moment, I couldn't

respond. But my anger welled within me and I gestured to the boy and said, "You have chosen this child over our friendship. So be it, Gunnr. This won't be forgotten."

I turned on my heels and stormed away from them, calling Yngvarr's name in the hopes he'd found Finn and we could return to Asgard. By the time I found him, I'd become convinced Gunnr had betrayed me, and all of the Valkyries were no better than their father, an untrustworthy god whose commitments meant nothing. Yngvarr listened to me ranting about her betrayal without interrupting then just shrugged and said, "You've known Gunnr a long time. Do you really think she intended to insult you, brother?"

"The Valkyries are charged with obeying us war gods in Midgard," I insisted stubbornly.

"Yes, but we are here on a personal mission. She didn't accompany us as a Valkyrie to retrieve our fallen heroes but to assist us in finding the brother of your wife."

"And how is she helping with that?" I cried.

"Havard," she said, startling me because I hadn't heard her approaching. When I turned around, I saw she had the boy with her, holding his hand protectively. He stared at me with wide eyes, his face smudged with the soot from the explosion I'd caused. "I'm taking him back to Asgard with me."

I flinched as if she'd struck me and stammered, "You're... *what?*"

"I will raise him myself, and when he's old enough to return to Midgard, I'll bring him home. Until then, you won't harm this child if you value our friendship at all."

"Gunnr—" I started, but she cut me off.

"I want your word, Havard."

"I thought I had *yours*," I hissed.

But she shook her head and insisted again that she wanted my promise not to harm the child she intended to raise.

When I didn't respond, Yngvarr asked, "How old are you boy?"

The boy's wide eyes turned to my brother, and Gunnr's voice became soft and gentle. "It's all right. Answer him, Áki."

"Five," he said in a voice so small, I had to strain to hear him.

"He's young enough that his mind hasn't been polluted by his father," Yngvarr told me. "Gunnr will teach him our laws, and he won't violate them. After all, he knows the consequences now."

Gunnr kept her attention on me, more determined and fiercer than I'd ever seen her. "How do you think Arnbjorg will react when she discovers you wanted this child murdered?"

Honestly, I hadn't considered that my new bride wouldn't understand the world of gods and how we handled transgressions against our laws. I glanced at the boy again and waved them off. "Go then. But if he returns to Midgard and violates our rules, I will hold you personally responsible."

Gunnr lifted her chin and narrowed her eyes just slightly, and when she acknowledged my command, her voice took a hard edge I'd never heard before. "So be it, my lord."

She led the boy back toward her winged horse, and Yngvarr resumed his search for Finn, already over Gunnr's decision to bring this mortal child to Asgard to raise as her own. But I couldn't let it go as easily. "What do you think Odin will say about this child in a Valkyrie's home? They're forbidden from having children."

Yngvarr lifted a shoulder in response, completely unconcerned about Odin's response or the boy's fate. "They're not allowed to have children. She didn't bear this child, so technically, she hasn't disobeyed her father."

"Don't you think it's awfully close, though?"

"What do you care, brother?" he laughed. "You wanted the child dead, and a moment ago, you were ready to sever your friendship with her."

That was true, but with my anger receding, I realized I didn't really want to terminate my friendship with my favorite of the Valkyries. We'd been through too many battles together, too many adventures. I didn't understand her reaction here, but I hadn't lost my respect for her after all.

"We should hurry," I decided. "I don't think we should allow her to face Odin's wrath alone."

"Probably not," he agreed. "And we may need to lie for her and claim we supported her decision."

I grunted in response, but he was right. Odin wouldn't challenge two powerful war gods, but not one of his daughters was so important to him that he would hesitate to cast her out of Asgard forever. Or worse, she may not survive his punishment.

"There," Yngvarr said, pointing to a gully at the edge of the wheat fields.

As we neared its edge, we heard the sounds of feet landing in shallow water, the attempts to quietly cross, and the occasional hushed whisper to encourage a speedy escape. These mortals only wanted to live, so I used that to my advantage. "Stop," I shouted. "We're only after one thrall, a young man called Finn. Surrender him, and the rest of you are free to do as you please."

Silence answered me, then more hushed whispers as they deliberated whether or not to surrender the young man we'd come for. Finally, someone said, "My lord, he is here. None of us have knowingly harbored a mortal who's offended you."

I peeked into the gully where the slaves had taken refuge and immediately saw the young man they were attempting to push up the bank, hoping that his surrender would spare them from a similar fate as their now deceased owner.

Yngvarr reached down and pulled Finn out, and we both looked him over quickly. This boy was clearly related to my wife, but his months of captivity and hard work had made him thin and he looked so much younger than his fifteen years.

"Do you know who I am?" I asked him.

He nodded. "You're the god who took Arnbjorg away from us."

"I'm the god who married your sister," I said. "Which makes you family. We've come to bring you home."

Finn's mouth opened then closed as if he couldn't understand what I was telling him. "My lord..." he breathed.

"We should hurry," I said. "Arnbjorg doesn't know we've come for you, and a friend of ours likely needs our help."

He nodded and followed us wordlessly, perhaps convinced his liberation was only a dream and he'd soon awaken to find himself back in the squalor he'd been forced into. I helped Finn onto Sigurd, who wasn't as particular as Magni had been but still seemed to eye me warily as if he couldn't understand why I'd put a stranger on his back. So I arched an eyebrow at him and told him, "You'll behave, Sigurd, and treat this boy as you would me."

Sigurd stamped a foot and whinnied, but that was the extent of his protest. I laughed and patted him gently, then mounted the saddle and we began the long journey back to Asgard.

As soon as we passed through the gates into our world, Arnbjorg called my name and began running toward us. But she must have seen that I wasn't alone on Sigurd, because she stopped and stared at us as if we were only apparitions, a deception of a cruel mind fast asleep. I dismounted and reached for her. "Love, I couldn't tell you where we were really going out of fear we'd fail. I couldn't get your hopes up."

Her eyes never left her brother who slid off Sigurd somewhat clumsily. He swallowed and took a deep breath. "Arnbjorg," he said quietly. "You're well then?"

The spell that had kept her fastened to the ground broke and she threw herself at her brother, wrapping him tightly in her arms as she cried, "I thought you were dead!"

Finn held her just as tightly, and I averted my gaze, wanting to allow my new bride this private moment of reunification of what could possibly be the only blood-relative she had left. After a few minutes, I said, "Can you help him to the palace and see that he gets a good meal? I must find Gunnr and make sure she's all right."

Arnbjorg nodded but before I could leave, she turned and threw her arms around me, thanking me for rescuing her brother and begging me to extend my thanks to Yngvarr and Gunnr as well. So I told her that both Yngvarr and Gunnr hadn't ventured into Midgard on my behalf but hers, that all of Asgard had grown to love her as if she'd always been one of us and one of the most precious of the Aesir at that. But always humble, Arnbjorg refused to accept her adoration among the gods here and wouldn't allow me to leave until I'd promised to deliver her message.

As I reached Gunnr's home in Valhalla, I could hear the arguing from within. Odin had already discovered Gunnr's new ward. I didn't bother knocking. Odin's method of confrontation was always an attempt at intimidation, so I wanted to send the message to him I was not now, nor would I ever be, intimidated by *him*. "All-Father," I said, my voice icy, "we could hardly leave the child in Midgard after destroying his home and guardians."

"You should have destroyed him with the others," Odin barked. "You know this, Havard. Asgard is *not* an orphanage."

I glanced at Gunnr who stood defiantly in front of her father, keeping Áki behind her as a clear signal she would defend the boy even at the expense of her own life. "Gunnr has served us faithfully for centuries," I countered. "And she's asked for nothing in return. She wanted to spare this child's life, and I will support her decision to do so, as will Yngvarr. If you harm either of them, we will *both* consider it an act of aggression against us."

Odin's nostrils flared slightly, knowing I was challenging him directly, daring him to react violently. From the doorway, Yngvarr's voice joined my defense of the Valkyrie who had most likely always had too good a spirit for a world like Asgard. "This child will not interfere with her duties to you," he told Odin. "And we will help her if necessary. I believe your business here is done now."

Odin's single eye flared, but he was no more powerful than me, let alone Yngvarr *and* me. But his gods so rarely disobeyed him or challenged his commands that he didn't seem to know how to handle our insubordination. "Keep him then," he finally told Gunnr. "Just remember you are responsible for every word and action from this child."

There was a clear, implicit threat in Odin's words, a signal that he would be searching for any transgression that could justify his revenge. Yngvarr closed the door behind the All-Father, and Gunnr attempted to calm the child she was risking her life to save. Yngvarr took a deep breath and whispered, "I hope we're doing the right thing, opposing him so openly like this."

But I only smiled and told him, "Opposing him is the biggest benefit."

He snickered but watched Gunnr and Áki warily. "We should prepare ourselves for a rebellion, recruit as much support as we can now in case Odin decides he won't tolerate this."

We'd tried to speak in hushed tones, but Gunnr overheard anyway and looked up from the floor where she'd knelt beside the small child. She still wore the same determined, stony expression as if, for the first time in her life, she'd discovered a cause for which she would willingly die. "Be discreet about who you approach but seek an alliance with those you trust. But know that you will have every Valkyrie at your side."

"This could be war then," I said carefully.

Yngvarr nodded. "Perhaps, brother, it's time to crown a new king."

CHAPTER NINETEEN

I'd spent the entire flight back to the States stealing glances in Keira's direction, and she'd occasionally catch me and ask what the hell had gotten into me now because I'd gone from looking at her like she was the anti-Christ to a starry-eyed adoration like she was Mother Theresa. So I just told her I couldn't help myself—slaying giant boars obviously made me a bit horny and she was a far better choice than Tyr's ugly ass.

Tyr snorted and shrugged. "Not exactly my type anyway, Gavyn."

I'd only been joking, of course, but I'd regretted the words as soon as they tumbled out of my mouth and decided I wasn't just the village idiot, I was more like the Shanghai-sized idiot, because I just *knew* someone would mention Freyja's ability to cure my horniness problem, and Keira had finally seemed to be moving past my brief affair with the goddess.

I sulked for a bit as I steeled myself for the inevitable teasing, but to my surprise, no one brought her up and Keira didn't even shoot me one of her, "*Why* do I even tolerate you?" looks. In fact, considering the spate of bad news we'd been delivered lately, she still seemed to be in a fairly good mood. She smiled and lifted an eyebrow at me and said, "Well, I slayed the dragon, you know. And really, how many people get to brag about slaying a dragon?"

Now I *really* pouted. "I want to slay a dragon. When do I get to become a dragon slayer?"

"Are you seriously hoping we'll fight another dragon?" Tyr asked. "One wasn't enough?"

"As long as he doesn't have a flaming zombie monkey friend, I'm totally down for dragon slaying," I replied.

Agnes opened one eye and hushed us from across the aisle, so I leaned forward and hushed her back. "Shouldn't you be hunting down some eye of newt or blood of a righteous man?"

"Those exist?" Keira asked a little too quickly.

"No," I answered. "Because Agnes hunted them all down and forced their extinction."

Keira laughed, which only strengthened my resolve not to mention this latest dream until we reached Baton Rouge. I selfishly wanted to enjoy these hours of an almost-happy Valkyrie who, for once, didn't seem to be carrying the weight of the world on her shoulders.

Once we were settled in our hotel again, I summoned the courage to ask Keira about Áki. I wasn't sure if she'd remember him or not since he was so closely connected to Havard, but I had to at *least* let her know she'd risked her life to save this child I'd accused her of murdering. She opened her door and waved me inside, immediately returning to her suitcase to finish unpacking and chatting about Frey's latest update with the CIA. Apparently, he was considering a career change.

She handed me a stack of neatly folded t-shirts and asked me to put them in the dresser, and I could feel that courage

I'd summoned slowly slipping away. If I didn't bring up this dream now, I'd keep this one secret forever. But honestly, I'd been putting it off because I suspected this child, if she remembered him, could be such a painful memory for her and I already knew I'd rather die than hurt her.

"Keira, I had another dream about Havard while we were in Russia," I said.

Her hands froze above her suitcase, and she gaped at me. "Why didn't you tell me?"

There was an unspoken implication, maybe an *accusation*, in her voice that she'd been desperately hoping for some piece of information that she hadn't done something so utterly despicable, something *my* ancestor had ordered her to do. And those genes were inside me, sometimes so powerful that I wasn't even sure what was Havard and what was me anymore. Sure, he'd eventually done the right thing, but only because Keira had stood up to him. And that terrified me, because I still wasn't convinced I wouldn't become this god whose power was so great, he somehow lived on in me.

I took a deep breath and closed the dresser drawer. "Because I was in awe of you. Because I was worried I'd upset you. And because when I see you like that, so brave and fierce and powerful and compassionate, I realize I'm utterly helpless against falling in love with you."

Damn it. I hadn't meant to say that last part. It'd just slipped out along with my admittedly lame explanation as to why I'd kept this dream a secret for days.

"Gavyn," she whispered.

But I shook my head and asked, "Did you once know a child named Áki?"

Her eyes widened and she gasped. "What did he have to do with Havard?"

"So you remember him?"

"Of course I remember him. He was my son."

"Keira, he was the child Havard wanted you to kill."

Her hands rose to her mouth and she backed away from me like *I* was the one who'd ordered her to murder a child she'd come to love as her own. "How did you think he'd become your ward?" I asked.

"I found him," she whispered. "Wandering alone in Midgard."

I recounted the entire dream for her, and when I finished, she gave me a confused look and admitted she remembered little about his childhood. "It was so long ago... but maybe I can't remember more because of this curse."

"Or maybe it's both," I offered. "But he survives? Odin doesn't kill him?"

Keira shook her head. "No, he never liked him, but he largely left us alone."

"And there was obviously no rebellion," I added.

"There might have been," she answered carefully. "But as far as any of us know, the gods of Asgard became angry that Odin wouldn't confront mortals who were turning away from us as Christianity spread through Midgard."

"Odin won? I mean, he's still at the head of your pantheon, so he had to have won, right?" Thanks to Havard's overbearing genes, I was incredibly disappointed that Asgard's civil war hadn't displaced him.

Keira's eyebrows pulled together as she searched for an answer and she finally shrugged and said, "I can't really remember. When you've lived thousands of years, memories have a way of becoming muddled, even without a curse."

"But you're sure Áki grew up? Did you ever bring him back to Midgard?"

"Yes, I'm sure. I couldn't forget that. He grows into such a handsome man with a generous heart and courageous spirit. I think you would have liked him."

"Probably," I agreed. "But let's be honest: I would have annoyed the hell out of him."

Keira smiled and lifted a shoulder. "He had a great sense of humor. I doubt you would have annoyed him at all."

"Keira, the way you stood up to Havard and your father... that was incredibly brave. I'm sorry I assumed you'd acted like a monster before."

"Don't be," she hurriedly said. "You can't control how much of these memories you relive. I would've thought the same thing."

I impulsively reached across the narrow space between her bed and the chair I occupied, taking her hand in mine. "How does your prophecy tie into mine, and why won't you tell me about it?"

"Gavyn," she sighed, but she didn't pull her hand away from me.

"You don't have to protect me. Okay, maybe you kinda do, but only until we defeat the Sumerians, right?"

She seemed on the verge of relenting about how secretive she'd been over this prophecy, but a knock on her door interrupted our conversation. I scowled at it and whomever was on the other side and their audacity to prevent Keira from *finally* opening up to me and revealing why she wouldn't be in a relationship with me.

Tyr's voice seeped through the door. "Gunnr? Is Gavyn in there with you?"

"It's Keira," I shouted back. "And no."

But Tyr had sounded worried, so I opened the door anyway. As soon as I saw his face, I backed away so he could enter. Something was obviously wrong.

"Freyja just called," he said. "She can't reach Frey."

"We just talked to him," I replied. "I'm sure he's fine."

"That was yesterday," Tyr argued. "And when half the supernatural world is attempting a violent comeback, going radio silent is concerning no matter how little time has passed."

"I thought he was still with the CIA," Keira said. "Surely, they'd let us know if anything happened to him."

"That's the thing," Tyr said. "The agent he's been working with has also disappeared. And they *did* let someone know. They called Freyja."

Keira and I finally began to share Tyr's concerns. "We shouldn't have gone to Russia," I said. "If we'd come back, we might've known Frey was in danger."

"How?" Keira asked. "He has a number of gods and demigods with him, not to mention one of the most powerful intelligence agencies on Earth. What could we have possibly done to prevent this?"

"I don't know," I admitted. "But maybe Frey's disappearance is retribution for—"

"Gavyn," Tyr interrupted. "We're squaring off against gods from all over the world and trying to be the good guys here. If we start second-guessing every decision, every fight, every action we make, we'll paralyze ourselves. The world needs us."

"No pressure," I mumbled.

Tyr ran his good hand over his jet-lagged eyes and sighed. "If he's dead, there's obviously nothing we can do. But if he was captured as a ransom, whomever took him will be calling us soon."

"And where do we stand on negotiating with terrorists?" I asked.

"It's Frey," Keira cried. "We have to get him back, even if that requires negotiating with terrorists!"

"Yeah, but not if it means sacrificing the entire planet," Tyr countered. "He wouldn't want that."

Tyr's phone rang and we all jumped at the unexpected sound, *and* the remarkably apt timing of the call. He didn't pull it out of his pocket right away, so I felt a bit pervy staring

so close to his crotch, which was really his fault for not immediately answering his phone. But I could tell by his expression
as soon as he glanced at the screen that this caller was the
god we'd all silently expected.

Tyr put it on speakerphone and eyed me warily, as if
knowing I'd likely say something dangerous or stupid and I
really wanted to ask the guy if he'd just met me because I
always said something dangerous or stupid. Ninurta's voice
slithered from the phone, and my fingers instinctively curled
into fists. *Man*, I hated this guy.

"I assume," Ninurta said, "you're with Gavyn?"

"And I assume," Tyr replied, "you're with Frey."

"I have a proposition," Ninurta said. "You want your god
back, surrender your heroes."

"No," Keira immediately answered.

"Gunnr," Ninurta cooed. "I hardly think a Valkyrie is in
any position to negotiate with a god."

"I'm going to kill you," I snapped. "Just thought you
should know."

"Oh?" Ninurta laughed. "Like you killed me when you
stabbed me with Sharur?"

"You were my leverage, dumbass. If I'd killed you, your
demigods would've had no reason not to shoot me."

I could almost see the Sumerian war god waving me off
like I was only making excuses for my incompetence. "I want
your heroes, Tyr. Or the next time you see Frey, it'll be in
pieces I ship to your door."

Ninurta disconnected before we could even ask how long
we had to make a decision. Keira kept frowning at the phone
as if Ninurta were actually in there, so to try to make her feel
as appreciated as she should, I told her there was no one
whose opinion I trusted more than hers. "Besides," I added.
"What does he know? The Valkyries are the most badass
warriors in any realm."

She glanced at Tyr then lowered her eyes again. "It doesn't matter," she murmured. "We have to figure out a way to help Frey."

"I know you won't like this," Tyr said. "But I have to call Odin. One of our own has been abducted. He needs to know."

I groaned but couldn't argue with him. I wasn't a god, and Frey wasn't my family. Tyr lumbered out of Keira's room, and I gently touched her elbow but she wouldn't look at me. "For so long, we were no better than slaves," she said quietly, and I could hear the shame in her voice. It physically hurt me. "The old gods will never see us Valkyries as equals."

"Even Tyr?"

She shrugged and I began to rethink my relationship with all of the gods, even Yngvarr. "I've always liked Tyr," she explained. "He's one of the good ones."

"What do you think Odin will do about Frey? As little as he's been doing to help us all along?"

"No," she said. "I think he'll come for Frey. He's too fond of him... and his sister."

"*What an asshole*," I thought, but I hardly needed to point that out to the woman he'd forced into millennia of servitude.

And not surprisingly, Keira was right. Tyr returned and announced Odin was on his way, and once he arrived, we'd decide what to do about Ninurta's ultimatum. But I already knew there was only one thing I *could* do to save Frey's life.

I would have to surrender to the war god who wanted me dead most of all.

CHAPTER TWENTY

Y ngvarr looked as happy as I felt to see the All-Father joining our ranks in Baton Rouge, but it's not like we could force the guy to leave. And besides, once the issue with Frey was resolved, he'd most likely be returning to Asgard because saving Midgard was clearly beneath him. I was a lot more relieved to see the arrival of gods I could trust a little more, like Thor and Ull and even Freyja, who was distraught over her brother's abduction and spent most of her time crying inconsolably. Even Keira regarded her with sympathy and offered her words of comfort and assurances that we would do everything in our power to get him home safely.

I hadn't told anyone that I was prepared to offer myself in exchange for Frey, and didn't plan on offering that information to anyone either. They'd only try to change my mind, and I couldn't let Frey die because of me. Sure, Ninurta had demanded the surrender of *all* the Norse heroes, but as Freyja was so fond of saying, everything was negotiable.

Yngvarr refused to sit with Odin in the room and stood in the corner with his arms folded tightly across his chest. Odin would occasionally steal glances in his direction, as if waiting for the younger war god to snap and leap across the room in an attempt to strangle him. And honestly, I thought Yngvarr could definitely take him, and I kinda wanted to see it.

John, our CIA contact here in Baton Rouge, opened his laptop and pulled up a list of possible locations where Ninurta was keeping Frey. They were all in the U.S., which only reinforced our belief that the Sumerians had no intention of reclaiming what used to be Sumer. They were aiming far higher and had targeted one of the most powerful countries in the world. They wanted to rule America.

"So are you guys planning some sort of Bin Laden raid on each of these complexes?" I asked.

He blinked at me in that incredibly annoying way of his then returned his attention to the screen. "Since I've been assured you gods can't teleport, the most likely location is close to where Frey was when he disappeared, which would put him in Chicago."

"Chicago," I repeated.

"Yes," John answered slowly. "You know... the city in Illinois?"

"I know where Chicago is, smartass," I snapped. "It's just a huge city and we have no idea where to even *start* looking. Hell, by the time we get there, Ninurta will know we're after him instead of rounding up heroes to hand over to his perverse evil lair."

"Perverse?" Tyr asked. "Why perverse?"

I shrugged. "It's Ninurta. You just *know* he's a total pervert." I probably shouldn't have said that in front of Freyja, because it only led to a new round of uncontrollable sobbing.

Odin shot me a "You really *are* a world-class dumbass" look and put his arm around the goddess he'd long coveted. And I couldn't help thinking this was all a ploy to try to get

Freyja into bed with him, which only reinforced what a lowlife creep the bastard was.

"Hey," I said, trying to mitigate the damage I'd caused, "I was kidnapped by this asshole, too, and not only did I escape, no one even hurt me. They drugged me, which kinda sucked, but it eventually wore off and I'm totally fine."

"You're a lot of things, Gavyn," Yngvarr added helpfully, "but I don't think totally fine is one of them."

So naturally, I flipped him off before reminding him that I *had* been perfectly fine before two women showed up at my door, kidnapped me, and hauled me off to *Iceland* so I could fight a bunch of pissed gods who thought they deserved to rule the world. And I was pretty sure *everyone* who thought they deserved to rule the world didn't actually deserve to rule the world. And the Sumerians, in particular, seemed grossly under-qualified.

"Are you done?" Tyr asked me.

I thought about it for a few seconds then nodded. "Think so. Unless you'd like to rant about the Egyptians for a few minutes, too."

"Actually," Odin interjected, "I'd like to give you something."

Both Yngvarr and I tensed over Odin's "gift," assuming whatever it was couldn't be good. But he flipped open a large case, and even though I was terribly curious as to what the All-Father would bring *me*, I asked anyway. "How the hell did you get *that* through customs?"

He glanced at me and shrugged. "You'd be surprised at what we can convince humans they're seeing or not seeing."

"Aha!" I exclaimed, pointing an accusatory finger at Agnes. "*That's* how you got Hunter and me on the flight to Iceland."

She just shrugged, too. "Of course. You didn't think we *actually* had your passports, did you?"

Well, yeah, actually. I mean, witches could do magical shit like that, couldn't they?

But Odin pulled a dull shield from the case and handed it to me. I turned it over in my hands, but no matter how many times I flipped it, the damn thing remained a shield. And not just *any* shield but a rather useless one considering it was made from *wood*. "Um... this had better be for sledding."

"Don't worry," Odin assured me. "It's far sturdier than it looks. It's enchanted."

"Enchanted how? Can it make me invisible? Because I'll be honest: I'd let Keira emasculate me again if I could become invisible." I thought about it then shook my head. "No, never mind. Considering I *just* got them back, I'm keeping my balls, but I *would* like to be invisible."

"Gavyn," Keira groaned.

"What?" I asked innocently. "You're the one who did the emasculating, so you can't really complain about it now. Let the next guy you kidnap keep his—"

"Gavyn," Tyr sighed.

"Hold up, one complaint at a time."

Odin tapped the shield, painted a dull blue with yellow runes around the edge, and hurriedly explained its enchantment before I could continue my ridiculous speech about emasculation and how difficult it was to achieve re-masculation. "The enchantment makes this shield far stronger than it appears. It *looks* like wood but is stronger than steel. No weapon will be able to penetrate it."

"What about a bullet?" I asked.

"No, that's a weapon," he answered.

So just to be a smartass, I decided to test him. "Okay, but what about a grenade launcher?"

Odin sighed and said, "Still a weapon, Gavyn."

"A missile?"

"Gavyn—" he started, but I was on a roll now.

"A *nuclear* missile. Surely, it can't withstand a nuclear bomb. Or would the bomb just obliterate me and everything around me but the shield would just fall to the ground, completely unharmed? And what's the point of having a shield that can't be scratched or broken if I still get blown off the face of the planet?"

Odin glanced at Agnes and asked, "Has no one really figured out a spell to keep him quiet yet?"

"I tried. Apparently, his tongue is more powerful than our magic."

"Hey," I protested. "You tried to put a spell on me?" But I replayed her words then smiled slyly at Keira. "Did you hear that? My tongue is more powerful than your magic."

Not surprisingly, she rolled her eyes at me and crossed the room to sit by her father. I would've been a little offended if I weren't totally aware I'd deserved that.

"Just keep the shield with you when you engage in any battle from now on," Odin instructed. "It could save your life."

"Okay, two questions," I said, and everyone in the room sighed loudly. I ignored them and asked anyway. "Why didn't anyone give me a shield *before* now considering I've been out there fighting gods and giant wolves and flaming zombie monkeys?"

"Flaming... what?" Odin asked.

"And secondly," I said, still ignoring him and everyone else. "No one ever trained me to fight with a shield. It seems like it'll just get in my way. And I haven't yet had a dream in which Havard had a shield."

"Havard had an enchanted sword," Yngvarr pointed out. "He didn't need a shield."

"And you?" I asked. "Where's yours?"

Yngvarr smiled and said, "I'm a war god. I don't need one."

"Men," Keira mumbled. "Your egos will get you *all* killed."

I nodded in complete agreement.

"So..." John said. "Can I remind you all now that I'm still here and we'd kind of like to find your missing god and our missing agent?"

"Depends," I replied. "Do you have a better solution then sending us to Chicago?"

"No. You're going to Chicago."

"*You're* going to Chicago," I muttered.

He blinked at me again then turned to Tyr. "How do you put up with him?"

"He's an acquired taste," Tyr joked, but I couldn't *not* say something about *that*.

"Dude! You are *not* allowed to taste me. Ever."

So Tyr blinked at me then turned to John. "Never mind. Let's leave him here, and the rest of us will go to Chicago to find Frey."

"All of you shut up!" Freyja cried. "Do I really need to remind you that my brother is in Ninurta's hands, and he will *die* if we don't rescue him soon?"

"We know," I assured her. "And I'm sorry."

John's cellphone rang so he excused himself from the room to answer it. The rest of us waited quietly, staring at our shoes or the floor or anything that would allow us to avoid Freyja's accusatory glare, which we obviously deserved. Or mostly me. After a few minutes, John stormed back into the room, cursing and looking very much like he wanted to either throw something or punch someone or maybe both.

"Chicago will have to wait," he said.

"Great," I sighed. "What now?"

"We've got company," he explained. "And this lion goddess wants revenge."

～

WE'D ENTERED a vicious cycle of battles, deaths, and a desire for vengeance, and the only way out seemed to be the complete annihilation of one side. Sure, the Sumerians had started it—and now, the Egyptians, Incans, and Russians had joined in—but that hardly seemed to matter to any of them. All they could apparently understand was that one of their own had been killed and they needed to avenge that death.

And Menhit had tracked me down to avenge Willy's death.

"Some of you should still go to Chicago, try to narrow down where Ninurta is keeping Frey," I suggested. "I'll stay behind to deal with Menhit."

"As will I," Keira immediately said.

Yngvarr wasn't far behind her. "And me."

"A demigod, a Valkyrie, and one war god," Odin muttered, and he made it sound like our particular grouping was a *bad* thing. "Ull should stay with you as well."

But now, I felt like I just needed to prove something, so I shook my head and pretended to be polite about the whole thing. "Frey should remain our top priority. Send everyone else after him, and we'll join you as soon as we've taken care of Menhit."

"She won't be alone," Odin argued, but I had no intention of allowing him to insult us further.

"Considering we've been here dealing with these assholes the whole time while you've been safely tucked away in Asgard, I think we're well aware of how they operate," I snapped. "And we can handle it. Go to Chicago. We'll see you in a few days."

I marched past him, wanting to slam the door on my way out, but it had one of those hydraulic hinges on it and I only managed to tweak my elbow in my effort to storm out properly. Keira and Yngvarr were close behind me though and by

Yngvarr's expression, I could tell he was quite pleased with my overly dramatic outburst and exit.

Keira, though, was still the pragmatist, always carefully calculating our odds and strategies. "Maybe we should've taken him up on keeping Ull here. It couldn't hurt, and he's an expert archer."

Damn it. I'd forgotten Menhit wasn't only a lion goddess but shot flaming arrows at her enemies. Presumably not as a lion though. But at this point, accepting Ull's help was just a matter of pride, so I offered a compromise. "Let's get Joachim to stay. He's almost as good as Ull."

"Works for me," Yngvarr agreed. "He's certainly got talent."

Joachim wasn't even put off that we'd made this decision for him rather than letting him decide if he should go to Chicago or face Menhit's wrath. He just grabbed his bow and quiver and nodded toward my shield. "That'll come in handy."

"I'm assuming it'll repel *flaming* arrows, but I didn't ask," I said smartly. "Pretty sure it repels the regular kind though."

Joachim grinned and lifted his bow. "Want to test it out?"

I arched an eyebrow at him. "Of *course* I want to test it out."

I jogged to the end of the hall and spun around, holding the shield in front of me while Keira and Yngvarr grunted impatiently at the two demigods who thought playing with a new toy was far more important than hunting down a lion goddess who would probably start prowling the streets of Baton Rouge soon. But really, what was the point in having new toys if we couldn't play with them?

Joachim unleashed a volley of arrows in my direction with that lightning speed of his, and the shield deflected each one. They didn't embed in the wood like I'd expected, but bounced off its surface as if there were a force field around the wooden planks that had been fitted tightly together to form a solid barrier. When he'd emptied his quiver, we both stared at the arrows that had piled around my feet and mumbled, "Holy shit."

"I want one of those," Joachim decided.

"There's only one," Keira said. "And it belongs to Odin. He's loaned it to Gavyn."

Joachim pouted for a few moments then shrugged. "Okay, then Gavyn, you have to fight beside me from now on."

"Deal," I said. "Although I'm not gonna lie. If we get attacked by a flaming zombie monkey again, I'm not above ditching you and running."

"Can you at least leave the shield before running?"

"That'll just unnecessarily slow me down," I pretended to argue.

"This conversation is unnecessarily slowing us down," Yngvarr pointed out.

"Probably," I agreed, but I didn't bother elaborating or even moving from behind the wall of arrows that had amassed by my feet.

Joachim finally joined me at the end of the hall so he could refill his quiver but he kept eyeing my shield. "Want to hold it, don't you?" I asked.

"So much," he admitted.

I handed it to him and he admired it for a few moments then shot me a sly grin. "Want to see if it deflects swords, too?"

"Oh, hell yeah!" I exclaimed, motioning toward Yngvarr so he'd give me my sword. But the bastard shook his head and reminded us again it was time to act like the grown men we were supposed to be and find the pissed off lion goddess whose flaming arrows would give us plenty of opportunities to test out the new shield.

"Damn," Joachim and I sighed in unison.

But we followed Keira and Yngvarr out of the hotel, and

headed toward the Garden District where John had told us Menhit had been spotted. I'd never even thought to ask if she'd been spotted as a lion or goddess shooting arrows at random houses and people, but it probably didn't matter. She was obviously luring us into a trap, and we had no choice but to walk into it.

We parked at a tennis court near the entrance to the Garden District and decided to venture into the old neighborhood on foot, assuming she'd soon learn of our arrival and try to ambush us.

And we'd been right. We'd only made it a block when a hail of flaming arrows rained down upon us, and the roars of what sounded like an entire pride of lions echoed through the streets. As we hid beneath the enchanted shield, waiting for the arrows to finish falling from the sky like a meteor shower, the lions leapt from the shadows of a nearby building, and we discovered Menhit hadn't recruited an army of demigods to exact her revenge.

We'd walked right into a battle with an army of full-fledged gods.

CHAPTER TWENTY-ONE

"That's a lot of lions," I said smartly.

Joachim nodded and began counting in German. "Eins, zwei, drei..." but apparently, Egyptian lion gods didn't *like* German because they roared and stalked toward us, the muscles in their flanks rippling beneath their golden fur.

"Try another language," I suggested.

"Okay," Joachim agreed. "Un, deux, trois..."

But they seemed to like French even less, because that only made them stalk faster. Joachim nocked an arrow and Keira held a knife in each hand, ready to throw them at whichever lion god provoked us first. Even Yngvarr held his sword ready to attack while I stood there silently deliberating what a bunch of Egyptian gods had against the French and if it was only their language or all things French. And if it was all things French, it was probably because they'd tried to convince us eating snails was a good idea.

For the record, it's not.

"Gavyn," Keira hissed. "Snap out of it!"

"You have to tell me that an awful lot," I whispered back.

"I can't imagine why," Yngvarr also whispered.

"So we're doing this whispering thing again?" I whisper-asked.

"Apparently," he whisper-answered.

But lions must've hated whispering more than German and French combined. Several of them lunged toward us, and Joachim's arrow and Keira's knives flew toward them. The other lions that had surrounded us took that as their cue to attack, so Yngvarr and I spun around to protect our small group from all sides. I briefly wondered how this damn shield would deflect lions, and I had a terrible suspicion I'd soon find out.

One lion in particular had me in its crosshairs, and I assumed it was Menhit. And honestly, I felt kinda weird about fighting a female lion and wished I could trade places with Keira, whose lion had a mane so was presumably male. I mean, I'd spent my whole life being taught not to fight girls, but maybe the rules were different when she was a goddess and a lion and was trying to kill me.

Menhit leapt at me, long claws spread wide as if warning me she wouldn't leave limbs still attached. My shoulder had *just* begun to heal, and I was going to be incredibly pissed if she ripped it off now. I held the shield in front of my face, and the impact of a four-hundred-pound lion, which I later learned was huge for a female, knocked me on my ass. Fortunately, I didn't have the pistol tucked into my waistband this time. Landing on a handgun probably hurt like hell... especially if it discharged and shot the person in the ass, which I was actually still waiting to happen to me.

But the impact also knocked Menhit on *her* ass, and as I lowered the shield to get back on my feet, I saw a woman instead of a lion rising to hers. And this woman held a bow with arrows that flickered like white-hot stars. "Um..." I stammered. "Joachim, is there any way you can light your arrows on fire?"

"Even if I could, it's not going to stop her from shooting us with—"

Menhit didn't bother waiting for him to finish his sentence. She released the flaming arrow at us, and I raised my shield. But instead of falling to the ground like Joachim's arrows had in the hotel, a wall of fire erupted as it hit the invisible barrier this shield created. We stared at the flames for a few moments before I yelled, "That's cheating, asshole!"

Menhit didn't seem to care. She unleashed another arrow, and a second wave of fire ignited on our left. Keira gasped and cried, "She's going to surround us!"

"Yeah," I agreed, "but what the hell are we supposed to do about it?"

None of us were weather gods that could control the rain, and I doubted this shield would miraculously protect us all from a fire collapsing in on us. But if we *knew* a weather god...

"Keira, please tell me there's a Norse god in town who can make it rain," I said.

"Thor," she and Yngvarr answered at the same time.

As far as I knew, though, the famous god of thunder wasn't in Baton Rouge. I'd last seen him in New Orleans, and even if he'd decided to hang out in the Big Easy for a while, we wouldn't survive long enough for him to get here. But Keira had already pulled out her phone as Joachim kept the lions at bay since she was momentarily defenseless. She began typing a text, and I wanted to just stand there staring at her like this was *literally* the most insane battle in supernatural history—and really, it *had* to have been, considering we were being attacked by a pride of lions and surrounded by magical fire, yet she was taking a break to send a text—but Menhit launched another arrow at us, and I had to deflect it as well. The only good thing about having an angry Egyptian goddess shoot flaming arrows at us was that Egyptian lion gods apparently weren't immune to fire. The more flames encircled us, the more they had to keep their distance. Of course, burning to a crisp was *definitely* not an epic way to die, and I didn't want to be the loser asshole in Valhalla having to admit I was brought down by a burning arrow.

I was just about to tell Joachim that, too, when the sky opened up above us with a sharp crack. Seconds later, rain fell in heavy sheets, immediately dousing the flames that had spread uncomfortably close. But with the fire extinguished, the lions could pounce.

I'd be willing to bet most people have never battled a lion, whether it's a regular lion or a god pretending to be a lion. I'd already decided I hated it. And Menhit must've decided her arrows would be useless against my shield, because she transformed once again, which would have been pretty cool to watch if she weren't trying to kill me. But as soon as her paws touched the wet pavement, she sprang at me, even though the last time she tried that, we'd both ended up on the ground. And go figure: this time, it didn't work out any differently.

But Yngvarr cried out in pain, and I quickly rose to my feet. Something inside me, that same force that sometimes took over my body and often confused me with its emotions, cried out for him. One of the largest lions had managed to get close enough to swipe his leg, and his shredded jeans were covered in blood. Even the puddle at his feet was turning crimson. My stomach turned and my head pounded as I ran toward the lion, dropping the shield in the process so I could hold the hilt in both hands. He roared at me, exposing unnaturally long fangs, and I held my sword above my head and jumped, driving the blade into the lion's throat as he leapt at me, too.

Searing pain ripped through my chest as we collided, and Keira screamed my name. I was vaguely aware that I was falling then the impact of my back hitting the hard ground took my breath away. I pushed the beast of a lion off me, not even realizing it must have weighed half a ton and it shouldn't have been possible, and tried to get to my feet again. Keira was beside me, hooking her hands beneath my arms to steady me, and I gently touched my chest then stared at my fingers, wondering if I were already dead, and if I were, why the hell did Asgard have to look like Baton Rouge now? And why was it still raining?

But there was no blood where I *knew* blood should be. I'd felt the lion's claws sink into my body and rip it apart. The long gashes in my shirt were still there, the pain was still there, but I wasn't bleeding. And I obviously wasn't the only one who found that incredibly strange.

The remaining lions morphed into their human forms and backed away except for Menhit who narrowed her eyes at me and hissed, "What sorcery are you bringing into battle? And you dare call *me* a cheater?"

Now, granted, I hadn't been in a lot of fights with either mortals *or* gods, but I was pretty sure taking a break to *talk* to the person you were just trying to kill wasn't normal, so I decided to ignore her. It's not like I had an answer for her, anyway. I grimaced from the pain as I leaned over to whisper in Keira's ear. "Is this like a truce? Can I not kill her now?"

"You can still kill her," she told me.

"Oh," I said. "In that case..." I scooped my shield from the ground and swung the blade of my sword at the goddess's head, separating it permanently from its body, but before I could turn on the next god, they retreated, backing into the obscurity of the heavy rain.

Yngvarr groaned as Joachim lifted him, and I grabbed his other arm. "We have to get him to a hospital," I said. I wondered if gods' bodies worked the same way as humans' and if one of our hospitals would even be able to help him, but I couldn't lose him. I wasn't sure why, but I felt that I owed it to Havard to keep his brother alive.

Keira wanted to run ahead of us to get the car, but I wouldn't let her go alone in case the Egyptians were just hiding, waiting for the chance to separate us or catch us with our guard down. That's what I would have done, and I was basically an infant when it came to this fighting stuff. So we trudged carefully back to the tennis court where we'd left our car, and just as carefully laid Yngvarr on the backseat. Joachim and I exchanged a quick glance as we both realized seating was now at a premium, and I grinned mischievously at him and asked, "How much do you charge for a lap dance?"

"No offense, but you're not really my type," he said. "But if you were, fifty bucks."

"Damn," I pretended to argue. "You're expensive."

"Hey, you get what you pay for."

"Oh, my God," Keira muttered. She tossed Joachim the keys and pushed me toward the other side of the car. "Get in and *don't* get any ideas."

"You're kidding, right?" I retorted. "The most beautiful woman that's ever lived is going to sit on my lap, and I'm not supposed to get *any* ideas? I already have about three hundred and we're not even in the car yet."

"Gavyn," Yngvarr begged, "would you shut up and get in the car before I bleed to death?"

And because I actually *was* worried he'd bleed to death, I shut up and climbed in the car, but as soon as Joachim pulled onto the street, I smiled at Keira and said, "I just got about nine thousand new ideas."

Keira glanced at Joachim and asked, "Can't you drive any faster?"

I gave him directions to the nearest hospital, and as soon as we pulled up to the ER, Keira jumped out and hurried inside to get help for Yngvarr. I twisted in my seat to check on him and reminded him, once again, "You're not allowed to die on me, or I'll send Agnes after you in whatever afterlife you gods have."

Yngvarr, who'd paled considerably since we left the Garden District, offered me a faint smile. "As long as she's the young, hot Agnes, I'm totally fine with that."

So I shook my head and insisted, "Only the old witchy one who probably gave birth to the Grim Reaper."

The doors opened and a few employees pushing a gurney emerged. Joachim and I waited silently as they ensured he was stable enough to move then lifted him from the backseat. Part of me screamed to get out of the car and follow them inside, but I couldn't move. The pain in my chest had returned, but I doubted it was any more real than the original wound that lion had inflicted. I touched my chest anyway, just to see if I'd suddenly begun bleeding and if I'd be following Yngvarr inside as a patient dangerously close to death.

As Yngvarr disappeared inside the hospital, Joachim took a deep breath and said, "How the hell are you okay?"

Was I supposed to know the answer, or was that just one of those rhetorical questions, something that likely bothered my friends as much as it did me? Because I *shouldn't* be okay. Maybe I shouldn't have even survived. And no one, not even Odin himself, could cast a spell to protect someone from death. Wasn't that the whole *point* of their Ragnarok stories, that even gods couldn't escape their fates?

And that's when it hit me. I knew exactly why I was still alive.

"It wasn't my time," I said, but I was numb and really wanted to go home and forget this day and everything in it. "My death has already been fated, and it just wasn't my time."

WE TALKED in hushed whispers as Yngvarr slept in a hospital bed, recuperating from his injuries. I'd learned that gods were apparently not so different than mortals, and even our blood types were shared. Keira had pointed out that we had to be similar in order to have children together, but I'd never really thought about it. All I knew was that my dead godly ancestor had such powerful DNA that he passed his memories and emotions on to me, and I wasn't even a first-generation descendant.

"The others have arrived in Chicago," Keira whispered. "I think you should join them."

"No way," I insisted. "I'm not leaving you and Yngvarr here alone."

Keira shot me a sly smile and asked, "You think I can't handle the Egyptians if they show up?"

That sounded like a trick question. My brain panicked but my mouth blurted out, "You'd be outnumbered and defending an invalid." I *heard* what my traitorous mouth had said, so I quickly added, "But believe me: I know you're a badass of epic proportions."

Keira's smile turned genuine, and she gently touched my chest where I should have deep claw marks. "Don't start thinking you're invincible, Gavyn. There are forces far more powerful than the gods you know, and there's a plan for you... but it doesn't make you immortal."

"I haven't forgotten," I assured her. "And you're certain the seer didn't tell you exactly how I was going to die?"

Keira shook her head and pulled her hand away from me. It had been a completely innocent touch, nothing sexual at all about it, just the touch of a concerned friend, but when it came to her, I doubted anything would ever be completely innocent in my mind. I was sure now that I loved her, and I'd never been in love like this. I'd never loved a woman so much that I would've been content to just remain in her presence and be with her, even if that meant taking sex out of the equation. "Even if I knew," she finally said, "I see now there's nothing I could do to prevent it. The gods will march into Ragnarok knowing exactly what will kill them, and they'll go anyway. Is that brave or stupid?"

I snickered and shrugged. "You're seriously asking me if something is stupid? I'm the king of stupid. Plus, all the stupid men of the world got together and elected me spokesman."

"You're not stupid, Gavyn. And I'm serious. If you knew how you were going to die, would you still go? Would you still fight the god or hero that's destined to kill you?"

I didn't need to think about it. Havard's own prophecy was so similar to my fate, and like him, I'd discovered there were things in all the worlds worth dying for. "Yes," I said. "If it meant defending those I love, I wouldn't hesitate. I still don't know who killed Havard, but I'm sure he died defending Arnbjorg and their children."

Keira lowered her eyes and stared at the back of her hands, which she'd folded in her lap. "And if the people you loved didn't want you to die for them?"

"I'd do it anyway. How could I live if I didn't?"

"Gavyn—" But Yngvarr stirred and interrupted her, so we both rushed to his side, eager to help him with whatever he needed. He opened his eyes and asked me, "You're still here?"

"Of course. Where else would I be?"

"Chicago," he said. "You have to help them find Frey."

"Yngvarr, I can't leave all of you here."

"Yes," he insisted, "you can and you will."

So I crossed my arms stubbornly to remind him he couldn't possibly out-stubborn me. "And what are you going to do about it?" I grimaced before he could even answer me and cursed my traitorous mouth again. I knew *exactly* what he was going to threaten me with, and he didn't disappoint.

"Keira," he said, "call Agnes. Tell her Gavyn is being a pain in the ass and needs an escort to Chicago."

"Don't," I immediately begged then squinted at Yngvarr and hissed, "I *will* kick your ass as soon as you can get out of that bed."

Yngvarr just smiled at me and repeated, "You're going to Chicago."

And he was right: I was going to Chicago.

CHAPTER TWENTY-TWO

Tyr looked entirely too happy to see me, which kinda freaked me out, so I scowled at him and warned, "Knock it off, you perv."

He laughed and said, "Still not my type, Gavyn. Just relieved you're still alive after the mauling."

My chest actually still felt bruised and sore, so I told him that and he just nodded as if none of my miraculous survival surprised him. "I suppose being attacked by a monstrously huge lion will do that."

"Can these Sumerian gods shapeshift? Because I'm really tired of fighting monstrously huge animals."

"Some can," he told me. "Shapeshifting gods exist in every pantheon of the world."

I grunted as a way of expressing my intense displeasure that I'd likely find myself battling more vicious creatures that attempted to literally rip out my heart. Which was also not an acceptable way to die, and I thought Tyr should know that.

"What *is* an acceptable way to die then?" he asked.

I had a brief flash of a memory, a god kneeling before a

faceless man who held a beautiful, powerful sword in his hands. And I knew I would meet the same fate, and somehow, I was all right with it. "By my sword," I told him. "By the Sword of Light."

"I suppose we'll have to find it then."

I couldn't tell if he was just patronizing me, but it didn't matter. I had every intention of finding Havard's sword—*my* sword—even if I'd die by its blade. It was just in me, every cell of my body, every memory and thought and action. Whether it had always been there or had only recently surfaced no longer mattered. It was defining me now, and I would find the Sword of Light and defeat Ninurta with it. And in the end, it would lead me to Valhalla where I'd never give up hope that my Valkyrie would change her mind and allow herself to love me, too.

But first, we had to find Frey.

"Any leads on where we're supposed to be looking?" I asked.

John, the somewhat annoying CIA agent who didn't seem to think I was any kind of hero, and honestly, I kinda agreed with him even though I'd killed a few asshole gods, handed me what appeared to be a map or blueprint. I wasn't even sure. I flipped it over a few times, sniffed it—simply because I didn't know what the hell else I was supposed to be doing—then handed it back while he stared at me like I really was too stupid to live, let alone save the world. When he didn't reach for the piece of paper, I shook it a little, but the bastard just kept gawking at me.

So I glanced at Tyr and said, "Okay, I give up. What am I supposed to do with this?"

"Um, Gavyn, it's the blueprint for the hotel where they're keeping Frey."

"I don't read blueprint."

"You don't..." He sighed and snatched the blueprint from

my hand. "What exactly is so confusing here? John has even marked where the CIA thinks Frey is being held, where each of the gods and demigods are staying, and our best routes of escape once we get in there and grab Frey."

Well, now I really did feel like an idiot, but I couldn't let them know this wasn't all part of my act to convince the world I had no business playing superhero, so I pointed to the paper and asked, "If it's a blueprint, why isn't it blue?"

"Why—" John started, but Tyr interrupted him.

"Don't fall down that rabbit hole. You may never get back out."

I shrugged and decided to run with it, because the day I couldn't embrace my title as the Dumbest Man Alive would be the day I finally caved and just became Havard Jr. "I'm just saying, it's a misnomer. It shouldn't be called a blueprint when even the print isn't blue."

"Please stop," John begged.

"You know," I said instead, "you remind me of my high school biology teacher. He never let me ask questions either. And I'm not even trying to get you to discuss animal genitalia."

John glanced at Tyr and said, "Didn't you mention he's terrified of Badb? Go get her."

"Do it and I'll jump out that window," I fake-threatened, which turned into a completely hollow fake threat since Tyr snorted and dared me to try. In my haste to avoid being cursed by Agnes, I'd forgotten hotel windows were always sealed shut.

"I need to get her anyway," Tyr said. "We can't keep wasting time. Any minute now, Ninurta will call and demand an answer from us about surrendering our heroes."

And I still planned to go if it saved Frey, but I had no idea how to communicate with Ninurta privately. If Tyr found out what I was going to do, he'd probably whisk me off to Asgard and I couldn't cross the veil alone. I'd be stuck in their realm until he allowed me back on Earth. "So translate this whiteprint for me," I said.

"The name doesn't..." He sighed again and rubbed his eyes. I thought I deserved some sort of medal for being able to make him do that so often. "Just stay with me, okay?"

"Got it, but if any giant wolves show up refusing to allow themselves to be bound unless someone sticks a hand in their mouth, I'm out of there."

But he'd apparently decided not to let me throw him off his game anymore. He lifted his prosthetic hand and said, "I can always buy another one."

And really, once your friends stop allowing you to annoy the hell out of them, it's not even fun to *try*. But as we stepped into the hallway, I pulled on his arm to stop him and quietly asked, "Has Agnes mentioned anything about Yngvarr?"

His eyebrows pulled together and he answered, "She's concerned as we all are."

"Yeah, but... is she *more* concerned than everyone else?"

"Gavyn, if you're worried about them resuming some affair they began a long time ago, you're just going to have to get over it. It's completely unfair for you to expect them to feel or act differently just because it bothers you."

"It doesn't bother you?" I shot back.

"No, why should it?"

I didn't actually have a good reason for that. Maybe my reaction was just residual resentment over my kidnapping and resulting emasculation, and the only reason I'd forgiven Keira was that I'd fallen in love with her. "Fine," I hissed. "But when they have little witch babies that take over Asgard *and* Earth, just remember I tried to stop this."

Tyr nodded as if that were completely reasonable. "I'll make sure nobody blames you for the witch-baby-pocalypse."

Agnes, who joined us as her young, hot self, kept shooting me strange looks, so I shot *her* a strange look and told her to stop hitting on me. She tossed her bright red hair over a shoulder and lifted her chin, but when she asked me how Yngvarr was doing, I could tell she wasn't nearly as nonchalant about it as she wanted us to believe. So even though I cringed as I answered her, I assured her he'd be fine.

It seemed totally bizarre to me that we were just going to *drive* to this hotel and walk in, but that's basically what we did. John insisted it was the safest way to get us to the hotel, and that we'd just blend in with other visitors. If we'd shown up in a helicopter or tank or *something* worthy of a Michael Bay movie, we'd not only alert Ninurta and his followers we were there, but we'd likely get Frey killed. And we were kinda trying to avoid that.

We parked in the garage and rode the elevator to the hotel's lobby, but I couldn't shake the feeling something wasn't right. I initially brushed it off as an, *"Of course* something isn't right. Ninurta and his evil minions are here." But a nagging little voice kept whispering that wasn't all, and if we attempted to walk through those doors into the hotel, we'd all die far sooner than we'd planned. Not that I thought John had planned his death or anything, but the rest of us with destinies and prophecies kinda had no choice.

The glass doors taunted me, practically begging to be opened and discover just what was so wrong about this hotel. Agnes stepped toward them, but I grabbed her arm and stopped her. I'd never seen her look so surprised, but she didn't pull her arm away from me. "Something's up," I whispered. "Haven't you noticed *no one* else is here? Where are all the guests and employees?"

Tyr scratched his chin as he stared thoughtfully at the empty lobby. "Come to think of it, did anyone notice if there were any other people driving through the garage? A hotel of this size, surely someone would be checking in or out?"

And that was *exactly* the problem. It was far too quiet. "It's a trap," I said.

"If Frey's here, we have to go in anyway," Agnes said.

"I don't see how dying will help him," I argued.

"What do you think will happen if we open the door?" Tyr asked. "Explosion? Buckets of acid above our heads? Charged by rhinoceroses?"

"Dude," I retorted, "rhinos?"

He just shrugged. "Ever gotten close to one? Those bastards are *mean*."

"You're a very strange man," I said.

John, who'd been quietly listening to us talk about traps and rhino invasions, announced, "Stay back. I'll go in first."

"I really don't think that's a good idea," I said, but he cut me off and insisted, "I'm expendable. There are billions of humans in this world, but a very limited number of gods and demigods and even fewer who are willing to stand up to those causing so much trouble. If anything explodes or I get mauled by a herd of rhinos, get out of here. There's always a chance our intelligence was bad, and Frey isn't even here."

Tyr and Agnes began arguing that the whole reason we were here is that *no* human life was expendable, which honestly kinda made me proud I considered them friends now, but John ignored their protests and headed toward the lobby. I hadn't been able to travel with my shield, so I had nothing we could hide behind in case the hotel *did* explode. We just stood there helplessly, watching a man march bravely to his death.

Except the lobby didn't blow up. The doors swung open and he stepped inside, and absolutely nothing happened. No acid rain, no rhino stampede. We all glanced at each other in a sort of, "Oh, what the hell—gotta die sometime, right?," moment and followed John inside.

But as soon as we entered the lobby, the doors slammed closed behind us. I spun around and tugged on the handle, but it refused to open, so Agnes struck the glass with a club that she'd magically produced from thin air—seriously, *how* did they keep doing that?—but it didn't shatter. We'd just been trapped inside the hotel with no way out.

A howling from the hallway on our left warned us we weren't alone after all, though, and I groaned, knowing I was about to end up fighting yet another freakish animal. What emerged from the hallway caught me off guard though, and as the pack of dogs, which weren't really dogs, flooded into the lobby, I might or might not have yelped a little. I wasn't scared of dogs or anything, I just hadn't been prepared for a bunch of canines with remarkably human features. Their eyes, mostly brown irises surrounded by a sea of white, just like a person's, were the most haunting aspect of these monsters, but their faces weren't a whole lot better. Instead of a snout like a regular dog, their faces were flatter, like a pug's but with a human's nose. They had the lips of a man but the teeth of a dog, and their ears were some unholy combination of the two.

The creatures snarled and barked, but beneath the normal canine sounds was a whispering of *words* that sounded like "die" and "eat." Goose bumps broke out all over my arms as I faced the pack of devil dogs. Of all the gods and monsters I'd already fought, none had scared the shit out of me like those mutants. The alpha fixed me with his disturbingly human eyes and *smiled*. I fought the urge to throw up or scream or both.

The alpha attacked, which apparently gave the rest of the pack permission to attack us as well. Like the lions in Baton Rouge, these canines had long claws, and he swiped at me as he lunged toward my neck. I swung my blade at his foreleg and only managed to nick him. Cursing, I stepped out of the path of his attack and brought my sword back to his body, which caused him to *scream* like a wounded man. So I screamed back at him. "Dude, *not* cool!"

Apparently, he didn't care that I found his human characteristics so disturbing. He bared his teeth and leapt at me again, entirely too fast because his claws got ahold of my arm this time. I swiped my blade across his paw, forcing him to let go, and backed away, bleeding all over the lobby's perfectly polished floor. "Son of a *bitch*," I complained, which apparently was a bigger insult when battling a dog because that *really* seemed to piss him off. He growled and lunged, so I growled back and ran my sword into his chest. His eyes widened like he was surprised I'd just struck a fatal blow, and I pulled my sword free, only then realizing I'd heard John firing his handgun when the dogs first attacked but he'd been far too quiet since.

Tyr speared the monster he'd been battling, and as the dog fell to the floor, I saw John's mangled body lying beside it. We'd warned him, of course, that bullets wouldn't work against gods, and presumably, any creature they threw our way. But John hadn't been a demigod with the knowledge of ancient weapons somehow embedded in his DNA. It had been our job to protect him, and we'd failed.

Agnes freed her blade from the last of the dogs still standing and cast an apologetic glance in John's direction. We'd have to leave him as we ventured farther into the hotel in the hopes of finding Frey, or at the very least, a way out. I stepped over the body of one of those freaks that would forever ruin my love of golden retrievers and followed Tyr into the hallway.

The elevator dinged as it reached the lobby, and we froze in anticipation of a new horror awaiting us behind those metal doors. When they finally opened, the car was empty. I was about to tell them we should take the stairs anyway when a mist began to fill the empty elevator, a thick white cloud that quickly filled the car and leeched into the hallway, tendrils of the vapor reaching toward us like it was alive. And not *really* being stupid, I backed away from it but not fast enough. Some of the milky white gas touched my bare arm, and I screamed as if it were fire burning off my skin.

Some of it must have touched Agnes as well, because she also screamed and bumped into me as we tried to get away from it. Tyr used his prosthetic hand to wave away the closest cloud, but the more he tried to disperse it, the thicker it seemed to coalesce until we were confronted by an opaque wall of poisonous gas. My forearm bore a bright red spot where the fog had touched me, and I couldn't imagine what it would do to our lungs if we inhaled it. I *could*, however, imagine it would be a terribly painful way to die.

Death by mysterious poison gas was also unacceptable, by the way.

We stumbled down the hallway and reached the stairwell, and I had a momentary lapse of sanity when I actually thought, "*Finally, we'll be safe in there.*" Of course, I immediately wanted to kick my own ass, but I had a toxic death cloud chasing me. Instead, I pulled the door open, and Tyr cursed and backed into Agnes, pushing her away from whatever lay beyond that door. I peeked into the dimly lit stairwell and muttered, "You have *got* to be kidding me," when I saw more of that strange white mist creeping down the stairs.

"We're trapped," Agnes breathed. "We're going to be killed by a *cloud*."

"No way," I insisted. "I'm only going to die one way and this ain't it."

In one of those rare moments of sudden Superman strength, I hurled my body into one of the closed doors, and the locks snapped, allowing us to spill into the cool, clean air of an empty hotel room. Agnes yanked the bedspread off and stuffed it at the bottom of the door while Tyr shut off the air conditioner. And me? I stood there rubbing my shoulder and wondering what kind of dumbass wouldn't have tried *kicking* the door down first then realized *I* was the kind of dumbass who wouldn't try kicking the door down first.

"I don't think Ninurta's here," Tyr sighed. "And neither is Frey."

"Help me break the window," I said. "If we stay here any longer, none of us will get out of here alive."

A ticking sound beat against the door, and each of us squinted at it like it was the door's fault something else was out there trying to kill us now. When the ticking sound became louder and more insistent, I shouted, "We didn't order room service."

"Gavyn," Agnes groaned.

But whatever was making that noise didn't appreciate my polite attempt to send them away. The door began to dent as those ticks became violent and incessant. "Is it just me or does that kinda sound like a million scarabs or something?" I asked.

"Not just you," Tyr agreed.

"And does anyone else hate bugs?"

Tyr slowly raised his prosthetic hand while keeping his eyes glued to the pockmarked door.

"Window," Agnes reminded us.

I pulled the curtain back and ran my fingers along the seam. "It's cemented closed."

"We don't have time to break the seal," she said. "We'll knock out as much glass as possible and try not to open a major artery on our way out."

The clicking of all those little legs against our door mixed with an unnerving whirring sound, like millions of beetles flapping their wings to take flight. Or worse, using their wings to communicate with each other. Tyr lifted a floor lamp and struck the glass until it shattered, then wrapped a towel around his good hand and broke off the jagged edges. So naturally, I reminded him to be careful that he didn't sever that hand, too.

The door burst open and a pulsing black mass swarmed into the room. I may or may not have screamed like a nine-year-old girl and dove out the window, but if I *did*, Agnes and Tyr were right behind me, and Tyr may or may not have landed on me, which would have been worse than the screaming like a little girl thing.

As we scrambled to our feet, prepared to run from the Hotel California, the weirdest thing happened. All those scarabs hit some invisible barrier where the window used to be and piled thicker and thicker against it. But not one of them escaped the hotel room.

"Enchantment," Agnes hissed.

"Do we have any kind of army of freaks?" I asked.

She shrugged and said, "We have you."

"Yeah," I pretended to agree. "But I'm not an army."

"No," she said. "You're not. And we're down one CIA agent and a powerful god while the Sumerians have the advantage of more and more distractions popping up all over the world."

"Then I guess," Tyr offered, "it's time we get an army."

ARNBJORG CHALLENGES ODIN

(And Áki has to be connected to Havard's fate)

For days, Arnbjorg moved around our palace as if in an enchantment, keeping her brother close during the day in case he might disappear again or she might wake up and discover his presence had only been a dream. She was happier than I'd ever seen her, and to me, that made our entire expedition and even Gunnr's insistence she bring this mortal boy back to Asgard worth it.

On the third day after Finn's arrival, Arnbjorg asked to meet Áki, the son of the wealthy farmer who'd purchased Finn and would now be raised by a Valkyrie. I'd asked a few gods, but none of them could remember a Valkyrie ever raising a child. But unable to tell my wife no, I brought her to Gunnr's home so she could meet the boy.

Áki had apparently won the hearts of many in Valhalla. We found him in the field where our fallen heroes prepared for Ragnarok, a few of them gathered around the small boy to teach him sword fighting skills and how to engage an enemy when disarmed. Gunnr watched him with so much adoration already that I felt guilty about our fight over his fate.

"Odin hasn't bothered either of you, has he?" I asked.

Gunnr's expression hardened and she crossed her arms, her eyes all fire and storms. "He says we'll put the boy's fate in Forseti's hands, but how can we know Odin isn't directing Forseti's judgment?"

"We can't," I answered. "He's always ruled fairly before, but no one has so directly challenged Odin before either."

"And if he decides that Áki cannot stay here?" she asked.

I was about to tell her that if we couldn't find a suitable home for him in Asgard, surely mortals would open their doors to the will of the gods, but Arnbjorg responded first and I wouldn't contradict my wife. "Then we will take him in," she said. "And we will raise him as our own."

Gunnr looked at me for confirmation, so I told her whatever Arnbjorg decreed, I'd support. Róta, another Valkyrie, called for Gunnr and waved us over. Before we even reached her, we could tell she'd summoned her sister because Forseti was ready to judge whether or not Áki could remain in her care.

As a god of justice who settled most disputes between us gods, we trusted Forseti's judgment and generally agreed to live by his decisions. But as we ventured to his palace so he could hear Gunnr's case, I was already scheming how I'd get Odin off his throne. By the time we reached Forseti's palace, the All-Father was already there, and he gestured angrily toward me, demanding I leave. "You have no business here. This doesn't concern you."

"It does," I argued. "Arnbjorg and I have agreed to raise the boy if Forseti's judgment is in your favor."

"And," Gunnr added, "Havard was with me when I decided to bring the child home. Forseti may wish to speak with him."

Odin wouldn't even acknowledge his daughter, which infuriated me, but what could I do? Forseti entered his hall and greeted each of us, even Arnbjorg, a human, and Gunnr, a

Valkyrie, all of whom most gods regarded as nothing more than servants of the All-Father rather than women with minds of their own. But Forseti was always fair to everyone, and this simple gesture of acknowledgment served as a reminder that his decision would be fair as well, although he followed our laws. And Gunnr *had* broken our laws.

He listened patiently as we recounted our destruction of Áki's father's farm, our rescue of Finn, and Gunnr's determination that this child shouldn't be punished for the sins of his father. When our story ended, Odin folded his arms over his chest and said, "She's a Valkyrie, and as such, she's forbidden to have children."

"But," I countered, "she has not had this child. She hasn't violated any law." It was a technicality, a flimsy hope that Gunnr could keep Áki over one word and its interpretation. And honestly, I couldn't see how this would end in her favor.

"It would set a bad precedent," Odin said. "The Valkyries have rules that don't apply to the rest of us—"

"Rules that *you* created and forced on them," I interrupted.

"But rules nonetheless," he insisted. "Do we gods not have rules that we've inherited and must live by even though we never personally agreed to them?"

I gritted my teeth and silently cursed him. Odin was a god of war *and* wisdom, and I was out of my depth in this hall... and he knew it. But Arnbjorg stepped forward and bowed politely to Forseti and addressed him. "My lord, may I speak?"

Forseti smiled and obliged her.

"Good men must live by two sets of laws, which don't always agree," she said. "One is the set handed down to us from the gods, and ignoring those laws can result in catastrophe, which is how Áki ended up in Asgard in the first place. But the second is just as important. It is the difference between good and evil, right and wrong. When our ancient laws compel us to do evil and we don't fight against it, we risk our own moral corruption. And tarnishing the soul is as catastrophic as any punishment from the gods."

Forseti raised an eyebrow and lifted a hand in Odin's direction. "And your rebuttal?"

Odin hardly seemed concerned that my wife's contribution could be anything but a delay in Forseti's judgment in his favor. "We aren't human. Our world doesn't operate the same way, nor do we."

"Do you not have souls?" Arnbjorg asked him. "Do you not have a conscience or a moral obligation to do what is right?"

Odin had the nerve to laugh at her as he said, "You're just a girl. What do you know of moral obligations?"

Arnbjorg remained as stoic as ever. "I *am* just a girl, and I don't possess your years of wisdom, my lord. But I know Áki is just a child in need of a home, and Gunnr is following her conscience. I've seen the way they look at one another, how much love exists between them already. And I know it would be an act of evil to separate them for no other reason than to abide by a rule that doesn't always make sense."

"Be careful, girl," he warned. "You forget to whom you're speaking."

"No, my lord," she responded. "But no man or god will change my heart."

Forseti rose from his chair before Odin could respond and declared, "I've reached a decision. We will proceed with the understanding that Valkyries are neither to bear nor adopt children, but Áki may stay until he is old enough to care for himself."

"Forseti—" Odin began, but the god of justice stopped him.

"This is my judgment, Odin. All of Asgard will uphold it."

Odin's single eye settled on my wife, narrowed and filled with loathing. My stomach turned, and a voice within me that sounded so much like my mother whispered, *"Kill him now, Havard. No harm shall ever come to your bride."*

But Odin turned on his heels and stormed out of the palace, leaving us with the god of justice who'd given Gunnr permission to become the only mother to ever exist among the Valkyries. She bowed respectfully and thanked him, but before I could follow Arnbjorg and Gunnr outside, Forseti grabbed my arm and told me, "Havard, Odin will most likely calm down. But you should have your wife attempt to reconcile with him."

"I cannot control her nor do I want to," I said. "I can convey your advice, but if she believes she owes him nothing then I will support her decision."

Forseti nodded as if he'd anticipated my response. "I don't disagree. Odin simply isn't used to anyone challenging him, and now, all three of you have in a very public way. Just encourage her to demonstrate a bit of humility toward him."

I promised I would even though I felt sick even thinking about it. Humility toward Odin? I'd rather die than subject Arnbjorg to such humiliation. But as I caught up to her and Gunnr, she took my arm and suggested, "Let's have a feast for Odin and Frigg as a thank you for their generosity in opening Asgard to Finn and me."

I laughed and told her, "Asgard doesn't belong to them."

"That hardly matters, Havard. We will keep the peace between our families."

So I smiled and assured her I would do my best to honor her wishes. We escorted Gunnr back to Valhalla where Áki still played happily in the field with our fallen heroes. The sun was beginning to set now, and soon, all of Valhalla would enter the dining hall and celebrate that the world continued on and Ragnarok had not yet consumed us.

"If becoming his mother kills me," Gunnr said quietly, "you should know it was worth it."

"Yngvarr and I will protect you," I immediately replied, but could we? We'd openly defied the All-Father and convinced Forseti to rule against him. We'd inflicted enough insults for him to use against us should he decide to raise an army, which meant there was really nothing we could do except raise an army of our own.

CHAPTER TWENTY-FOUR

W e'd survived Ninurta's Haunted Hotel of Horrors, so I assumed Frey wouldn't make it much longer, if he were even still alive. As soon as we returned to Baton Rouge, I checked on Yngvarr then pulled Keira into the hallway to find out what Odin was up to. He was still in town, and the more I dreamed about Havard, the more convinced I became that Odin was responsible for his murder.

But really, I had a lot of questions about Áki. "What happened to him?" I asked after filling her in on Forseti's decision and Odin's response.

"Nothing," she said. "He grew up and eventually returned to Midgard."

I wasn't sure *why*, but it seemed like we were missing a huge piece of Havard's and my puzzle, and Áki had played a big part in it. "Once he returned to Earth, did you visit him?"

"Of course, but I really don't remember anything unusual. He married and had kids and lived a normal, mortal life. I was always so proud of the man he'd become."

I sighed and ran my fingers through my hair. "Maybe the connection is just that Áki triggered this feud between

Havard and Odin, but it feels like there's more. I just can't figure out what."

Keira lowered her eyes and nodded. "I remember Forseti deciding Áki's fate, Odin's anger that he hadn't gotten his way, but I'd long thought it was directed at me, that I'd convinced Forseti to allow Áki to stay in Asgard and Odin resented *me* for it. Our relationship was strained for a long time, at least until Áki returned to Earth, then it was like I had to prove myself all over again."

"What do you mean?"

"I mean Odin wanted to ensure he had my loyalty again. I went into a lot of dangerous battles and questioning him just sent me back to square one. As messed up as it may seem, he's still my father... I can't help loving him, you know."

I didn't know that, actually, because it sure as hell didn't seem like he spent a whole lot of time worrying about his daughters, let alone loving them. But she must have guessed my thoughts based on my expression. "It's complicated, Gavyn. We can love and hate someone at the same time."

"If you remember *anything* about Áki that even might be important to uncovering Havard's secrets, let me know," I said. "But right now, we need to focus on finding Frey."

"Agreed." The elevator beside us chimed with the arrival of a car, so we fell silent as its passengers emptied into the hallway. But one of them made me want to start punching people, or really, just one guy but I wouldn't have objected to punching Ninurta either.

"I heard about the hotel in Chicago," Odin said to me. "It's unfortunate our intelligence was bad, but we may have another lead on Frey's whereabouts."

"If it's as helpful as the CIA's last lead, I'll pass," I retorted.

"This tip didn't come from the CIA but my own team," he said.

"Your team..." I repeated.

Odin nodded. "I've had every Valkyrie except Gunnr out looking for Frey, and they've got a pretty good handle on where he is. But rescuing him may be impossible."

"Oh, no," Keira whispered.

"What?" I asked. "Where is he?"

Keira took a deep breath and when her eyes met mine, I saw only sadness and regret. "He's in their world. The Sumerians brought him into their realm."

Well, great. I couldn't cross the veil on my own, so even though I still wanted to attempt a rescue mission, unless I had a god or Valkyrie to help me, Frey and I were out of luck. "Okay," I said slowly. "But we're always outnumbered here, too. We have to try anyway."

"Gavyn," Odin argued, "you're too important to risk on a mission like this."

For some reason, hearing Odin claim I was more important than other heroes, most of whom had gone to Iceland willingly, only solidified my decision to enter the Sumerian realm and find Frey. "Keira," I begged, "take me there. I'll bring Frey home. You *know* I can do this."

She opened her mouth to answer me, but her father spoke for her instead. "Absolutely not. I forbid it, Gunnr."

"I wasn't asking for your permission," I snapped.

"*You* may not need my permission, but *she* does," Odin responded. "And she won't be taking you."

"Then I'll take him," a familiar voice said, and honestly, it surprised the hell out of me. I glanced over my shoulder at Agnes, still appearing as her scorching hot redheaded self, and couldn't think of a damn thing to say. Did she just want to aggravate Odin? Did she want to bring Frey home as badly as the rest of us? She was an Irish goddess... why was such a dangerous mission for a Norse god so important to her?

"Badb," Odin started, but she cut him off.

"Don't argue with me, Odin. Gavyn has proven himself capable of tackling challenges that would kill or break most heroes. If we're not willing to risk everything for one of our own, why the hell are we even here?"

I'd never liked Agnes more than in that moment. Sure, she was still a witch and at some point, I expected her to turn me into a frog, which admittedly, I'd probably deserve, but maybe Keira had been right about her all along.

"If you do this, you're going without my Valkyries or any of the Norse gods," Odin warned. "Not all of the Sumerian gods support Ninurta's war here, and if you'd just let us negotiate—"

"Negotiate?" Agnes scoffed. "You think Frey has time for us to negotiate with a handful of gods who may be lying about their allegiance to Ninurta anyway?"

Odin looked prepared to continue this argument indefinitely, so I figured now was a great time to butt in with my own insistence we leave immediately. "If we can only go with Irish gods, see who's willing to come with us. You're right: if Frey's even still alive, I don't think he will be for long. We need to leave *now*."

Tyr stood in Yngvarr's doorway and folded his arms over his chest as he stared at Odin. "I'm going, too."

"Tyr," Odin sighed.

But I didn't want to hear anymore of Odin's objections either. "I want Joachim to come with us. Next to Ull, he's the best archer among us."

Agnes snorted and reminded me *she* was actually the second best archer among us, which was true, but as fantastic as she was with a bow, she was even better with a sword. And admittedly, I kinda understood why Yngvarr had once fallen so hard for her... not that I'd ever admit that to *her*. But both Agnes and Tyr agreed that Joachim should come with us if he was willing.

We returned to the hotel with Odin still objecting like that was going to change our minds or something. I'd anticipated Joachim agreeing to come with us, but we didn't have a chance to finish explaining where we were going and why before he stood up and asked us when we were leaving. I had a brief vision of that beautiful little girl in the picture, eagerly awaiting her father's return, and shook my head as if I could literally knock the memory out of there.

Agnes shot me a funny look as if she suspected I was doing something completely idiotic—which was always a safe bet with me—but she wisely decided to ignore it and brought us across the veil. We found ourselves standing in a wheat field, the shoots reaching past our waists. In the distance stood a walled city much like Asgard.

"Well, this was an oversight," I said smartly. "I doubt their Sumerian Heimdall is just going to open the gate for us."

Tyr nodded and said, "Be right back."

And the bastard actually disappeared, leaving us alone in the wheat field, gaping at a circle of broken stalks where he'd once stood. "What the hell?" I muttered.

But Agnes just shrugged. "Let's give him a minute. And we should probably sit so we aren't quite as visible in case anyone's watching this field."

I felt ridiculous doing it, but she and Joachim crouched below the wheat, so I crouched, too. And then I blurted out, "Who harvests all this wheat? Do you gods have harvesters or do you contract out?"

Agnes moved a handful of wheat stalks to gape at me, but being Agnes, she was also ready with a smartass response. "Every year, we kidnap the demigods who've pissed us off and force them to do farm labor."

"Sounds about right," I said.

Tyr returned and grunted at us. "What are you doing on the ground?"

"Hiding from Agnes," I answered.

"Don't blame you," another man's voice said. I quickly rose to my feet to see who else had joined us, and found myself staring at a Mjollnir necklace again.

Thor already held the hammer in his hand, and even though I was pretty sure Joachim and Agnes had already figured out why Tyr had brought him into our rescue party, I decided to point out the obvious anyway. "You're going to break through the wall."

"Yep," he said.

"And we're somehow going to get through it without being slaughtered by the Sumerians who will hear the commotion and come running," I continued.

"Yep," he said.

I squinted at him, but he didn't offer an explanation as to how we were supposed to accomplish that, so I gestured toward the city and exclaimed, "How are we even supposed to get to the wall without them noticing us?"

"We can't," Agnes explained. "We'll have to fight our way inside."

I groaned, but really, I shouldn't have expected anything else.

"Well," Joachim offered, "I don't see this ending badly at all."

I clapped him on the back and said, "It's been nice knowing you. Look me up when you get to Valhalla."

"Wouldn't we be going at the same time?" he asked.

"Actually, if we die here, I don't see how the Valkyries could retrieve our spirits to bring us there. I'm beginning to have serious reservations about this entire enterprise."

Joachim nodded but shrugged at the same time, which was actually kinda impressive... like that whole being able to pat your head and rub your belly and hop on one foot at the same time kinda thing. "There are worse ways to die than storming a supernatural kingdom."

"I don't think it's a kingdom," I pointed out. "They'd need a king for that."

"True," he acknowledged. "But it sounds better to say we're storming a kingdom rather than we're storming a city."

"One of these days, I really will figure out a spell to keep you quiet," Agnes threatened.

"Sorry," I hastily said. "I'm done."

She eyed me suspiciously but must have decided she'd just be wasting everyone's time if we waited on me to really keep my mouth shut. "When we get to the wall, Thor will break a section open. Joachim, you and I will deflect any attacks from above while Tyr and Gavyn prevent anyone from walking through."

"And how are we supposed to do that?" I asked, but Agnes shot me a look that told me I was three seconds away from being turned into a frog, so I said, "Never mind. We'll figure it out."

About halfway across the field, I began to wonder why we'd crossed the veil so far away from the city. I tried to ask, but Agnes shot me the same look so I closed my mouth and kept walking. About three-quarters of the way to the wall, I'd added, "Who *eats* all this wheat, anyway?" and "Why is their city so quiet?" to my growing list of questions. This time, I didn't bother asking, although I kept a mental catalogue in case we somehow survived.

Not surprisingly, the Sumerians attacked before we even reached the wall. Archers shot arrows in our direction, forcing us to hide behind our shields, unable to shoot back. I glanced at Agnes and asked if she had any other bright ideas, so quite naturally, she flipped me off.

And also quite naturally, I flipped *her* off in return.

"Gavyn," Tyr whispered, "your shield's enchantment offers

you greater protection than ours. Provide cover for Joachim so he can take out the archers on top of the wall."

I blinked stupidly at him before hissing, "This shield isn't big enough to cover two people, dumbass."

"Figure it out," Agnes hissed back at me.

I wanted to flip her off again, but Joachim was already nocking an arrow, preparing to stand up and pick off archers so we could invade their city. I rose with him, even though I still thought this idea was suicidal, and the Sumerians unleashed a hail of arrows on us. Instinctively, I held out my shield but braced for an arrow through my brain, which honestly didn't seem like a *terrible* way to die. I mean, it was a hell of a lot better than mauling by supernatural lion or whatever those mutant scarabs would have done to us.

As the arrows hit my shield, they made a *thumping* sound, which kinda surprised me. I'd expected more of a *plink, plink, plink*... not that the sound they made was important or anything. It just surprised me. It seemed like we'd never get a lull in their constant barrage, which would allow Joachim to fight back, but apparently, he didn't think we *needed* a break in the seemingly never ending storm of deadly projectiles. Bastard just stepped beyond the shield's protection, released his bowstring to send an arrow flying back toward the gods or demigods trying to kill us, and stepped back.

My mouth fell open and for a moment, I couldn't think of a damn thing to say. If I'd had vodka, I could've quickly solved that problem, but being vodka-less, it took a few seconds before my brain and mouth cooperated again. "Dude, are you *trying* to die?"

He shrugged and said, "It worked. We have one less archer to worry about."

"You can't do that again. They'll be expecting you now."

"Probably," he agreed. "They're also changing positions,

which will make it impossible for me to quickly hit someone anyway."

Agnes crawled closer to us and whispered, "I can still see them. I know where they've moved. On the count of three, we'll switch places. Gavyn, keep that shield up."

"Are you kidding me? I've got arrows attempting to turn me into another American Crowbar Case, and you think I'm going to just *drop* it?" I whispered back. Agnes muttered something that sounded an awful lot like a frog transformation spell so I grinned sheepishly at her and added, "I'll cover you."

She and Joachim switched places so quickly though that I almost failed in my promise. And true to her reputation as one of the most badass warriors among gods, she even released an arrow as she replaced Joachim. I heard the guy screaming as he fell from the top of the wall, so my mouth hung open again, only this time, my brain and mouth couldn't reconcile and I just stood there gaping at her like the total dumbass I'd apparently become. Or already was. Really, that changed minute to minute.

"On the count of three," she told me, "we're going to duck so I can shoot. Their arrows will go over us. Joachim, while I've distracted them, take out the archer on the far left. Tyr will cover you."

I hated everything about this plan, but most of all, I hated that my friends were taking such great risks and all I could do was stand there holding a shield. But I had to place *some* faith in Agnes's strategic genius. We all knew I hadn't inherited any of that.

Our progress toward the wall became painstakingly slow as she had to develop new maneuvers each time we executed one. But her plans actually worked, and one by one, the archers fell, and with each archer she and Joachim killed, the number of arrows shot at us became fewer, and eventually, we made faster progress. The silence within the city shattered when it became apparent the archers had failed and we'd enter the city soon, but the Sumerians made the fatal mistake of assuming we'd attempt to break through the gate. And that was likely the only reason we were able to enter their city at all.

Thor swung his hammer at the massive stone structure, which had to have been at *least* several feet thick, and we all had to hide beneath our shields as the debris exploded everywhere. Shouting erupted as the Sumerians charged, but we'd had the advantage of a surprise point of entry, which forced them to redirect their attack. As we walked through the opening Thor had created, I was greeted by several assholes attempting to either decapitate or impale me. I didn't think they'd be too picky about my cause of death. I parried the first attack then pivoted to deflect the second. But fending off *three* swordsmen would be impossible.

An arrow zipped past my ear and turned one of the gods who'd tried to either decapitate or impale me into a life-sized pincushion. Considering the chaos that erupted with our invasion into their kingdom—or goddom—I had a hard time figuring out where to focus my attention. All around me, the air seemed to pulse with the energy of battle, and we fought our way farther and deeper into their admittedly impressive labyrinth of a city.

After turning a corner into an empty street, my brain finally had a break, allowing it to start working again. I looked around at the tall buildings surrounding us, the identical streets, the twisting alleyways. And I realized we *were* in a labyrinth. "Shit," I sighed.

Everyone looked at me as if expecting I'd just offer an explanation for my sudden dropping of an expletive without prompting like they'd just met me. I mean, seriously, when were they going to learn that if I couldn't be a pain in the ass about something, it probably wasn't worth me doing it in the first place? So I ignored them and tried to mentally retrace our steps, but I couldn't figure out what direction we'd even come from, let alone how to get back to the hole in the wall Thor had created.

Finally, Agnes snapped, "Gavyn, *what?*"

I pointed my sword toward the street behind us then turned and pointed it toward the street in front of us. "We've been fighting our way into the heart of this city, or what we *thought* would be the heart of this city, for a long time. And I think we're just getting completely turned around but not actually going anywhere. Without Ariadne's thread, we may never get to Frey, let alone out of this place."

"Cut that out," Tyr warned. "It freaks me out when you correctly reference history or mythology."

I nodded in total agreement. "Just pretend like it's Havard and not me, because honestly, we all know it's not me."

I felt a little insulted when everyone immediately agreed, but it's not like I could deny the truth of it.

"So if we're really in a maze," Joachim said, "how are we ever going to find Frey?"

"What *was* our plan?" I asked. "Were we just hoping Ninurta would show up and hand him over?"

Tyr snickered and shook his head. "We're looking for one of the most heavily guarded buildings in this place. They're not going to hold a hostile god here without a *lot* of protection."

"And how do we know our presence alone isn't going to get him killed?" And why hadn't we thought about any of this *before* invading their stupid goddom?

"We don't," Agnes answered.

I waited for her to elaborate or offer some words of encouragement, something to indicate we hadn't just thrown away our lives for a futile rescue mission, but instead, she just headed toward the street in front of us, leaving me scowling at her back. Don't get me wrong: it was a nice view, but I was stuck in a Sumerian labyrinth and even if we found our way out, there was a fairly good chance it wouldn't be with Frey.

"Son of a bitch," I mumbled.

Joachim nodded and sighed. "Might as well follow them though. What else can we do?"

And he was right. What else could we do?

The street branched into a fork, and we argued about which direction to choose for a while then argued about what *method* we should use to determine our direction, and I finally convinced them there was significant scientific validity to eeny-meeny-miny-moe. Or they just got tired of arguing and agreed to shut me up. But since we landed on the road I'd wanted to take, I insisted the method was foolproof. None of us realized the street was getting narrower until we found ourselves getting closer and closer, and there was absolutely nothing pleasant about being sandwiched between Tyr and Thor. But when we turned to head back and try a different street, just in case this one crushed us to death or something truly bizarre, everything looked different and we couldn't even see the fork anymore.

It was like we were on a completely different street now.

"Um, does anyone remember taking a side street or...?" I asked.

"I hate magic," Tyr sighed.

Agnes nodded and suggested we keep going, but it was like we were on a *haunted* street or at the very least, a voodoo street, and I really didn't want to find out what they'd meant by "magic." I grew up an hour away from New Orleans; I knew better than to mess around with voodoo. But I had a horrible suspicion if I'd tried to walk back in the opposite direction, I'd find myself even more lost and alone, so I stayed with them on the voodoo street, where even our footsteps were soundless. I was about to complain about how much I hated magic, too, when something else caught my attention and I stopped walking.

"Guys?" I whispered then glanced at Agnes and added, "And witch?"

"What Gavyn?" she snapped.

I pointed down an alley on my right. "You mentioned we needed to find a heavily guarded building, right?"

The others glanced down the alley, which *looked* fairly short, but this street hadn't seemed endless when we took it either. And none of the guards seemed to notice us, which was kind of a big red flag, but if Ninurta had Frey in that building, we didn't really have a choice: we had to figure out a way to get to it. "Let's go single file," Tyr suggested. "But stay close behind whomever is in front of you in case they seem to fall off a cliff."

He nudged me forward, but how the hell did he expect me to go first after proclaiming falling through an alleyway was possible? "Send Thor first," I said. "He's large enough that he'll get stuck and we can just pull him back out." I looked him over quickly then decided, "If we can find a crane."

"Fine," Tyr said. "I'll go last in case anyone follows us."

I crept behind Thor through an alleyway that seemed a hell of a lot more confining than it had appeared from the street, but Tyr's large frame was blocking most of my view from the rear and Thor was blocking my view of the street ahead. I could do nothing except walk and hope it was all an illusion. Time worked as well as spatial observation in this place. My watch had stopped working long ago, probably as soon as we stepped through the hole in the wall, so I couldn't be sure how long we'd been searching for Frey or even walking down this alleyway. But at some point, I realized my legs were aching, not from walking or the sword fights, but it was almost like...

"A slope," I whispered. We'd been heading *downward* the whole time. "Everybody stop!" I yelled. But it was too late. We all heard the water rushing toward us, but we were trapped. There was nothing we could do except hold our breath and swim.

CHAPTER TWENTY-FIVE

As the water crashed into me, I thought, *"This must be what it feels like to get body-slammed by an eighteen wheeler."* The impact was so painful, I couldn't even struggle against the water to try to force my way to the surface. Of all the ways I'd imagined dying, almost all of which I'd deemed unacceptable, drowning had never even made it onto the list. The water carried me farther down the alley, bumping me into solid objects and walls, but I could neither hear nor see anything except the water. If my allies were still alive, I'd lost them.

A thick, strong arm wrapped around me, and instead of being propelled forward by the unceasing wave, I began to move at an angle. We broke the surface of the water and gasped for air, sputtering as the water I'd inhaled when the wave first crashed into me was forced from my lungs. Thor had to keep me from being dragged below the surface again, but he shouted at Tyr and I turned my head to see the war god pulling Joachim along with him. I looked around us, but I couldn't see Agnes anywhere.

I sputtered for a few more moments before I could call her name, but even with all of us shouting—and I even called out "Badb" instead of "Agnes" in case she hit her head and forgot who she was or something—she didn't answer. Ahead of me, I noticed a pipe running along the side of the building, so I gestured to it and told Thor, "There! Help me get to it, and I can hold on while you look for her."

He swam over to the pipe, and I grabbed it then watched as this giant of a god dove beneath the tidal wave attempting to drown us all. On the other side of the alley, Tyr and Joachim grabbed onto a drainpipe, but their weight apparently didn't agree with it. It creaked and bent, but I could tell by Tyr's face that he was exhausted. He couldn't fight this surge forever.

I couldn't even tell where all of this water was going. The heavily guarded building we'd been trying to reach was still there at what appeared to be the end of the alley, but none of the water reached it. Thor broke the surface of the water again and shook his head. He hadn't been able to find Agnes.

My arms ached and strained as I clung to the pipe, but I was also clinging to the naïve belief that it would *have* to end soon. But this wasn't a world like mine. Magic and illusions and impossible mazes and the complete dismantling of time all reigned here, and if there were any chance Agnes was still alive, we'd never get the opportunity to find her because this wave didn't *have* to end. Whatever, or more accurately, *whoever* controlled it could keep it flowing until we *all* drowned.

So I did the only thing I could think to do.

I let go.

Water crashed all around me and pulled me back under, but this time, I didn't fight it. I let it carry me toward the end of the alleyway, searching for Agnes's bright, unmistakable red hair. I slammed into what I assumed was the building I'd been clinging to, but as I tried to push myself away from it, the water suddenly fell through the stones that paved the alley. I gasped and coughed and crawled away from the wall of water where Tyr, Thor, and Joachim were still trapped, but a hand grabbed my arm and pulled me in a different direction.

If I'd had more air in my lungs, I may or may not have screamed like a little girl again, but who wants to barely survive a freakish encounter with possessed tidal waves only to get manhandled by some pervert of a god? And with my luck, I figured it would be Ninurta, the perviest of the perverted gods. But I found myself being hushed by a familiar voice, and I blinked a few times to clear the water from my eyes.

I noticed her hair first and threw my arms around her. I mean, sure, she was a witch and all, but she was *my* witch. "Holy shit," I whispered. "I thought you were dead."

"I'm not convinced I'm not," she whispered back, so I nodded. I felt mostly dead, too.

"Any idea how to get the water to shut off?" I asked.

"Asalluhi. Their god of magic. He must be controlling all of this."

"I can hardly move, and we have to track down a god and kill him?"

"He's a god of *magic*, Gavyn. How the hell would we kill a god of magic?"

I threw my hands up and sighed. "How would I know? I didn't even think magic existed until it tried to kill me fifteen minutes ago."

Agnes grunted at me and pushed herself to her feet. "You've been fighting wolves and lions and demonic dogs and have an enchanted shield, but you didn't think magic was real?"

So I shrugged and pushed myself to my feet, too, although

with a lot more complaining and groaning. "I figured it was just godly science."

She blinked at me and said, "I'm really too tired to even point out how incredibly stupid that is."

I glanced toward the alleyway filled with water and asked her how we could possibly save them, but we couldn't. We'd have to hope they'd either be able to hang on long enough or they'd get as lucky as we did and reach the end without drowning. But as we crept through the shadows toward the building where we suspected Frey might be imprisoned, I had another idea, as brilliant—or dangerous and reckless—as *all* of my ideas. "So if a god is controlling that water," I said quietly, "he's probably having to concentrate or something, right?"

"Maybe. He could have just created it with an incantation and released it."

"So would it do our friends any good to create a distraction or not?"

Agnes groaned and rubbed her eyes. "I really don't know. And we're both so weak right now, I don't think we should count on our ability to fight our way out of tough situations."

I glanced toward the alleyway again and told her, "Imagine how weak they must be."

Instead of calling me names or pointing out the numerous flaws in my admittedly stupid idea, Agnes just stared at me with weary eyes and took a deep breath. "Okay, Gavyn. Let's get their attention."

My fingers tightened around the hilt of my sword as Agnes grabbed an arrow from the quiver on her back that hadn't been there a second ago. I added, "Where the hell do you gods hide these weapons?" to my growing list of questions I wanted answered once we got back to Earth. As soon as she released the string, we'd have an entire army descending on us, so I kinda felt like we should share something really deep and meaningful. "Hey, Agnes?" I whispered.

"Yeah?" she whispered back.

"Don't tell anyone I hugged you."

"Ditto."

Her arrow coursed toward its target, impaling the guy through his temple, and as I'd expected, every guard around the building charged us. Agnes slung her bow over a shoulder in favor of her sword, which she was actually even more of an epically amazing badass with, and I thought about telling her it had been nice knowing her, but it seemed wrong to lie to someone right before their death.

Arrows whizzed past us with blinding speed, taking out the entire front line of guards before they even reached us. Aside from Agnes and Ull, there was only one person I knew who could shoot like that. "Joachim," I breathed. I wanted to search for him, but we still had a dozen guards about to attack us. I braced myself for the inevitable ass kicking I was about to receive and wondered why the hell Agnes had let me proceed with this ridiculous plan, but Mjollnir knocked one of the guards down, leaving a huge, disgusting hole in the guy's chest, while more arrows rained down on the stubborn guards who refused to retreat.

I'd just begun fighting one particularly stubborn guard who refused to retreat *or* die when an alarm sounded, echoing through the otherwise quiet and empty streets. It couldn't have been a secret that we'd entered their city, so why had they waited to sound an alarm? And what did it even mean?

Apparently, asking questions—even mentally to myself—had the magical ability to create nightmarish scenarios. I'd *just* thought, "What now?" when my question was answered by a loud screech that sounded suspiciously like... "A dragon," I whispered aloud.

I got a good hit on the guy I was fighting and pushed him

away from me then glanced over my shoulder, and sure enough, an honest-to-some-god *dragon* was flying toward us. "Get inside!" Agnes shouted.

But I was frozen as the dragon descended, bellowing one last time before fire shot toward me. The only reason I wasn't turned into a human torch was that Tyr grabbed me and dragged me with him to the entrance of the building. "A dragon," I exclaimed. "I was only joking when I claimed I wanted to be a dragon slayer. I never signed up to actually *be* a dragon slayer!" And really, I never signed up to fight anyone or anything, but I sure as hell hadn't signed up to fight *dragons*.

Agnes shook her head and said, "None of us are fighting their dragons. We can't kill them, because their bodies are filled with poison that only the Sumerian gods are immune to."

A strange sound escaped from my throat, some cross between a croak and a scream, but a dragon filled with poison? I mean, who thought *that* was a good idea? Okay, obviously the Sumerians did, but still.

"Come on," Thor urged. "Let's see if Frey's in this place."

I was so glad to see our allies had survived the wave in the alley, but I didn't have time to celebrate. The building seemed to be mercifully empty, which I didn't realize was strange at first, considering how many guards had been stationed outside. Yet I still had a horrible feeling this building was just as messed up as the rest of the Sumerian goddom, but honestly, braving whatever horrors it might hold was a better option than fighting a fire-breathing dragon filled with poison.

We were on the second floor, or at least what we *thought* was the second floor, before we realized this building was laid out just like the city itself. Circular streets, circular hallways, both of which brought us back to the same starting point. Or maybe they weren't circular at all, but the deception of their magic still got us turned around, unable to find a point B. I remembered going up stairs, but this floor was identical to the one we'd just searched. Even the mess we'd made in some of the rooms as we broke down locked doors and shattered mirrors, which I always thought was bad luck but it turned out that some gods knew spells to trap people *inside a mirror*, which was *Alice Through the Looking Glass* level bizarre.

"This isn't working," I complained. "Either Asshole is—"

"Asalluhi," Agnes interrupted.

"That's what I said. Either Asshole is messing with our heads, or we're really in some magical labyrinth and we can't possibly find Frey *or* get out."

"Perhaps," Joachim suggested, "we're going about this the wrong way. I once read about an Egyptian building that Herodotus described as a labyrinth. The upstairs rooms were a confusing network of rooms and courtyards, but the tombs below ground may have been different."

"The stairs only went up," I pointed out. "I don't think there *are* hidden rooms below us."

But Agnes shook her head and said, "We only saw the stairs going to the second floor. Or more accurately, we only *thought* we saw stairs going up but maybe they go down, too."

I blinked at her then turned to Tyr and waved irritably in Agnes's direction. "Translate. I don't speak witch."

"I think," Tyr said, even though he looked as confused as I felt, "we need to believe we're going down the stairs instead of up, and that'll change the direction we're actually going."

So I blinked at *him* before snapping, "That is *literally* the dumbest thing I've ever heard, and thanks to all of you, I've heard some really insane shit."

But Joachim shrugged and said, "It's worth a shot."

So we returned to the stairs and stared at them for a few seconds, and I even crossed my arms and demanded, "Okay, stairs. We're going to go *down* you, got it?" Then I grinned mischievously at Agnes and said, "That sounds totally pervy."

Agnes sighed but refused to allow me to be a pain in the ass. She approached the stairs carefully and began making movements like she was trying to walk downward, which meant she was staying on the first step, and I was about to glance at Tyr and ask him how long we were going to stand around watching Agnes walk in place when she disappeared.

We were silent for a second before we all muttered, "Holy shit."

And then we couldn't let Agnes descend into some-god-knows-what kind of terrors below, so we hurried to the first step and mimicked her walking downstairs movements even though the stairs only seemed to go *up*. And yeah, I felt a bit ridiculous, but only for a minute, because soon, we actually *were* going downstairs into a dark hallway where Agnes awaited our arrival.

Now, given that we'd just taken a secret, magical staircase into the dungeons of a Sumerian fortress, I expected an actual *dungeon*. But the hallways and rooms appeared just as modern as the upstairs rooms, so I pouted for a while as we resumed our search for our stolen god. Their dungeon, though, was just as quiet as the rest of the building, so I'd pretty much given up hope that we'd find Frey, and with a poisonous dragon waiting for us outside, I couldn't imagine how we'd roam the city looking for other possible prisons.

I could tell by the expressions on my friends' faces that they were giving up hope, too, and we began piecing together a possible escape plan. And that's when I noticed a door that seemed to have an excessive number of locks on it. "You know," I said, "if I were going to kidnap a god and keep him locked up, I'd literally keep him locked up."

"Gavyn," Agnes sighed, "*what?*"

I pointed to the door, which we'd overlooked, because

we'd been so sure we'd already searched this hallway. Thor had knocked down several doors already, and when we first stepped into it, we saw the exact same wreckage as before. But I was sure we hadn't missed a locked door on our last trip down this hallway considering we opened every single door we passed, which meant we'd somehow managed to escape the strange loop we'd been stuck in.

Thor took a deep breath and lifted Mjollnir. "Here goes nothing," he said then brought his hammer down on the door, which exploded beneath the impact. We all stood ready to battle in case some monster or Sumerian god had been hiding in there, but as the debris cleared and we were able to see inside, we lowered our weapons and rushed in. And there, standing against the back wall, miraculously unharmed and wearing a sly grin, was the god we'd all risked our lives to save. "It's about time," Frey teased.

Agnes laughed and hugged him then pulled away just as quickly, as if embarrassed by her temporary display of affection. Thor and Tyr, who'd known Frey for so many millennia they'd lost count of how long they'd been friends, quickly embraced him as well, but I was already fixated on what would come next. I clapped his back and offered him my own sly smile. "You have no idea what we went through to get here."

"Probably not," Frey agreed. "But I sure as hell hope you have a plan to get us out."

I shrugged and gestured toward the door, indicating we were about to find out. "We're in a labyrinth without Ariadne's thread."

Frey squinted at me and asked, "How do you know about that?"

So naturally, I flipped him off, but I suddenly realized why we hadn't met *any* opposition inside this building. Or perhaps it had been Havard who figured it out, but either way, it wasn't good news for us. "We're not only in a labyrinth, but we've got an entire army outside waiting to ambush us."

"Okay," Frey said slowly, "so what do we do?"

"The only thing we can," Agnes answered. "We fight."

END OF BOOK TWO

SWORD OF PROPHECY, book three of the *Heroes of Asgard* series

ALSO BY S.M. SCHMITZ

Sign up for my mailing list, which will keep you up to date on new releases and great deals when I put books on sale, here.

For more information, please visit my website at smschmitz.com.

Other titles by S.M. Schmitz

Shadows of the Gods, book one of *The Unbreakable Sword* series (fantasy & mythology)

As a powerful demigod, Selena has been running from the gods who control the government agency, the New Pantheon, for the past three years, but now, they've caught up to her.

When they trap Selena in an alleyway in New Orleans, she is ready to admit defeat. But an unfamiliar demigod rescues her, and the more she learns about Cameron, the more she discovers their common bonds may be the key to unraveling her own mysterious history.

In the first book of The Unbreakable Sword series, Selena and Cameron must not only evade the New Pantheon, which is ruthlessly hunting the remaining gods and their descendants, but an angry Aztec god that wants Selena's power to himself. And they will discover in the impending final battle of the gods, no one can be trusted.

Blades of Ash, an *Unbreakable Sword* series prequel

When Olympus is destroyed, the Tuatha Dé and their Greek

allies want revenge. But what their vengeance costs may haunt them forever.

Badb, one of the triune of Irish war goddesses known as the Mórrígna, is having a rough millennium: the mortals of Ireland have turned away from the Tuatha Dé, and now, the Sumerians have launched a disastrous invasion into Olympus.

Worse, the reason for the invasion isn't as straightforward as they first thought. With powerful players stoking the flames between the Irish alliance and their enemies, both sides may ultimately lose everything, including their own worlds.

The *Resurrected* trilogy, a science-fiction romance (also available in *The Complete Resurrected Trilogy Box Set*)

Awakened from death. Herself but no longer alone in her own body. Two lives merged into one.

A mistake. An aberration. A miracle.

And a company that wants her dead for existing.

When Dietrich's fiancée, Lottie, is killed in a car accident, he descends into his own personal Hell until he runs into her in a café two years later. Claiming she isn't really Lottie but only possesses some of her memories, the young woman offers him an unbelievable story then disappears.

Using his position as a CIA agent to track her down, Dietrich quickly discovers Lottie remembers far more about her past life than she'd originally let on. But his attempt to learn more about the planet she comes from or the woman she is now is disrupted by a group of men from the company that transports people from their home planet to Earth when they find out about her resurrection and attempt to murder her.

Because for Lottie, something went wrong, and her existence threatens their entire business on Earth. And Dietrich's ultimate second chance with the only woman he's ever loved will be threatened as well.

The Chosen, a *Resurrected* series novel

They promised her happily ever after. Instead, they gave her Hell. Now, she's getting revenge.

When Bella agreed to travel to Earth to start a new life with the man she loved, she'd been promised two things: healing dead human bodies so they could live on this planet always worked, and they could have the happily ever after forbidden to them at home.

But soon after arriving on her new planet, she discovers both of those promises were lies. And the consequences for trusting the wrong people are deadly.

After six years of hiding from the company that helped her cross over, she is approached by a beautiful but mysterious stranger who offers her a different kind of promise: the chance for revenge. And Bella's journey to end her own nightmare and to seek justice for the man she'd once loved is finally able to begin.

The Immortals series, a fantasy & mythology series (also available in *The Complete Immortals Series Box Set*)

When demons refuse to play by the rules, all Hell will break loose.

Colin and Anna have been hunting demons for a long time. But something is different in Baton Rouge. The rules are being broken and they're powerless against some of the greatest forces Hell can assemble. If they can't stop these demons from manipulating every rule of this war, then Heaven may lose the only battle that's ever really mattered.

The Golden Eagle, a romantic suspense

After a vicious second civil war in the U.S., the states that seceded are occupied, and the people there live by different rules.

Jon is the highest-ranking officer in an elite Task Force whose purpose is shrouded in mystery. Ava is just trying to survive the occupation after two years of brutal war. After meeting unexpectedly, they discover they are both willing to risk everything for the chance to love one another. But what those risks entail may be far greater than anything either could have imagined.

The Cambria Code series, a science-fiction romance

When a mysterious spaceship appears above Cambria, Zoe remains skeptical that it's anything but an elaborate hoax. By the time the first spaceship is joined by two others, Zoe reluctantly admits that Earth has been invaded, even though it's a pretty lame invasion: the aliens look remarkably human and keep to themselves. From what humans are able to learn about them, they seem incredibly arrogant and boring anyway.

After meeting Peyton, one of Earth's newest residents, Zoe feels an immediate attraction to him although she is reluctant to become involved with someone who isn't even human. But she soon discovers that these aliens are far more dangerous than they've led everyone to believe, and the secrets they are hiding may signal the destruction of her entire planet.

The Scavengers, a post-apocalyptic novella

When nothing is left, what will you treasure most?

In a world completely destroyed by adults, eleven-year-old Nic believes he is the only thing still alive after four years of isolation—the only thing except for the Scavengers.

When he meets Celia, another child in an empty world, they offer one another hope and the promise of an end to the kind of fear and loneliness that only a child abandoned on a dead and forsaken planet could understand.

But Nic's universe, for years centered around Celia, will be tested, and he'll discover just how far he's willing to go to protect them both.